Needled to Death

"[A] tightly stitched tale." —*The Best Reviews*

"Solid . . . Kelly is easy to like." —*Mystery Reader*

"Nonknitters and fiber fanatics alike will enjoy the yarn-shop setting." —*Romantic Times*

Praise for
Knit One, Kill Two

"Well-drawn characters and a wickedly clever plot—you'll love unraveling this mystery!"
—Laura Childs, author of *Blood Orange Brewing*

"A clever, fast-paced plot, with a spunky sleuth and a cast of fun, engaging characters. *Knit One, Kill Two* delivers the goods." —Margaret Coel, author of *Eye of the Wolf*

Berkley Prime Crime titles by Maggie Sefton

KNIT ONE, KILL TWO
NEEDLED TO DEATH
A DEADLY YARN
A KILLER STITCH
DYER CONSEQUENCES
FLEECE NAVIDAD
DROPPED DEAD STITCH
SKEIN OF THE CRIME
UNRAVELED

Anthologies

DOUBLE KNIT MURDERS

A Deadly Yarn

Maggie Sefton

BERKLEY PRIME CRIME, NEW YORK

THE BERKLEY PUBLISHING GROUP
Published by the Penguin Group
Penguin Group (USA) Inc.
375 Hudson Street, New York, New York 10014, USA
Penguin Group (Canada), 90 Eglinton Avenue East, Suite 700, Toronto, Ontario M4P 2Y3, Canada
(a division of Pearson Penguin Canada Inc.)
Penguin Books Ltd., 80 Strand, London WC2R 0RL, England
Penguin Group Ireland, 25 St. Stephen's Green, Dublin 2, Ireland (a division of Penguin Books Ltd.)
Penguin Group (Australia), 250 Camberwell Road, Camberwell, Victoria 3124, Australia
(a division of Pearson Australia Group Pty. Ltd.)
Penguin Books India Pvt. Ltd., 11 Community Centre, Panchsheel Park, New Delhi—110 017, India
Penguin Group (NZ), Cnr. Airborne and Rosedale Roads, Albany, Auckland 1310, New Zealand
(a division of Pearson New Zealand Ltd.)
Penguin Books (South Africa) (Pty.) Ltd., 24 Sturdee Avenue, Rosebank, Johannesburg 2196, South Africa

Penguin Books Ltd., Registered Offices: 80 Strand, London WC2R 0RL, England

This is a work of fiction. Names, characters, places, and incidents either are the product of the author's imagination or are used fictitiously, and any resemblance to actual persons, living or dead, business establishments, events, or locales is entirely coincidental.

PUBLISHER'S NOTE: The recipes contained in this book are to be followed exactly as written. The publisher is not responsible for your specific health or allergy needs that may require medical supervision. The publisher is not responsible for any adverse reactions to the recipes contained in this book.

A DEADLY YARN

A Berkley Prime Crime Book / published by arrangement with the author

PRINTING HISTORY
Berkley Prime Crime mass-market edition / August 2006

Copyright © 2006 by Margaret Aunon writing as Maggie Sefton.
Cover art by Chris O'Leary.
Cover logo by axb group.
Cover design by Rita Frangie.
Interior text design by Stacy Irwin.

ISBN: 978-0-425-20707-9

BERKLEY® PRIME CRIME
Berkley Prime Crime Books are published by The Berkley Publishing Group,
a division of Penguin Group (USA) Inc.,
375 Hudson Street, New York, New York 10014.
The name BERKLEY PRIME CRIME and the BERKLEY PRIME CRIME design are trademarks belonging to Penguin Group (USA) Inc.

PRINTED IN THE UNITED STATES OF AMERICA

10 9 8 7 6

Acknowledgments

First I want to thank Lee Ann Williams of Midland, Texas, for helping in my research on oil and natural gas deposits. My questions were many, and her answers were detailed and thorough. Thanks again, Lee Ann, for sharing your lifetime of experience in the business. My challenge was to weave specific details on the subject throughout the book without slowing the story—or boring the reader. I hope I've succeeded.

Next I want to thank all the talented fiber artists I spoke with while researching this novel. Like Kelly, I did not know that something called "wearable art" even existed until I actually saw it. I am astounded by the variety that is being created.

I also want to thank Sandy Dunn, a talented fiber artist from Santa Fe (now living in Colorado), who was kind enough to share her "artist's journey" with me.

Most especially, I want to thank Kristin Hansen of Kristin's Boutique in Santa Fe, which was the inspiration for the fantastic and fabulous boutique Kelly visits. Like Kelly, my jaw literally dropped when I first entered Kristin's. My poor descriptions do not do justice to the unbelievable variety of clothing and accessories I saw there. Thank you, Kristin, for providing that marvelous shopping experience and for answering my many questions.

Finally I want to thank Anne Murphy and Richard Dolph for contributing their wonderful recipes for Chiles Rellenos. Enjoy!

One

Kelly Flynn eyed the tempting appetizers spread out on the nearby buffet table. As hungry as she was right now, she could easily empty a whole tray of the tiny morsels. Balancing her glass of white wine, Kelly selected a creamy white cheese melted over a thin cracker and tasted, savoring the delicate Oaxaca cheese as she wandered the balcony of the restored Spanish colonial building.

Glancing out into the plaza of Old Santa Fe, Kelly could almost feel herself slip back in time. Most of the buildings surrounding the historic plaza still had the distinctive adobe architecture—sunbaked mud covered by stucco. Trees and benches dotted the graceful square, and Kelly imagined colonial ladies from yesteryear strolling with their long lacy skirts and parasols.

It was a charming picture, but Kelly was grateful she didn't live in those days. She was fairly certain she'd never make it as a "fine lady" in colonial times. She'd probably trip on her long skirts and fall face first onto the plaza—after she'd accidentally speared someone with her parasol, of course. Heck, she had enough trouble wearing dresses now.

"Have you tried that dip with the chili sauce, yet?" Megan asked as she came up beside Kelly.

"I don't know. Which one is it?" Kelly glanced back at the table, which was draped with colorful embroidered cloths. Platters of tropical fruit vied with the appetizers for space.

"Ohhh, you'd know it if you tasted it."

"Hot, huh?"

"Oh, yeah," Megan teased, with the self-confident grin of a veteran chili taster.

"Well, I'm starving right now. What do you say we go to dinner before I disgrace myself and gobble up all those Oaxaca cheese morsels when no one's looking."

Megan laughed out loud, her red wine sloshing in her glass. "That would be pretty tacky. Let's tell Allison where we're going first."

Kelly looked back through the open doorway into the spacious meeting room where she and Megan had just watched their friend from Fort Connor receive an award. "Southwestern Design Institute's Wearable Fiber Artist of the Year. Not bad," Kelly commented with a proud smile as she spotted Allison Dubois across the room, surrounded by other fabric and fiber artists.

Kelly had no idea that such a thing as "wearable art" existed until she met Allison. Megan had met the young weaver-designer when Allison was teaching a class at their favorite knitting shop, House of Lambspun, and introduced them one afternoon around the cozy knitting table.

Megan beamed. "Allison deserves it. She's super talented and works hard. You know, she told me it took her twice as long to get her Master of Fine Arts degree because she was working two part-time jobs to stay in school."

"Whoa, that's rough," Kelly said in admiration. "I don't know how she found time to create all that she has."

"She said she barely sleeps, and works way late each night, then crashes. Insomnia, apparently."

"And I thought my schedule was bad."

"I know. She's unbelievable. I don't know how she does it. I couldn't keep those hours." Megan waved towards Allison, who'd glanced their way.

"I didn't know how varied her work was until I saw her exhibition in Old Town," Kelly said, as Allison returned Megan's wave. "I mean, she started out with oils on canvas, then she went to painting on fabric, then weaving and designing."

Megan nodded. "And no matter how different each medium is, you can still see her design through them all. I guess that's her artist's eye. Me, I'd be happy to learn how to create one of those fantastic tops we saw today at Kristin's shop."

"Now, that place is truly another world," Kelly observed, remembering how she felt when she first stepped into the Santa Fe shop that specialized in wearable art.

Kelly's jaw had nearly dropped. She'd never seen clothes like that before. Every type of fabric and texture imaginable, combined into garments of all kinds. Gorgeous weavings, subtle and bold, vied with each other for attention. Handwoven shawls of silk and wool, linen and cotton, were wrapped with vibrant belts. Sinfully soft wools were woven into tops adorned with draping cowl necklines, knitted with lacy yarns and threaded with ribbons or colorful beads.

Everywhere Kelly looked, she saw one-of-a-kind art. Crushable velvets of antique bronze and dusky rose trimming a linen vest. Hand-dyed denim jackets with faux fur trim. Brocade bordering shirts, embroidered flowers and vines twining up shirt sleeves. Ribbons and beads woven into shawls, ponchos, and scarves. Hand-painted, long-fringed velvet shawls. Scrumptious chenille, springy linen, sensuous silk, sturdy denim, and suede as soft as a baby's cheek.

"She has fabulous things there. That's why I couldn't resist this," Megan said, stroking the vivid sapphire-blue woven shawl that draped her body. A turquoise and emerald hand-painted silk belt cinched the shawl, accentuating her small waist. "I took one look, and I had to have it."

"You look wonderful in that color, Megan. The whole look suits you," Kelly said, admiring shy Megan's bold fashion statement. Megan was still school-girl shy in most things except colors. With her almost-black hair and porcelain complexion, Megan looked radiant in all the bright colors. In fact, Kelly couldn't recall seeing her knit anything that wasn't in a vivid hue.

"And you looked great in that velvet shawl," Megan reminded her for the third time that afternoon.

Ever since they'd left Kristin's shop on San Francisco Street, Kelly had been having a mental argument over the beautiful black velvet shawl she'd seen there. She had to admit it did look striking on her when she'd succumbed and tried it on. *But where would she wear it?* her nagging voice had whined.

Now that she was telecommuting from Colorado to her Washington, D.C. corporate CPA firm, she no longer needed business suits or dressy outfits. She could sit in front of her computer in her favorite attire: Colorado-casual shorts or jeans, tee shirts, and sneakers. Furthermore, she was either working at the computer, knitting at House of Lambspun close to her home, or on the softball field with her friends. *Face it,* the voice nagged again, *that shawl would sit in the drawer.*

"It was gorgeous, wasn't it?" Kelly said with a sigh. "But, you know, I wouldn't have any place to wear it. It would just sit in the drawer."

"C'mon, Kelly, that's no excuse," Megan scolded.

"Sometimes we have to buy something simply because it's beautiful, and it's meant for us. That's all. No other reason. Besides, those clothes are art. Heck, you could always hang it on your wall."

Kelly was trying to think of a reply to that novel suggestion but was spared the effort when Allison rushed up to them, out of breath, her fair skin flushed, her blue eyes huge.

"Did you see her? Sophia Emeraud, the designer? I can't *believe* she came all the way here from New York," Allison exclaimed, brushing a lock of blonde hair from her face.

"That's because she loves your work," Megan reminded her. "Besides, she probably wanted to meet you. After all, you'll be joining her studio soon."

"Who would have thought those contest entries would be seen by so many designers," Allison mused out loud, as if she were still surprised at her good fortune.

"Hey, you deserve this break, Allison," Kelly spoke up. "You've worked hard, and you've developed an incredible portfolio. I was really amazed when I saw all those pieces in the Fort Connor gallery. If we can see your talent, you better believe a professional designer like Sophia recognizes it."

"And don't forget, she already used one of your weavings in her last show, and everyone loved it," Megan added.

Allison sighed. "I still can't believe she asked for one of my pieces."

"Believe it," Kelly ordered with a grin.

"She looks *fabulous*, doesn't she?" Allison gushed as she stared over her shoulder toward the tall brunette adorned in classic black. "I don't know if I'm up to this or not. New York is going to be filled with all these *gorgeous* people!"

"Yes, she's stunning," Kelly concurred with an indulgent smile. "But you're just as beautiful, Allison. You're a fresh-faced Colorado girl. And you're as tall and willowy as any New York model. So, don't be worrying about them."

"Kelly's right," Megan piped up. "And *you* are a designer. A New York designer, now."

Allison shook her head, golden hair brushing her shoulders. "It's going to take a long time for this to settle. I still feel like I may wake up and find this is all a dream."

"It can't be a dream, Allison, because Megan and I are in it, too, and I'm starving!" Kelly joked. "Hunger is as real as it gets. We were about to head for dinner, because we figured you'd be meeting with So-phee-ah." She deliberately dragged out the syllables.

"We're going to have dinner at the restaurant in her hotel, so why don't I meet you guys afterwards," Allison suggested. "Where're you heading?"

"I'm leaving it up to Megan," Kelly said. "She's the expert in New Mexico cuisine."

Megan grinned. "I thought we'd try the old Spanish colonial hotel restaurant with the gorgeous patio. They have great food. Kelly needs to sample more sauces."

"Nothing too hot, promise?" Kelly warned as they turned to leave.

Allison glanced back toward her future employer. "Okay, I'll see you later, guys," she said with a wave as she walked back into the adjoining room.

"I can't believe that dare-devil Kelly Flynn is afraid of a tiny little chile," Megan teased as she and Kelly headed downstairs to the exit.

"I'm not afraid of them," Kelly countered. "Let's just say I'm wary. They may be little but they're powerful, and they always travel in a group."

Kelly leaned back into her high-backed wooden chair, having devoured the last morsel of her dinner. Chiles rellenos con queso. Delicate, mild, sweet green chiles stuffed with rich cheeses and simmered in a delicious sauce. Yum.

The marvelous dinner had been worth the wait. She and Megan had arrived at the popular Santa Fe restaurant to discover that others had reservations, while they had none. Ravenous already, Kelly had lobbied to leave for another restaurant, but Megan insisted this one was worth waiting for.

She was right. Everything from the wine list through the delicate soups to the delicious entrees—Kelly savored it all, much to the friendly waiter's delight. Now she was fairly bursting, but the dessert tray looked tempting. Maybe a cup of coffee would help, she thought as she uttered a contented sigh.

Megan laughed softly. "I take it you enjoyed the food?"

"Absolutely," Kelly said then drained the last of her sauvignon blanc. "Megan, you can choose restaurants for me anytime we travel together."

Megan gave a modest nod. "Thank you. I do appreciate good food."

"And I love to eat," Kelly said with a laugh. "So, I'll just follow you around."

"You up for dessert?"

"I'd love some, but I think I'll need a few minutes and some coffee first." She glanced around the gracious patio-style restaurant with its colorful Spanish tile, hanging plants, and vivid paintings. All the tables were filled with diners who looked as contented as she felt.

Megan gestured to the waiter. "Well, you can have your coffee. I can't wait another moment for one of those yummy caramel custards."

Kelly chuckled as she watched Megan order dessert and coffee. "I don't know where you put it all, Megan. You never gain an ounce. I'm going to have to double my workout after we return home tomorrow."

"Just lucky, I guess. Oh, look," she said, glancing over her shoulder, "here comes Allison."

Allison wound her way through the patio to their table. "Hey, guys, how was dinner?" she said as she sank into one of the empty chairs.

"Fantastic, thanks to Megan's suggestion," Kelly answered, noticing that Allison still radiated excitement. "How did your dinner meeting go with Sophia?"

"Great, I think, but I was so excited I can barely remember what we talked about," Allison enthused. "All I remember for sure is that I need to be in New York three days from now." She glanced down at her purse. "Oh, before I forget, you've got to see these handmade beads I found on the way over here. The shop was about to close, but I begged him to stay open." She withdrew a small packet and carefully unwrapped the layers of paper. "Aren't they great?" she said, dangling the beads.

"They almost look like they were carved in another century or something," Kelly said, observing the strand of bone-colored beads, their shapes decorated with curving lines and jagged angles.

"Wow, I've never seen anything like that before," Megan remarked.

"Neither have I, but I've already got an idea how I can use them in a design," Allison said, her eyes alight.

"Look out New York, here she comes," Megan said with a laugh.

"Do you have a place to stay in New York?" Kelly asked.

"I'll be sharing an apartment until spring," Allison replied. "Sophia has a cousin who's studying at one of the city universities, and her roommate moved out, so she needs someone. It works perfectly, because I can't afford New York City rents right now. I'll be earning apprentice-like wages for quite a while."

"Well, maybe you'll be able to keep on sharing," Kelly suggested.

"Boy, this Sophia sounds like a fairy godmother," Megan said. "Kind of like she's taken you under her wing."

"I'll say," Kelly agreed.

Allison glanced at the table. "I've thought the same thing, guys," she admitted. "She's making all of my dreams come true. I still can't be—"

"*Believe* it," Kelly finished with a laugh. "I swear, Allison, I'm going to make a cardboard sign saying 'Believe it!' for you to wear around your neck all the way to New York."

"Okay, okay," Allison said, joining the shared laughter. "I'm working on the self-confidence."

"We'll work on you all the way back to Fort Connor tomorrow," Megan teased, gesturing for the waiter to bring their check. "And speaking of tomorrow, we'd better head back and get to sleep. Gotta leave early tomorrow if we want to stop by some of those yarn stores in Denver."

Allison closed her eyes and groaned. "Ohhhh, just the thought of all that cleaning and packing I have to do when I get back. Brother! My apartment is a mess."

"Don't worry," Megan reassured her as the waiter approached with dessert and coffee. "I can come over Monday morning and help all day if you need me. My work is caught up until Wednesday."

Kelly wished she could say that. She'd stolen time away from her corporate accounts to take this road trip to New Mexico and into another world. In Santa Fe, with its vibrant art scene and distinctive architecture everywhere she looked, Kelly felt as if she'd briefly stepped into a whole new world. Unfortunately, the old world of corporate accounts and bulging email inboxes was awaiting her return.

"Thanks for dropping me off, Kelly," Megan said as she leaned on the car window, backpack over her shoulder.

"No problem," Kelly said. "See you in the shop later to-morrow. I'll have to catch up with the office work first."

"I may not get in at all. Depends on how much cleaning there is to do at Allison's." Megan turned toward her town-house gate. "Say 'hi' to the others for me." She walked through the gate, lugging backpack and knitting bags.

"Will do," Kelly called as she drove off into the evening twilight.

The return trip to Fort Connor had gone smoothly and super easy with three drivers taking turns. She wasn't even tired. Of course, the brief stops at three different yarn shops were also great energy breaks. Almost as good as coffee. All three of them had been unable to resist buying more yarn. Even Allison had succumbed, and she was packing for a move.

Now, all Kelly had to do was find the time to make all those new scarves. Her yarn purchases were starting to pile up at the little cottage left to her by her aunt. It was her home now, and it was filled with bags of future projects. After years of seeing Aunt Helen's bags of yarns waiting to be used, she understood why all knitters talked about their "stash bags." Gorgeous yarns they'd purchased but had yet to find time to knit.

Another memory intruded. Allison, subdued and red-eyed, after a phone call to a friend while Kelly and Megan were buying fast food in Denver. She'd waved away their concern and said she was simply tense and upset about all she had to do before leaving.

Kelly had exchanged a quick glance with Megan, then changed the mood entirely by announcing she'd decided to buy the beautiful velvet shawl after all. She promised to call Kristin's shop first thing in the morning. Thank goodness for plastic, they all agreed, and broke out into laughter.

TWO

"**HOW** was the road trip?" Lisa asked as Kelly dropped her knitting bag on the library table.

"Fantastic," Kelly said, sinking into a chair. "I had no idea how beautiful Santa Fe would be. And, of course, there's the food." She took a deep drink from her coffee-filled mug and watched her friend work her usual needle magic on a fluffy pile of yarn in her lap.

"Ah, yes, the food," Lisa said with a grin, brushing a wisp of blonde hair from her forehead. "What'd you eat? I love New Mexican cuisine, so I'll live vicariously through your descriptions."

"What *didn't* we eat?" Kelly corrected with a laugh. "I ran double distance this morning to get a head start on the fat."

Kelly pulled out a circlet of rose-colored silk and cotton yarn from her knitting bag. Her half-finished sweater-in-the-round. The neglected circlet lay there, forlorn, its circular needles dangling like puppydog tails. She stared at the strange-looking needles. It had been months since she'd even pulled out this piece. Good thing that knitting-in-the-round only called for the knit stitch. Were those cobwebs on the yarn, she wondered?

She examined the vibrant rose yarn she'd chosen months ago, surprised she'd been so easily lured away from this lovely piece by the seductive summer temptations of the flirty eyelash yarns that filled the shop's bins.

Spilling from crates, scattered across antique tables, stacked in squeezable bundles on shelves, the little balls of soft yarn were everywhere. Bold, spiky, lollipop colors and silky fringed palettes of aged cognac and vintage cabernet. Kelly had been unable to resist and succumbed to what Lambspun's knitting regulars called "fiber fever." Meanwhile, the rosy silk and cotton circlet was shoved into the bottom of the project pile—forgotten once more.

Kelly let her mind drift from fiber memories back to food. "Let's see, we had chiles stuffed with this yummy cheese, and there were these wonderful fruits everywhere, and desserts."

"Oh, good, I came at the right time," Jennifer announced as she plopped her knitting bag on the table and sat down. "Keep talking. I'll just sit here and gain weight while you describe the desserts. Flan, right?"

"Oh, yeah," Kelly nodded. "And some other delicate white confections I can't remember."

"Probably meringues," Lisa spoke up. "What about the chiles? Did Megan introduce you to some of her favorites?"

"One or two, but I was too chicken to try them all," Kelly admitted with a laugh.

Jennifer made a noise as she pulled out a pumpkin-orange yarn. "Don't remind me. She tempted me with one of her favorites, and I swear I couldn't feel my lips for a week."

"That'll teach you to eat first and ask questions later," Lisa teased. A lacy bluish-gray creation was forming on her needles.

"What are you making?" Kelly pointed toward the soft pile of yarn on Lisa's lap.

"One of those shawls I saw in a knitting magazine. It's the same one Mimi has hanging in the yarn room."

Kelly turned and surveyed the renovated farmhouse's former dining room, now filled floor-to-ceiling with colorful yarns and fibers of every description. She spotted the lacy shawl draped along the wall, six inches of fringe edging the entire length. It was even prettier finished. Kelly recognized the siren song of temptation again and glanced at the rosy silk and cotton circlet in her lap. It stared back accusingly.

"Kelly, you're back!" Mimi said in a delighted voice as she hurried into the room, notebook in hand. "How was the trip?"

"Wonderful, of course," Jennifer piped up. "She was telling us about the food, and we were gaining weight listening. Except for the skinny Scandanavian, of course." Jennifer wrinkled her nose at Lisa, who was shoving her knitting into its bag as she pushed back her chair.

"Gotta run," Lisa said, skirting the table. "Clients at five o'clock. Don't forget we have ball practice at seven tonight, Kelly."

Kelly smacked her forehead. "Ooooo, thanks for the reminder. Forgot to check my daytimer. I've been glued to the computer all day."

"I'll bet Carl was happy to see you," Mimi said as she straightened a yarn bin.

Remembering her dog's excited barks and welcoming howl, Kelly had to laugh. "Oh, yeah. I got lots of Rottweiler kisses. Big, wet, and slurpy. Was he good while I was gone?"

Mimi gave a dismissing wave. "He was fine. A perfect gentleman."

That didn't sound like Carl. "You didn't go to another

cottage by mistake, did you, Mimi? We're talking about Carl, remember?"

"Yes, we're talking about Carl. He was waiting patiently for me in the kitchen when I came each morning," Mimi said before she headed into an adjoining room.

"Well, I'm impressed. I'll have to give him an extra doggie treat for being a good boy," Kelly said, picking up the neglected circlet of yarn. Okay, where did she leave off? she thought, as she examined the stitches.

Jennifer began to cast loopy pumpkin-colored stitches onto a large needle. "What does Steve get? He's being a really good boy, too."

Kelly stopped in the midst of counting between stitch markers. What? She must have missed something in Jennifer's last comment. "Steve? What does he have to do with doggie treats?"

"You mentioned Carl would get an extra doggie treat because he's been a good boy while you were gone," Jennifer commented as she scrutinized the orange yarn. "So, I wondered what Steve would get. He's been a very good boy for a very long time. Months, actually."

Watching Jennifer's intense concentration on the yarn, Kelly had to hand it to her. Jennifer was smooth. But Kelly was way ahead of her. She knew where this conversation was headed, and Kelly wasn't about to go there.

"I agree. Steve's a really good guy," she said nonchalantly.

"Great guy, actually," Jennifer added.

"Yes, a great guy."

"Good-looking, smart, great personality, runs his own business, good sense of humor, great athlete just like you." Jennifer rattled off the litany in time with her stitches.

Kelly tried to hide her smile. "All true."

"And talk about being a perfect gentleman," Jennifer continued. "Steve has Carl beat. I mean, he may not be waiting in your kitchen every morning, but he might as well be. All you have to do is crook your finger, and Steve's right there. Waiting *patiently*, I might add."

"A slight exaggeration, don't you think?"

"*No?*" Jennifer turned to her with an astonished gaze. Kelly didn't think Jennifer could look that innocent. "Steve handled the golfers when Carl chased golf balls, then he went with you to question Curt Stackhouse when you were poking around after your aunt's death, then he came up to Wyoming with you to help with all that cattle and ranch stuff. Every time you need someone to help, Steve's there. Heck, when you went charging off to Stackhouse's ranch all by yourself last spring, it was Steve who rushed to the rescue."

"Hey, I didn't *need* rescuing," Kelly retorted. "I didn't ask him to come out. You guys did."

Jennifer turned back to her stitches. "You're missing my point."

"Which is?" Kelly was feeling decidedly prickly now.

"Steve is sending some very strong signals that he's seriously interested in you, and you just ignore him."

"I don't ignore him. Steve's one of my friends just like you guys. He knows that."

"I can't believe you're missing this, Kelly. It's obvious to all of us that Steve would like to be more than 'just another friend.' How come you can't see it?" Jennifer asked as she methodically added another pumpkin orange row.

Kelly bit her tongue to keep from blurting her first response. Of course, she'd noticed Steve's attention. And his interest. But she'd be darned if she admitted it now.

"I mean, the least you could do is go out for pizza with the guy once in a while. Heck, you could always take Carl along, so Steve wouldn't get any ideas."

Kelly had to laugh at that. "I'll think about it," she replied, deliberately not admitting that she and Steve had already had several pizza dates as well as three really enjoyable evenings at a favorite jazz cafe in Old Town. No way would she admit to that. Not yet, anyway. So far, no one knew she and Steve had ever gone out. Except Carl, of course. Carl could keep a secret.

She wasn't exactly sure why she didn't want to tell her friends. Kelly had an idea, but she didn't want to examine that too closely, either. So, all of those bedeviling thoughts and ideas went into the I'll-think-about-it-tomorrow drawer in her mind. Kelly had too much on her plate every day to spend time on distracting thoughts like that.

"I suggest you do more than think. A guy like Steve won't be waiting around forever," Jennifer tweaked again.

"You can stop now."

"Okay, okay," Jennifer acquiesced with a sigh. "I'll change subjects. What are you hearing from your boss lately? Is he still making noises about your working away from the office so long?"

Kelly exhaled a long breath. "Unfortunately, yes. I talked to him last week and tried to explain why Aunt Helen's estate settlement is taking so long, but I got the distinct feeling he thought I was exaggerating. That's what I sensed, anyway. He gets this tone in his voice when he wants to show his displeasure." She made a face.

"Sounds like a really fun guy to work for."

"Ohhhhh, yeah."

"Did you tell him Helen's estate is not just your simple everyday settlement? I mean, your cousin Martha's property in Wyoming is mixed in with all of Helen's property as well. Heck, it confuses me just to hear you talk about it."

Kelly nodded. "I did my best, but it's kind of hard to explain all that over the phone. I may have to take another trip out there. Talk to him in person."

"Sounds like a good idea. And while you're there, why don't you tell him you quit," Jennifer advised.

"I can't, Jen," Kelly said, fingers getting their rhythm back with the circular knitting. "I need that salary every month. I wouldn't have a prayer of paying that whopping mortgage Helen put on the cottage before she died."

"Haven't you done some consulting, though? I thought you were helping Debbie Claymore back in July."

Other memories flooded back. It was hard to believe so much had happened since she'd come here last April. "Yes, I did and was paid handsomely for it by the estate lawyer, too."

"Well, there you go."

"But consulting is off-and-on, Jen. I can't depend on it to pay my bills. I need regular income. You know what I'm talking about."

Jennifer sent her an ironic smile. "Actually, I don't. There's no such thing as 'regular' income in real estate. Sometimes it's feast, other times it's famine. Thank goodness I work here at Pete's. That's about as regular as I get." She gestured to the cafe at the rear of the knitting shop.

"I rest my case."

Jennifer checked her watch. "Speaking of working, I'd better run over to the real estate office and check some listings for tomorrow."

"Hi, there," Megan called out as she rushed into the room and collapsed into a chair beside Jennifer. "Boy, I'm beat. Allison and I have been working like maniacs all day. She wasn't kidding when she said her apartment was a mess." She wrinkled her nose.

"Bad, huh?" Kelly said.

"Well, not bad *dirty*, just bad *cluttered*, if you know what I mean."

"Careful. You're describing my place," Jennifer said as she rose from her chair and headed for the door. "Hey, Megan, when you're at practice tonight, make sure you work with Kelly, okay? She's really dropping the ball." She shot a wicked grin Kelly's way, which Kelly studiously ignored.

"Huh?" Megan stared blankly after their departing friend. "What was that about?"

"Ignore her. She's being annoying. We've got practice at seven. Will you make it, or are you going back to Allison's?"

"I'll be there." Megan leaned back. "We were able to clean the entire apartment and pack up almost everything. Allison said she'll handle the rest later tonight. She has to go to a university awards dinner for the Fine Arts program. So I guess it'll be another long night for her."

"I'll bet she's excited," Kelly said.

"That's an understatement," Megan replied with a laugh. "I had to restrict her coffee and sugar intake this afternoon, she was getting so hyper. We'd run out of boxes, and Allison just panicked. I grabbed several bags from the trunk of my car and loaded them up, then I put them all back in my car."

"Are you going to store them for her?"

Megan nodded. "Just until she gets settled. She said there's no hurry because it was all odds and ends. We'd already packed up her most important stuff, except her design portfolios. She was going to carry them with her."

"I can imagine. Those portfolios are—"

"Oh, I almost forgot," Megan interrupted, sitting up straight. "I'd told Allison I'd take her to the airport, but one of those idiot lights flashed on my dashboard today, so I have to take my car to the dealer tonight. Would you be able to drive Allison tomorrow, Kelly? I know it's a lot to ask when you're catching up with your accounts and all."

Kelly ran through her mental daytimer. "Sure, I'll be glad to. Is it a morning flight?"

Megan nodded. "Eleven thirty. I think I'll come along, too. That way we can treat her to breakfast first then send her off to the Big City with some loud cheers."

"Sounds good," Kelly said, smiling at Megan's enthusiasm. She'd noticed that Allison's encouragement seemed to be working. Megan had already sent one of her knitting designs to a national magazine.

"Oh-my-gosh, I've got to run to the dealer before it closes," Megan said as she sprang from her chair. "Listen, tell Lisa I may be a little bit late tonight, but I will be there."

Kelly tucked the circlet of yarn back into her bag and rose to go. Her earlier vision of a quiet evening watching the sun slip behind the Rockies with Carl's head on her knee had disappeared with Lisa's reminder of practice. "I'm right behind you," she said, following Megan out of the shop. "See you later."

Actually, the thought of practice had reawakened Kelly's softball instincts. Watching sunsets could wait for another day, her muscles commanded. What she needed tonight was exercise—running the bases and chasing down balls. Who knows? Since Megan wouldn't be there for a while, she might actually hit a homer to an empty right field.

Kelly tugged at the brim of her USS *Kitty Hawk* cap, shifted her stance in the batter's box, and waited for Lisa's next pitch. If she was lucky, it would be low and to the right. Kelly'd been studying Lisa's pitching habits since she started playing with the team last spring. Every pitcher had habits. Little things that tipped you to the next pitch, if you paid attention—and Kelly always paid attention.

Lisa wound up and let fly, her long armed motion sending the ball exactly where Kelly hoped. She connected with a satisfying crack, and the reverberation of ball meeting bat shot through her forearms with an electric charge. Kelly was already off the base, bat dropping from her hand, when she spotted the ball sail high out into an empty and Megan-free right field. *Sweet.*

Three

Megan balanced her coffee and pointed across the street. "That's Allison's building on the right."

Kelly checked traffic and made a swift U-turn on the nearly empty street, bringing her car flush up to the curb in front of Allison's apartment building.

The red-brick, three-story building was one of several that spread around the corner and down the street of this older neighborhood nestled close to the foothills. Older buildings and cheaper rents attracted college students and struggling families alike. Kelly glanced at the chainlink-encircled playground and noticed a bedraggled and broken tire swing dangling from its playground chain. The only children Kelly spotted were a few toddlers on the slide with young women keeping watch, be they mothers or caregivers.

A long-ago memory flashed briefly before her eyes. Her dad fixing her roller blades one sunny Indiana Saturday morning. He'd used gray duct tape to hold the wheels in place so she could catch up to her neighborhood friends, the "pack" he called them. Kelly smiled at the memory. Her dad used duct tape to fix everything. Once again, she felt the bittersweet tug of loss.

Megan left her coffee in the cup holder and pushed open the car door. "I'll run up and get Allison. Her cell phone died yesterday, and she gave it to me to buy new batteries." Megan patted her jacket pocket. "Problem is, I forgot all about it when my car light went on. I didn't remember until this morning. I feel terrible that I didn't get it back to her right away like I promised."

"Don't worry. Allison was probably glad not to have any interruptions while she finished. I'll bet you did her a favor," Kelly reassured.

Megan gave a rueful nod and sprinted up the concrete apartment steps. Kelly shifted her gaze to the nearby foothills. Nestled this close, the houses on the far west side of town didn't have the same views of the Rockies looming behind the ridges that the eastern edge of the city provided. Spectacular views, usually accompanied by higher price tags.

Listening to Jennifer talk about the rise in real estate values in her hometown, Kelly knew sticker shock drove many families of modest means to head for the western edge. But Kelly actually liked these views. The houses were tucked protectively into the foothills, whose colors changed as the sun tracked across the sky. Peach and rose at dawn, gray-green in the glare of midday, purple at sunset, disappearing into deep blue-black at moonrise.

Kelly spotted the early October hint of autumn on the ridges, a subtle glimpse of an orange bush or a swath of golden aspens. Fall. She loved the colors, the smell of falling leaves, the early morning chill in the air, the hint of winter to come. Maybe she'd take Lisa up on her offer to go camping one weekend. She could handle a moderate hike. Of course, Lisa's idea of moderate might not . . .

"*Kelly!* Kelly, come up here, quick!" Megan's shrill voice cried out, startling Kelly from her autumnal musing.

She leaned down to peer through the open passenger window, but didn't see Megan at the front door. Glancing up, Kelly spotted her at an open second-floor window. "What's the matter?" she called.

Instead of answering, Megan beckoned frantically. Kelly shut off the engine, pocketed the keys, and raced inside the building. Taking the steps two at a time, she grabbed the banister and hurried up the stairs leading to the second floor. A white-faced Megan was waiting for her at the apartment door.

"What's the matter?" Kelly demanded as she strode into the nearly empty living room. "Where's Allison?"

She quickly scanned the room and saw nothing unusual, except for the absence of Allison. Two scuffed black suitcases sat in the far corner next to three packing boxes. There was another half-filled packing box sitting open. Several of Allison's portfolio drawings were spread out on the floor next to the leather carrying case. The rest of the room was empty except for two metal folding chairs and a battered metal office desk and a rolled-up sleeping bag.

"She's . . . she's . . . oh, God, Kelly," Megan said in a choked voice, wringing her hands. Kelly had never seen Megan like this before.

"Megan, where's Allison?" she asked again.

Instead of answering, Megan pointed a shaking finger toward the desk. That's when Kelly got a cold feeling. Part of her didn't want to see what was on the other side of the desk. The other part of her couldn't stop herself. She had to see what had terrified Megan.

Kelly cautiously approached the desk. That's when she saw the legs. Black pants, brown sandals. Kelly recognized those sandals. Allison had worn them on the drive home from Santa Fe. Kelly edged around the desk and felt the visceral punch of recognition hit her in the gut.

Allison lay on the floor, head turned to the side, blonde hair spread out around her in a halo, blue eyes staring wide and lifeless. A multi-colored wool shawl lay across her body. Kelly recognized the beautiful piece as one of Allison's recent weavings. Was she wearing it when she fell, Kelly wondered?

"She's . . . she's dead," Megan whispered behind her. "I checked her throat for a pulse. And there isn't any." Her voice broke off.

Kelly quickly surveyed the area around Allison, looking for something, anything that might explain this. Did she fall and hit her head on the desk? There was no trace of blood on the floor. No implement of any kind lay around Allison's body, either. Only a coffeehouse paper cup with corrugated sleeve, dribbling what was left of its contents, lay beside her empty hand.

"Oh, God, I'm gonna be sick," Megan croaked.

Kelly quickly turned and placed her hands on Megan's shoulders. "Megan, go sit down right now and put your head between your knees," she ordered. "I need you to pull yourself together."

Megan did as she was told and collapsed into a nearby metal chair, her head dropping between her knees. Meanwhile, Kelly drew closer to Allison's body, sank to the floor, and carefully placed two fingers on Allison's throat. Maybe Megan missed the pulse. Kelly held her fingers there for nearly five minutes, hoping to feel a faint flutter. Nothing.

The cold sensation that Kelly had experienced months ago when she'd been the one to walk in on a similar scene ran through her. She held her crouching position and scrutinized her dead friend, forcing away the revulsion.

There was no visible mark on Allison's face, and no mark on her forehead either. Could she possibly have fallen and struck her head so severely the blow would kill her? Kelly's logic rebelled at that thought. Besides, she was lying approximately three feet away, facing the desk. If she'd hit her head, wouldn't she have fallen closer?

Suddenly, the image of her friend, Burt, from the shop popped into her head. Former police investigator Burt would probably smile at her amateur analysis. Still, Kelly felt compelled to observe everything she could, remembering how important small details were in the previous investigation.

She gingerly lifted the woolen shawl covering Allison's torso, half-expecting it to be hiding a bloody wound which would explain how a young, talented, and vibrantly alive Allison could be lying here dead. Kelly held up the shawl, intently surveying Allison's white cotton shirt. There was no trace of any stain, bloody or otherwise. She gently lowered the shawl back to its original position.

Rising from her crouch, Kelly slowly circled the body at her feet, scanning the bare wood floor surrounding her. There was nothing on the floor except Allison and the cup of spilled coffee. She stared at the back of Allison's head and saw no trace of blood peeking through the pale gold curls.

What in heaven's name caused this! Kelly's mind screamed. Allison was embarking on the first day of her new career, a career for which she'd sacrificed and worked long and hard. How could this happen? Did she have a heart condition or some other hidden health problem?

"Megan, did Allison ever mention a health problem?" Kelly asked.

Megan slowly raised her head, face still pale. "I . . . I don't think so," she said. "Do you think that's what happened?"

"Well, something awful happened," Kelly said, frowning at the floor. "Either she had a life-threatening health problem, or she fell and hit her head on the desk and died. I mean, there's nothing here, no blood, no weapon to indicate she killed herself—"

That last comment seemed to rouse Megan. Color returned to her face in a flush. "Kill herself?" she retorted. "Allison wouldn't do that, Kelly! You know her. I mean, she had everything to live for." Megan's hand jerked out expressively.

"I know that, but there has to be some explanation for this," Kelly answered, then looked at her friend solemnly. "Listen, Megan, I'm going to call the police now, but first I want you to take a careful look around and see if you notice anything different in the apartment. You were here with Allison until late in the afternoon. Anything you notice could help the police. I learned that much from Burt."

Megan stared in the direction of Allison's body. "I don't think I can look at her again, Kelly. I swear, I can't."

"That's okay. Don't look at Allison," Kelly instructed as she pulled her cell phone from her jeans pocket. "Just take a good hard look at everything else. Floor, desk, boxes." She gestured to the nearly empty room. "Don't touch anything. Just look around. It's important, Megan."

"Okay," Megan acquiesced and rose shakily from the chair. Taking a deep breath, she turned her back to the body and started walking through the apartment.

Kelly thumbed through her cell phone's directory until she found a name from the past. Lieutenant Morrison of the Fort Connor police department, the taciturn detective in charge of her Aunt Helen's murder investigation. She hesitated before she punched in the number, wondering if Morrison had ever forgiven her for solving her aunt's murder and capturing the real killer.

Kelly watched Megan tour the apartment as an official sounding voice came on the phone. She was relieved it wasn't Lieutenant Morrison, but another officer. Kelly carefully explained where they were located and how they had arrived and found their friend dead. The young officer's voice crept up the scale in apparent excitement as he took the information and assured Kelly that investigators would be there shortly, advising her to stay put. Kelly promised she and Megan would be waiting.

"Nothing's missing, Kelly," Megan announced. "Only the portfolio drawings are out of the carrying case, that's all. The suitcases are packed, and there are the boxes she wanted me to ship to her once she called with the address. She was packing the last one."

"What about the desk?" Kelly gestured toward the cluttered desk. "It looks like she hadn't finished going through things here."

Megan stared at the desk as Kelly shoved the phone back into her pocket and checked her watch. These past few months had given her a taste of how long police investigations and questioning could take. Last summer, she and Jennifer had been kept in nearby Bellevue Canyon for hours as police combed through a murdered friend's home. Of course, interviewing the vanload of visiting knitters had been the real slowdown, she remembered with a grim smile.

"The beads," Megan spoke up in a quiet voice. "The hand-carved beads Allison bought in Santa Fe. They're gone." She pointed toward the desk. "They were right there on the desk yesterday, I remember. Allison spread them out, showing me some of the design ideas she wanted to use with them."

Kelly stared at the desk. There were various papers scattered about and a purse she assumed was Allison's. There was also a checkbook and pen, but no beads. "Are you sure, Megan?"

Megan nodded. "Positive. She was trying to explain this design. She wanted jagged lines running through the fabric, or something like that."

"Do you have a pen with you?"

"I think so," Megan said, searching her back pocket and drawing out a ballpoint.

"Good, now use that and carefully lift up the papers on the desk and check to see if the beads are hiding underneath. You've got me curious."

Megan leaned over the desk, clearly hesitant to disturb anything, and slowly slid the ballpoint beneath the closest pile of papers. No beads were visible. She lifted the other papers scattered across the desk. Again, no beads. "They're not here, Kelly."

"Maybe she packed them already," Kelly mused out loud.

Suddenly the sharp sound of a siren in the distance cut through the air. Megan jerked back from the desk with a gasp, face draining of color once again.

Kelly reached over and took the pen from Megan's shaking hand before she dropped it. "Take it easy, Megan," she reassured her friend, placing a hand on Megan's shoulder. "It'll be okay. The police won't bite. Just keep picturing friendly old Burt."

The cold cement steps outside Allison's apartment were getting harder and harder the longer Kelly sat there. She and Megan had been sitting on the steps ever since they were first questioned by the responding officers. The two uniformed policemen had been polite but firm. Kelly and Megan were to remain there until the criminal investigation unit had finished examining Allison's apartment. Lieutenant Morrison, head of the investigation, would want to talk with them.

Oh, joy, Kelly thought. That should be fun. She remembered Morrison's brusque manner after she'd questioned his conclusions about her aunt's death. Morrison could be intimidating. She could handle Morrison, but he was bound to scare the daylights out of Megan.

Kelly glanced at her friend, who was hunched in a semi-crouch on the concrete. Her face still pale, eyes darting about, watching every movement as investigators ran up the steps beside them. In and out of the apartment—some carried cameras, others held small cases or briefcases. All of them running up the concrete steps with grim determination. Megan stared wide-eyed at each group.

Reaching over to her friend, Kelly patted her arm. "Don't worry, Megan. This will all be over in a little while. That lieutenant will take our statement again and ask us some more questions, then we can leave."

Megan chewed her lip. "I hope so. This is all so awful."

Kelly was about to agree when she watched what little color that had returned to Megan's face drain away in an instant as she stared past Kelly's shoulder.

"Oh, God—" Megan whispered.

Jerking around, Kelly saw two medical personnel maneuver their way through the apartment building doorway, carrying a stretcher. Allison. Covered now with an institutional shroud instead of her colorful woven shawl, her body was carefully carried down the steps. Kelly and Megan leaped to their feet to clear the way for their friend as she was taken to the ambulance. They both continued standing until the ambulance had closed its doors and pulled away from the curb.

That's when Kelly heard a distinctive gruff voice behind her. "Ms. Flynn, I understand you and your friend were the ones to discover the victim, correct?" Morrison asked.

Megan jumped around with a squeal, clearly startled by the detective's sudden appearance. Kelly met Morrison's stern gaze and answered. "Yes, Lieutenant. Megan went into the apartment first while I waited in the car out front." She pointed to her parked car. "We were planning to take

Allison to the airport and send her off to New York. Then Megan yelled to me from the apartment window and told me to come up."

Morrison had listened attentively to Kelly's repetition of what she'd previously told the officers. Then, he turned to Megan. "Ms. Schmidt, you previously told officers that the door was unlocked when you arrived, and you entered after knocking without hearing an answer. Was Ms. Dubois in the habit of leaving her apartment door unlocked?"

Megan stared as if transfixed by Morrison's gaze for a few seconds, then stammered, "I-I-I don't know, Lieutenant. I've rarely been over here before today."

Morrison scribbled in his notebook, and Kelly tried to catch Megan's eye to give her a reassuring smile. But Megan was still staring, clearly ensnared in Morrison's authoritative spell.

"When Ms. Dubois didn't respond to your calling her name, that's when you found her on the floor?" he continued in a low voice.

"Y-yes, yessir!" Megan squeaked, then cleared her throat. "I started walking around the apartment, calling out, and I-I saw her—on the floor. It was horrible!"

"Yes, I imagine it was," Morrison said in a tone that could pass for reassuring. Kelly could barely believe her ears.

"Tell me, did you notice anything that had been disturbed or out of place in your absence? I understand you were here with Ms. Dubois helping her pack until nearly five yesterday afternoon."

Megan cleared her throat, and Kelly noticed she looked slightly calmer. "Her portfolio drawings were out of the case and on the floor. And some hand-carved beads that Allison bought on the way home from Santa Fe are missing. She had them on the desk yesterday, and they're gone now."

Morrison bent over his notebook. "You said you were

acquainted with Ms. Dubois from the knitting shop that you both frequented. Did you ever see her with any of her other friends? From the university or elsewhere?"

"No, sir," Megan said, shaking her head. "Allison was involved in lots of artist groups all over town, not just the university. But I—" She gestured to Kelly. "I mean, Kelly and I only knew her from the knitting shop."

"But you knew each other well enough to take a trip to Santa Fe over the weekend, right?" Morrison's eyebrows furrowed together in a look Kelly remembered. "That's a long drive. Did she talk about having problems with anyone? A boyfriend, perhaps?"

Tired of being completely ignored, Kelly jumped in. "She did mention her boyfriend once or twice, Lieutenant. But she said she'd broken up with him."

Morrison's bushy eyebrows arched at Kelly's comment, but he studiously wrote it down.

"Ohhhhh, yes!" Megan spoke up in an excited voice. "I remember now! She did break up with him. His name's Ray, and he called yesterday while we were packing." Megan's wide blue eyes got even wider if that were possible, and her voice dropped to a dramatic whisper. "And Allison was really upset, too. He was yelling at her over the phone. I could hear it! She finally hung up on him and turned off her phone."

"Do either of you know this Ray's last name?"

Kelly and Megan both shook their heads.

Morrison scribbled then checked his watch. "Well, thank you ladies," he said as he slipped the notebook into his coat pocket. "You've been very helpful. If we have any further questions, we'll be in touch. We'll also be contacting the family once we locate them."

"Please, Lieutenant, could you tell us when you've found the family?" Megan asked. "I'd like to express my condolences to them personally. I think Allison said they live in southwestern Colorado, near Durango."

"I'll be sure to let you know, Ms. Schmidt," Morrison said in a kinder voice.

Realizing that Morrison was clearly leaving her out of the loop, Kelly once again spoke up. "We'd also appreciate knowing if there's to be a service of any kind. Allison had a lot of friends who would like to pay their respects."

"Certainly," he said with a nod, then cocked his head as if remembering something. "Oh, yes, one last thing. Do you know if Ms. Dubois was depressed or distressed about anything in her life?"

Megan spoke up before Kelly could open her mouth. "Good heavens, no! She was just starting out on a new life, a new career that she'd been working for. She was so excited she could barely sit still."

Morrison didn't reply, simply nodded. "Perhaps this new life had become overwhelming for her," he suggested. "Perhaps her boyfriend didn't want her to leave. Did she ever voice any conflicting thoughts about this new life?"

"Absolutely not!" Megan retorted with an emphatic nod. "This was the chance she'd been working and waiting for."

Kelly sensed where Morrison was going with this and was amused by how forcefully Megan was refuting the detective's theories. "What are you suggesting, Lieutenant?" Kelly said, cutting to the chase.

Morrison turned his stern gaze to hers. "I'm merely offering the possibility that this death may be the result of a suicide."

"Impossible," Megan declared vehemently, crossing her arms as if squaring off with the detective. "We're her friends. We would know."

Morrison gave Megan a weary smile. "Sometimes a person's friends are the last to know," he said as he turned to walk away. "We'll be in touch."

Four

Kelly concentrated on the deep rose circlet of yarn, stitches rhythmically adding row after row to the sweater-in-the-round. She'd been sitting at the shop's library table for over two hours this morning. Just like yesterday, she'd found herself unable to start on her usual morning routine at the computer. She'd work on client accounts later. Right now, Kelly wanted to be surrounded by the warmth of the shop, where she could talk to friends and people she'd grown to care about these last six months. She needed to be here.

It had been two days since Allison's death. Two days of answering horrified questions from her knitting friends and others at the shop who knew Allison. Everyone was shocked. Allison was so full of life, so creative, so talented, so young. How could she be dead? She was only twenty-seven. Two years younger than Kelly. Much too young to die.

Kelly took a deep drink of the dark, rich coffee that was the cafe's specialty. Strong coffee was a daily essential to Kelly, like her morning run along the river trail that meandered through the normally quiet college town. She doubted she could get through all those corporate accounts without Eduardo's potent brew.

She glanced about the empty room that had once been her Uncle Jim's and Aunt Helen's farmhouse living room. The library table dominated the room now, and open bins and wooden crates were stacked everywhere, crammed with yarns. Frothy mohairs draped along the wall, intricate weavings hung over the fireplace, and colorful patterned socks moved in the breeze from the open window as if they were dancing.

Bookshelves bulged with knitting books and magazines on every fiber topic imaginable. Kelly'd been surprised there were so many fiber artists. Knitters, spinners, weavers, quilters, fabric designers, wearable artists, and needleworkers of every persuasion. How did people do all those intricate projects, she wondered, after paging through some of the magazines.

"Hey, there," Megan said in a subdued voice as she approached the table. Collapsing into the chair across from Kelly, she withdrew a navy blue yarn and needles from her knitting bag.

"How're you doing?" Kelly asked her friend, noticing that Megan lacked her usual spark. She seemed drained of energy ever since Allison's death. She'd even abandoned her usual bright yarns. Somehow Kelly couldn't picture lively, energetic Megan wearing a subdued, dark institutional blue.

Megan sighed. "Okay, I guess."

"Have you heard from Allison's parents yet?" Kelly asked, aware that Lieutenant Morrison had given only Megan's name to Allison's mother and father when they arrived yesterday.

"I called over to the police this morning to see if Allison's parents had arranged a funeral or something, and the detective said her parents were taking her back home to Durango for a private family burial. They're not having anything here at all."

Kelly watched Megan try to hold her emotions in check, but tears pressed on her voice. "Maybe that's for the best, Megan," she suggested softly.

"But what about her friends?" Megan protested, her eyes glistening. "We wanted to say goodbye." Her fingers seemed to stumble with the drab blue yarn, as if Megan's nimbleness had deserted her.

"I know, Megan," Kelly tried to soothe. "But maybe that was simply too much for her parents. They're devastated, no doubt. And heartsick."

Megan glanced down at her needles, slowly moving through the knit stitch. "Maybe you're right. I confess, I've only been thinking about how much we'll miss Allison."

The tinkling sound of the shop's doorbell sounded over the usual morning hubbub of customers searching for yarns and the helpful shop staff bustling about to find what they needed. Kelly sat without speaking, letting the quiet meditative feeling settle over her. She'd become addicted to the peaceful sensation that knitting brought with it. Her thoughts became more ordered. New ideas popped into her mind. As her fingers worked the familiar motions with the colorful yarn, Kelly found herself solving problems that had eluded her before. Strange. Even the knottiest problems seemed to untangle all by themselves as she knit. While she added row upon colorful row, solutions magically appeared. Now she understood fully what Mimi meant whenever she said she'd "knit on it."

"Excuse us," a woman's voice said from the adjoining room. "But is one of you Megan Schmidt?"

Kelly swiftly turned to see a middle-aged couple standing hesitantly in the archway. There was something familiar about the woman's face, even though Kelly saw dark shadows beneath her eyes. The balding man at her side stared at the floor.

"Yes, I'm Megan Schmidt," Megan spoke up, clearly surprised that someone was looking for her at the shop. "How can I help you?"

The woman slowly approached the table, both hands tightly clutching a brown purse. "Lieutenant Morrison at the police department said we might find you here. We're . . . we're Allison's parents."

Both Kelly and Megan came to their feet at that. Being closer to the couple, Kelly extended her hand first. "Mr. and Mrs. Dubois, I'm Kelly Flynn, and I was a friend of Allison's. I cannot tell you how sorry I am for your loss."

Mrs. Dubois clutched at the breast of her beige knit dress and glanced away. "Thank you."

Megan scurried around the table, hands reaching out. "Mr. and Mrs. Dubois, I am so, so sorry. We're all just heartbroken to lose Allison." She grasped Mrs. Dubois's hand with hers, her pale face radiating concern.

Mrs. Dubois's mouth tightened and her shadowed eyes glistened. "Thank you," she whispered. "Lieutenant Morrison said you were the one to find Allison. I'm so glad it was a friend and not some stranger." She fumbled in her purse and withdrew a handful of tissues. "It's just so tragic. What a loss . . ."

Megan nodded, seemingly unable to put her grief into words, so Kelly spoke up. "I understand you're taking Allison back to Durango for a family service. Is there an address where we can send flowers?"

Mr. Dubois stepped forward then and took his wife's elbow. Kelly looked into a stern face. Lines drooped down from his mouth indicating a lifetime of frowning. "Flowers won't be necessary. We want to keep this quiet. Allison will be put to rest in private." Jerking his wife's arm, he said in a gruff voice, "Come along, Mary. We've got a long drive ahead of us."

Kelly held her tongue. Mr. Dubois was clearly uncomfortable in their presence.

Megan, however, took in her breath in an audible gasp. "Oh, but you must let us send something. Flowers, or a gift to charity. Something in Allison's name."

Mrs. Dubois reached out to pat Megan's arm. "That's sweet of you, dear. But under the circumstances, it would—"

"Mary, that's enough!" Mr. Dubois snapped.

Mrs. Dubois closed her eyes and took a deep breath. "These are her friends, Fred. They cared about Allison."

Fred Dubois spun on his heel. "I'll be in the car," he barked and stalked from the shop.

Kelly watched Mary Dubois take another deep breath as if steadying herself. Curious at her last comment, Kelly ventured, "What circumstances are you talking about, Mrs. Dubois?"

"Lieutenant Morrison told us that the medical examiner had found a lethal dose of barbiturates in Allison's body and in the coffee she was drinking." Her eyes sought the floor as her voice dropped. "They think Allison may have committed suicide with sleeping pills."

Megan sucked in her breath, both hands flying to her breast. "No! That can't be true! Allison wouldn't . . . she couldn't . . ." The rest of Megan's protest died on her lips.

Mary Dubois looked up again, and Kelly flinched inside at the raw grief on her face. She instinctively reached out and patted Mary Dubois on the shoulder. "I'm so sorry. It's a shock to hear that, Mrs. Dubois. Allison had everything to live for."

That comment seemed more than Mary Dubois could bear, and her face betrayed her pain. She squeezed Kelly's hand as she turned away. "Yes, she did. Thank you, girls, for . . . for being her friends," she said before she ran to the door and out of the shop.

Kelly stared after her, her heart aching for the mother's grief she'd just witnessed.

"I can't believe that, Kelly," Megan whispered, shaking her head as she stared blankly into the adjoining yarn room. Somehow the colorful yarns looked muted now. "There's no way Allison would kill herself."

"I don't understand it, either, Megan," Kelly admitted with a sigh. "But the evidence speaks clearly that she died of barbiturate poisoning. Either it was accidental or deliberate."

Megan pursed her mouth in a stubborn expression that Kelly recognized. "No. It couldn't be deliberate. Maybe she drank a lot at that awards banquet and got confused with the pills. She told me she always took sleeping pills when she needed to crash. She *must* have been confused. It couldn't be deliberate."

Kelly held her tongue. She knew that right now Megan couldn't accept any other possibility for Allison's sudden death. Megan needed time to process everything they'd learned. In fact, Kelly felt a part of her own mind rebelling at the thought that Allison would take her life. They both needed time to let the awful events settle.

She placed her hand on Megan's shoulder. "Do you want to go into Pete's for some coffee? We can see if Mimi can join us," Kelly suggested. They could both use some of Mimi's maternal nurturing.

Megan shook her head. "Not right now, Kelly. I need some time alone. I need to think. Maybe I'll take a walk."

"That sounds like a good idea. Why don't you head out on the river trail where I run every morning? There's an entrance on this side of the golf course." She pointed toward the far end of the shop.

"Maybe I will," Megan said as she scooped her knitting back into the bag. "We'll do that coffee another time."

"It's a deal. Say hello to Carl when you pass by, okay? His feelings get hurt when people ignore him," she joked.

That brought a small smile to Megan's face, which was Kelly's intention. "Will do. See you later, Kelly," she said as she headed for the door.

Kelly stood alone for a moment, letting the familiar sounds of the busy knitting shop wrap around her like a comfortable sweater. Then, she grabbed her empty mug and headed for the cafe. With or without friends, it was coffee time.

Rounding the corner that lead from the shop into the cafe, Kelly spied the cafe's owner, Pete, standing near the kitchen talking with two men. Both men wore red shirts with DUGAN CONSTRUCTION printed in white letters.

"Hey, Pete. Are you remodeling or something?" Kelly said as she leaned over the counter and dangled her empty mug. After six months, Pete's staff were well used to her coffee routine.

Pete turned his friendly grin her way. "We're adding on, Kelly. These guys are going to enclose the porch and build a new one so we can add more seating."

"Whoa, that's great to hear, Pete," she said, remembering her small business clients from years past. Most went belly-up within five years. "That means business is good."

"It's been really good, Kelly," Pete said with a nod. "In fact, I'm thinking of adding a dinner menu. What do you think about that?"

Kelly's accounting lobe fairly vibrated with pleasure. Pete's business must really be doing well. She grinned. "That's fantastic. I'm so happy for you. Pete's Porch is definitely the success story accountants love to hear."

"Here you go, Kelly," the young waitress said, handing over the mug.

Kelly inhaled the aroma and sighed. "Thanks, Sara. You guys keep me going."

Pete turned to the builders and grinned. "See, we get our customers addicted to the food and coffee, and they have to keep coming back."

Kelly waved goodbye as she returned to the shop. Checking her watch, she knew she had to return to her accounts before noon, or she wouldn't keep up. As she rounded the corner, however, she nearly bumped into someone she hadn't expected.

Curt Stackhouse jumped back before they collided. "Whoa, sorry, Kelly. I guess I wasn't watching where I was going," he apologized.

Kelly stared at Curt, shocked at the difference she saw in him. Big, sturdy Curt, the epitome of the Colorado rancher had lost a lot of weight. Curt had been in good shape for a man well into his sixties. Now, he looked positively skinny. That's not all that had changed. Curt's face looked more careworn than could be explained by decades in the sun.

"Curt, how are you?" she exclaimed. "When did you get back from traveling with your son?"

"About a month ago, I guess," Curt answered, glancing to the side. "I've been staying over at my daughter's since then."

"I've wanted to call you, but Mimi said you were still out of town," Kelly said, noticing even more differences in her stalwart friend. Subtle things. Even his voice didn't have its usual firm self-assured sound.

The sudden death of Curt's wife, Ruth, from a heart attack last summer had clearly knocked Curt off his feet. After over forty years of what Kelly figured was an exceedingly happy marriage, Curt was all alone. The pain of loss was visible on his face, etched in with the windswept lines of Colorado's rangeland. She'd heard that Curt's son and daughter had taken their distraught father into their homes, hoping to ease his loss.

Curt shifted his stance and stared at the floor. "That's good of you, Kelly, but I . . . I didn't really want to see anybody for quite a while, if you know what I mean."

Kelly's heart ached for him. Curt had always looked imperturbable, as solid as the boulders that formed the Poudre Canyon. She placed her hand on his arm. "I understand, Curt. We all do. You needed to take some time to get back on your feet. I've just missed seeing you, that's all."

"That's nice of you to say, Kelly," Curt said, meeting her gaze for the first time. "I'm not sure I'm too steady on my feet, yet, but I'm better than I was."

She glimpsed a hint of Curt's old sense of humor, a wisp of it, in his last comment, and she grabbed the opening. "In time, Curt. It took me more than a year to get over my dad's death, and I still miss him. I probably always will. Little scenes keep flashing into my mind." She hoped her openness would strike a chord within her heartbroken friend.

"Yeah, I know what you mean," Curt said, glancing away once more. "Listen, Kelly, if you've got a minute, I thought I'd go over some information about that Wyoming property of yours. I'm sorry it's taken me so long to get back to it—"

"Hey, don't apologize," Kelly interrupted. "You had more important things on your mind. Besides, the estate took forever to be settled. What with everything going from Cousin Martha's husband to her, and then through Aunt Helen's estate to me. In fact, it was only yesterday when Mr. Chambers called me to say it's finally official. So you'll have plenty of time to check into things."

"Don't depend on it," he countered. "Where there's land with potential for oil and gas, things can go pretty quick. Especially since you own both the land and the mineral rights below. That's not often the case." He pointed behind her to the cafÇ's empty alcove. "Why don't we pull up a chair, and I'll give you an update."

They settled at a nearby table, and Kelly signaled the waitress to bring Curt some coffee. "Chet still appears to be happy managing the ranch, at least according to Mr. Chambers."

"Yeah, Brewster's doing real well up there. The boy's got a good head on his shoulders, and he's managing the herd according to the plan we set up back in July. We're selling off a lot of the cattle so we can reduce some of the expenses for leasing extra grazing land and hiring extra ranch hands to help Chet, especially in calving season. Things like that. Chambers and I also discovered some past-due bills that had accumulated, so we needed to increase cash flow." He gave Kelly a little smile.

"Sounds like a good plan, Curt."

"Chambers took my place and went with Brewster to the cattle auction and said they got a pretty good return, considering the market." Curt murmured his thanks to the waitress when she brought his coffee. "We've also decided to sell Cujo. He'll fetch a fair amount of cash. Plus, we've got plenty of other bulls."

"I'm sorry to be burdening you with all this Wyoming business, Curt. I know you've got a ranch of your own to manage," she said, suddenly feeling guilty for adding to Curt's problems. "I'm sure Mr. Chambers could find someone for me, if you don't want to bother with all this."

Curt sat up straighter, it seemed to Kelly, and gave a dismissing wave of his hand. She glimpsed some of the old Curt in the gesture. "Wouldn't hear of it, Kelly. I like being busy. My place runs like a Swiss watch, so I actually enjoy getting a new spread in order. Sort of a challenge, if you know what I mean."

Kelly knew exactly what he meant. Curt's voice had even regained its former self-assured timbre when he talked about the challenge of organizing her ranch. It was clear that Curt needed something to engage him completely, especially now after Ruth's passing. And, if his spread ran like a Swiss watch, then maybe what he needed was something he could tinker with. Fine-tune and adjust. Cousin Martha's property would provide Curt with many months of tinkering. And if challenge was what Curt needed to find himself again, then Kelly would be more than happy to oblige him.

"Boy, Curt, that's a relief to hear," she said, leaning back in her chair. "You know I don't have a clue how to manage a cattle ranch, let alone one that may have oil and gas on it."

"Don't forget the sheep and alpaca," Curt said with a grin.

Delighted to see the familiar spark return to his eyes, Kelly feigned memory loss. "Ohhhh, brother, almost forgot about them. See, Curt, I need you to keep track of these things. Who knows what would happen if I was in charge? I might forget to feed the animals or something."

"Boy, you have forgotten a lot since July," Curt teased. "Cattle graze, Kelly. They're not like Carl, waiting for his food dish every day."

Kelly laughed. "Maybe that's what Carl needs. A couple of weeks of cattle boot camp. Grazing off the land."

Curt relaxed visibly and leaned against his chair, balancing the coffee cup. "Another thing you've forgotten, Kelly, is that you *are* in charge. This is your spread. Chet Brewster works for you."

She wrinkled her nose. "Don't remind me. It's still a scary thought."

"Don't worry. Chet is dependable, and you've got me to help you out. And, Steve. Think of us as your consultants."

"Consultants," Kelly nodded her head. "Consultants I can handle. I'm used to them."

Curt grinned at her over his coffee. "Well, just don't handle us too tight. Men like Steve and me, we like a loose rein."

Kelly threw back her head and laughed at the image of trying to "manage" the likes of Curt and Steve. "Hey, I wouldn't dream of it. I'm throwing the reins to you. Do with it what you will, Curt. I trust you implicitly."

"Well, that's mighty kind of you to say, Kelly. Meanwhile, I expect we may be hearing from some oil and gas folks shortly. Chambers and I both made a few phone calls back in July. Let's see what happens. Right now, we're looking at a cattle spread with some sheep and alpaca thrown in. But if those folks are interested, the whole picture chsnges."

"You'll have to explain it to me. That's an entirely different world."

Curt nodded. "I have a hunch you'll pick all that up pretty quick. Meanwhile, I wanted your permission to contact the preservation groups you mentioned. We have to know exactly what sort of arrangements are available to donate a portion of land."

"You've got it, Curt," Kelly said with a nod. "If they want a paper signed, I'll do that, too."

Curt drained his cup and pushed back his chair. "That's all I have for now, so I guess I'd better be going. Got a lot of errands to run in town. Some for me and my daughter."

Kelly checked her watch, and her accounts nagged louder. Time to get to work, she thought as she reluctantly rose and accompanied Curt back to the shop.

She couldn't help noticing once again how much thinner Curt was now. No longer his robust sturdy self. His broad shoulders and chest drooped uncharacteristically.

Suddenly Kelly got an idea. Steve had mentioned going to dinner this Saturday night at their favorite cafe, Jazz Bistro. Maybe they could take Curt along. Steve wouldn't mind. Once she explained it to him, of course. Curt needed some companionship and good food. A lot of good food. Remembering how his mood had lightened over a few minutes of coffee, Kelly was convinced that she and Steve could definitely help Curt regain more of his old demeanor.

Curt paused in the foyer. "I'll stay in touch, Kelly, okay?"

"You'll do better than that, Curt," Kelly pronounced, crossing her arms over her chest authoritatively, in a pose she knew would amuse Curt no end. "You're coming to dinner with Steve and me this weekend. No excuses. Your daughter has had you all to herself. She's just going to have to learn to share." She gave an emphatic nod.

"I'll think about it, Kelly," Curt said with a grin.

"Not good enough, Curt. Steve and I will show up at your daughter's place Saturday at six and kidnap you if we have to."

That caused a familiar spark to dance in Curt's eyes once again. "You think you can handle that?" he challenged.

Kelly assessed him head to toe and gave a smug nod. "Absolutely. You're looking positively puny, Curt. We can take you, no problem," she taunted. Maybe that would spur the return of Curt's appetite.

Curt chuckled, clearly amused by her threat. "We'll see about that. Okay, Saturday at six. But I'm not wearing a tie, understand? Probably not a coat, either. So let's not go anywhere fancy." With that, Curt was out the door and gone.

Kelly returned to the library table long enough to grab her knitting bag before she headed for the door and the return to responsibility. Corporate accounts no longer were content to nag. They screamed. Kelly pushed open the shop's heavy oak door and raced down the brick steps, heading for her cottage across the driveway, a mirror image of the knitting shop.

She was already sorting through accounts in her mind when a familiar voice called out behind her. "Hey, Kelly."

Kelly spun around to see Steve Townsend approach, dressed in his normal workday clothes: jeans, denim shirt, and workboots. Exactly the same as his workcrew. "Hey, perfect timing," she said.

"Was that Curt I saw driving off?" Steve asked, gesturing toward the busy street that bordered the shop.

"Yes, and I need to run something past you," Kelly plunged in. "I wanted to ask Curt to join us for dinner this Saturday. Actually, I've already asked him. He looks awful, Steve. Positively skinny, and you know, that's not like Curt. I think he's wasting away after Ruth's death, and we can't let him do that. So, that's why I asked him to dinner. We are still going to dinner this Saturday, aren't we?"

Steve grinned, clearly unfazed by the onslaught. "It's still on my daytimer. And sure, we'll take Curt along and give him a good meal. Maybe we'd better take him someplace else, though. I may be wrong, but I don't think the bistro is Curt's speed. He'll take one look at the tapas bar and bolt."

"Yeah, you're right," Kelly admitted. "Maybe some small family place like—"

"We could always go to your place, and you could fix him a home-cooked meal," Steve teased.

Kelly sent him a withering stare, which withered when it reached Steve. "Riiiiight. Unless I can microwave it, it isn't gonna happen."

Steve laughed. "Okay, we'll pick one of those family places south of town. One that has blueberry pie, how's that?"

"Now, you're talking. Stroke of genius, Steve," Kelly congratulated

"Do you want to follow our usual routine and meet at the restaurant, or should I pick you up here? In the interest of time, that is," Steve asked with a sly smile.

Kelly debated. She'd been scrupulously careful these

last few months to make sure no one at the shop saw Steve
taking her out. Again, she wasn't entirely sure why she always insisted on their meeting at the restaurant. The only
thing she knew was that she didn't want to think about it.
Not now, anyway. She was much too busy.

"I mean, it might look a little funny if both of us drive
up to Curt's daughter's house, don't you think?"

"Okay, okay," Kelly acquiesced. "You've got a point.
Pick me up before six then."

"Here?"

Kelly exhaled an impatient breath. "Yes, Steve. Here."

"In broad daylight?"

She didn't respond to that one, simply watched Steve
laugh.

Steve glanced up into the noonday sky, sunlight filtering
through the cottonwood trees. "Sure I won't be struck by
lightning?"

"I'll strike you with one of Carl's golf balls if you don't
stop," she threatened as she turned toward her cottage.
"Gotta get on the computer now. Swamped with work. I'll
see you Saturday night." And she raced up the cottage steps
before Steve could tease her again.

Five

Carl leaped about the kitchen, dancing on his hind legs, as Kelly poured doggie breakfast into his food dish.

"Carl, you act like you haven't been fed in weeks," Kelly chided her excited dog. "I'll bet you didn't act like this for Mimi. She said you were 'waiting patiently' in the kitchen every morning." Kelly ladled another scoop of dry dog nibbles into the dish.

At the familiar sound of crunchy beef-chicken-turkey nibbles rattling his plastic dish, Carl's dance grew more frenzied.

"Hey, look out," Kelly scolded when Carl stomped on her bare toes. "Careful with those big Rottie feet. Perfect gentleman, my eye."

She quickly set the dish on the outside patio and closed the glass door. Watching Carl inhale his food as if it were his last meal, she was glad dogs didn't get indigestion. Or did they?

"I bet he saved all his good behavior for Mimi," Kelly said as she slipped on her sandals and checked her watch.

If she was careful, there was time for a quick stop for Eduardo's coffee and a knitting break. She had to watch her time, though. Yesterday's accounts took longer than she'd thought, and once again, Kelly had been working until past midnight to make up for yesterday's "knitting break." Brother, she'd have to buy a watch with a timer to stay on schedule, she thought, as she grabbed her knitting bag and coffee mug.

Was it her imagination or had her client load gradually increased these last few weeks, Kelly wondered? Up until this month, she'd congratulated herself on managing all the corporate account analysis her Washington, D.C. CPA firm assigned her. And, to her surprise, she'd also found time to visit with her new friends every day, join a coed softball league, and take several wonderful hikes in nearby Poudre Canyon. In short: she got herself a life. Kelly couldn't remember the last time she'd had one. During that time, she'd also managed to involve herself in investigating two separate murders—Aunt Helen's and alpaca rancher, Vickie Claymore's. Without police permission, of course.

Closing the cottage door behind her, Kelly sped across the driveway and wound through the gardens surrounding the shop, aiming for the cafe's patio entrance. Once inside, Kelly filled her mug and headed through the hallway that led to the shop. Pausing at the doorway that opened into the largest yarn room, Kelly stood for a moment and let the warm atmosphere settle over her. It felt so good here. A lot better than sitting at her computer with those blasted corporate accounts.

Guilt gave a little twinge, but Kelly sloughed it off as she headed for the library table, wondering who might be there this morning. When she turned the corner, she had to smile. Lizzie and Hilda von Steuben. Spinster sisters, retired school teachers, and master knitters. If there was a knitting hierarchy, Lizzie and Hilda had already ascended to the top of the golden stairs. Kelly was still fumbling on the lower rungs.

"Good morning, ladies," she greeted, more formally than she would anyone else, and chose a chair between the two.

"Ah, Kelly, how good to see you," Hilda pronounced in her can-be-heard-in-the-back-of-the-room voice.

"You're teaching a class today, Hilda?" she asked, noticing the gray and black tweed forming into a long scarf on Hilda's swift needles. Was that alpaca, Kelly wondered?

"Advanced knitting," Hilda said with a nod. "Something you'll be doing after a while."

"Not yet. I still feel like a novice," Kelly demurred as she reached over and squeezed the soft scrunchy wool. "Alpaca, right?" she asked the teacher.

"Yes, indeed. I must get busy on my holiday knitting. Two nephews and three nieces have moved to colder climes and have begged me for winter scarves," Hilda replied without looking up.

"I must say you're looking brighter, dear," Lizzie commented as she observed Kelly over the wire rims of her glasses.

Kelly knew that was Lizzie's way of referring to Kelly's subdued mood since Allison's death. "Thanks, Lizzie. What are you making?" She indicated the peach froth forming on Lizzie's nimble needles.

"Hilda's right. It's time to get busy on holiday knitting if we want to have gifts ready on time." Needles moving at warp speed.

"I'd be afraid to give my knitting to anyone," Kelly joked as she withdrew the deep rose circlet from her knitting bag. Several inches of stockinette stitches covered the circle now. "I'm not sure they would consider it a gift."

"Don't be silly, dear. You're coming along fine," Lizzie verbally patted her on the head.

"Ahhhhh, the forgotten sweater-in-the-round," Hilda decreed, peering at the growing circlet. "I was wondering when you'd return to that lovely piece."

"Blame it on Mimi," Kelly announced, as Mimi sped into the room. Hurrying to the backroom, no doubt. "She keeps buying those scrumptious yarns that seduce me and everyone else. If I don't finish this sweater, it's all Mimi's fault."

Mimi tossed a smile over her shoulder as she paused to straighten a bookshelf. "I'll tell Rosa to cancel this month's order, then. We can't be responsible for unfinished sweaters."

Kelly was enjoying the light moment and the laughter when she noticed Megan standing in the archway to the yarn room. Megan beckoned to Kelly anxiously. Kelly knew something was up from the expression on Megan's face, so she dropped her knitting on the table.

"Excuse me, ladies," she said and followed Megan's retreating figure. "What's up?" she asked after Megan hastened through the foyer and outside onto the front patio. Clearly, Megan didn't want to share whatever was concerning her in front of the others.

Megan looked up into Kelly's face. "Kelly, you've got to tell me if I'm off base. I've . . . I've found some information and . . . and . . ."

"What kind of information?"

"I completely forgot about Allison's things in the trunk of my car until yesterday. I felt really bad about it, because I know her parents took everything else from Allison's apartment when they were here. So, I was about to call the police and get their address when something stopped me. I . . . I saw her diary sticking out of the top of one bag, and I got this crazy idea that maybe, just maybe, Allison might have mentioned someone who was bothering her or giving her trouble, or would want to hurt her."

Kelly stared at her friend. "Hurt her? You mean, like—"

"Like *kill* her," Megan said in a dramatic whisper, even though they were outside with no one around.

"What! Megan, are you serious?"

"Yes, I'm serious," Megan insisted, leaning forward. "There's no way Allison killed herself. I know it, Kelly. I can feel it. Someone killed her. I don't know how, but they put all those sleeping pills in her coffee."

Kelly stared at her friend, not bothering to hide her incredulity. "But who would do that? Who would want Allison dead?"

Megan glanced over her shoulder. "That's why I wanted to talk to you. I spent the rest of yesterday and last night going over her diary, and I want to show you what I found. Allison talks a lot about her boyfriend, Ray. He was threatening her! And there's this other student, Kimberly, who was jealous of her and—"

"Whoa, Megan," Kelly said. "Slow down, this isn't making any sense."

"I know, I know. That's why I want to show it to you, Kelly," Megan pleaded. "I mean, it looks suspicious to me, but I want you to see it, too. Then you can tell me if I'm completely off base." She patted her knitting bag. "I've got the diary right here."

Kelly watched her afternoon computer time go flitting away like a swallow at sunset. But Megan was a friend, and a sensible one, too. She wasn't one to go off on a wild goose chase. If Megan was concerned about these entries in Allison's diary, then they merited Kelly's attention.

"Okay. I'll take a look. Why don't we go over to my place where we can have some privacy, okay?" Kelly gestured toward her cottage. "I'll go back and get my things from the shop."

"Thanks, Kelly," Megan sent her a relieved smile. "I knew I could count on you."

Kelly reached for the shop door, then remembered something. "Hey, did you find those antique beads by any chance?" she called back to Megan who was halfway to the cottage. "Mimi said she would weave a piece in Allison's memory and use the beads."

Megan shook her head. "No sign of them, Kelly. I'm hoping the police found them."

Back in the shop, Kelly found the library table empty once more. Sounds of Hilda and Lizzie riding herd on their knitting students came from the adjoining classroom. Kelly shoved her knitting back into the bag, grabbed her coffee mug, and scurried out of the shop again, nearly bumping into Burt as she left.

"Oooops, sorry Burt," she said. "I seem to be bumping into everyone lately."

"Means you're in a hurry, Kelly," Burt said with his indulgent smile. "Work piling up over there?"

"Oh, yes. It's getting harder to balance it all, too," she admitted. "I'm having to stay up later and later at night to get it all done."

Burt gave her a fatherly pat on the shoulder. "Don't push yourself so much, Kelly. You can learn to slow down. I did." He grinned.

Kelly wasn't sure she'd know how to slow down even if she tried. There were not enough hours in the day. And this image of a ticking clock was constantly in her head. "I'll keep that in mind, Burt," she said, returning his grin.

"Oh, incidentally, I'm really sorry about your friend, Allison," Burt said, sobering. "That was tragic, just tragic. Mimi told me Megan was taking it particularly hard."

Kelly glanced towards the cottage, picturing Megan still worrying about Allison, even in death. Was Megan overreacting?

"Yeah, Burt, she did take it pretty hard. She'd grown really close to Allison this last year, apparently. And Allison had helped Megan with her own designs. So, it's been a big loss."

"It's particularly hard when someone that young takes her own life, too. Believe me, Kelly, I've seen more of that than I care to."

Kelly saw the empathy in Burt's gaze and risked revealing her true feelings. "Well, for the record, Burt, both Megan and I find it difficult to believe Allison would take her own life. She was about to start this whole new career that she'd been building for years."

Burt nodded compassionately. "I understand that, too, Kelly. Better than you think."

She believed him. "Listen, Burt, could you check with your police partner and see if the detectives ever found any antique beads in the apartment? They were special to Allison, and Megan says she saw them on the desk the evening before Allison died. But they weren't there the next morning. Mimi says if we find them, she'll weave something in memory of Allison and use the beads."

"Sure, Kelly," Burt reassured. "I'll be glad to ask. They were probably discovered on the floor and catalogued with other items. I'll check for you."

"Thanks, Burt, you're a sweetheart," Kelly said with a wave as she headed for her cottage.

"That's what you gals keep telling me. I'm gonna believe it after a while," he joked.

Kelly leaned back into her desk chair and took a long drink of coffee. She stared at Allison's diary, laying open on the table in front of her. Kelly'd been amazed at the passages she'd read.

Allison's artistic career may have been blossoming, but her personal life was a mess. Her boyfriend, Ray, had threatened her several times since she'd thrown him out.

Twice, he'd come over in a drugged state and forced his way into her apartment. Unbelievable as it was to Kelly, Allison still felt guilty for throwing him out, even though Ray hadn't paid his share of the rent for six months.

"Well, am I crazy or what?" Megan asked, across the table.

"No, you're not crazy," Kelly said, shaking her head. "This Ray guy sounds like really bad news. I mean, forcing his way into the apartment . . . brother, I'd have called the cops on him."

Megan nodded somberly. "I know, and she said his drug habit was getting worse, too. Maybe he came over that night in a rage because she was leaving and . . . and killed her."

"Who knows, Megan. All I know is that the police need to see this diary. We should show it to Burt."

Megan let out a loud sigh. "Thank you for saying that, Kelly. I was thinking the same thing." She leaned over the table and riffled the pages. "What do you think about that other designer who was so jealous? Sounds like she was pretty mad about losing to Allison all the time."

Kelly shrugged, remembering the passages referring to a Kimberly Gorman, who was always finishing second best to Allison in show after show. "Jealous, yes. And angry. But it didn't sound like Allison was afraid of her."

"But she was definitely afraid of her boyfriend, Ray," Megan offered. "You could feel it coming off the pages."

Remembering some other diary entries, Kelly swirled the last of the coffee in her mug and stared through the patio door. Carl was monitoring a squirrel's fancy footwork along the top of the fence. "There was someone else Allison was afraid of," she suggested. "This guy named 'Brian.' Did she ever mention him to you, Megan?"

"Never," Megan shook her head. "What makes you think Allison was afraid of him?"

"Hard to explain. It's just a feeling I have. Her whole mood changes when she writes about him. Little cryptic passages about how Brian is disappointed in her and says she's not appreciative and how much she owes him. I don't know, it made me uneasy to read it."

"You'll take this to Burt, then?"

Kelly nodded. "First thing Monday morning." Glancing at her watch, she realized she had half an hour to get ready before dinner with Steve and Curt. Feigning work pressure, Kelly bolted from her chair. "Brother, I have got to get back to my accounts. Listen, Megan, hate to throw you out, but I've gotta get to work."

Megan swiftly grabbed her things and sped to the door. "Sorry to dump all this on you, Kelly, but I knew I needed someone I could trust to check this out. Thanks so much."

"I'm glad you did," Kelly said. "We owe it to Allison to help the police find the truth about her death."

Kelly watched Curt toy with the slice of blueberry pie in front of him. In the last five minutes, he'd taken only one or two bites. If it had been Ruth's pie, that whole slice would be gone by now.

"I know it's not as good as Ruth's, Curt, but some vanilla ice cream will camouflage that," she suggested, leaning over the red and white checkered tablecloth.

"I'm not sure it will, Kelly," Curt observed with a wry grin. "Once you've been spoiled by the best, it's hard to settle for less."

"Well, you need to gain weight, so we'll smother that pie if we have to," she said, signaling the waitress.

"Better humor her, Curt, and eat the pie," Steve said with a chuckle. "She won't stop till you've gained at least five pounds tonight."

"Did Ruth have a cookbook?" Kelly asked, after the waitress hurried away with their ice cream orders.

"Look out, Curt, she's going to try to cook for you," Steve warned.

Kelly eyed him. "Not for me. It's for Megan. She's a darn good cook, as you guys remember from our road trip to Wyoming. I was thinking maybe she could take a shot at Ruth's pie."

"Sure you don't want a take a crack at it?" Steve tempted.

Kelly sent him a condescending stare, which always seemed to make Steve laugh. "Trust me, you wouldn't want to sample my efforts. Even Carl would pass, and he'll eat anything." She leaned out of the way so the waitress could deposit three heaping bowls of vanilla ice cream in front of each of them. Kelly ladled several big spoonfuls over the remnants of her pie, remembering that the last time she'd seen Ruth was over their dinner table.

"Mimi told me you and Megan lost a close friend this week," Curt interjected as he swirled ice cream over the less-than-the-best blueberry pie. "I'm sorry to hear that. She was pretty young, wasn't she?"

"Two years younger than I am," Kelly answered after swallowing. The pie might not be Ruth's, but smothered in ice cream it was darned good.

"How's Megan doing?" Steve asked. "Jennifer mentioned that Megan was taking the suicide pretty hard. She and Allison were pretty close, huh?"

"Yeah, they were, but Megan's coming along. She's working through it pretty well now." Kelly swirled her fork through the purple puddle, weighing her next words. Then the sugar kicked in, and caution melted into the cream. "Neither Megan nor I believe Allison killed herself."

"Maybe it was accidental, Kelly. With sleeping pills, who knows?" Steve offered before he devoured his last bite of pie. He'd switched from a fork to a spoon, she noticed, obviously averse to missing a morsel of dessert. Maybe Megan should make Steve a pie, too.

"What are you suggesting, Kelly?" Curt probed, eying her across the table.

Kelly hid behind a heaping forkful of pie, which was dripping purple cream. "Nothing," she said after a moment. "Except there are some loose ends that bother us."

"Uh, oh, I've heard that tone of voice before," Steve said and dropped his spoon onto the empty plate. He leaned back into the end booth they'd found at the coziest family restaurant in town. "You're up to something, Kelly."

"I don't know what you're talking about," Kelly replied in her most innocent voice, which was a little strained since she didn't use it that often.

Steve gave her a knowing smile. "Come on. 'Fess up. What are these 'loose ends' you're talking about."

Kelly studiously ignored him while she polished off the remnants of pie.

"She knows something," Curt observed. "I can tell."

Kelly glanced up to see the old Curt observing her across the table. Good. If it took her getting into trouble to help Curt plug back into life, then she'd gladly push the limits. Pushing limits was what she did best, anyway.

She gave an exaggerated sigh and leaned back into the red vinyl cushions. "Megan found Allison's diary in some things she was packing up for Allison's parents. There are several entries in there that raise suspicions. Allison's boyfriend had threatened her physically several times, and he had a drug problem. Megan showed me the diary today, and I agree with her. I'm giving it to Burt first thing Monday morning. The police need to see it."

"Good girl. Let the police handle it," Curt decreed with an authoritative nod.

Kelly nodded obediently. "Absolutely."

Steve just smiled his lazy smile. "I'll believe that when I see it."

"I think you're seeing things that aren't there," Kelly jibed, holding her coffee cup so the waitress could refill it. "Have you been up on the roof with your guys all summer? You ought to stay in the shade more, Steve."

"I'll stay out of the sun the day you stay out of trouble," he countered.

Kelly was content to sit and sip her coffee while both her male companions laughed.

Six

Kelly strode across the driveway toward the patio entrance of Pete's Porch. The afternoon sun angled over her shoulder, slipping between the canopy of cottonwood leaves that spread overhead, lemon yellow, veined with green and mottled with brown. Early October's warm sunny days and crisp cool nights brought the color rising through the massive trunks and shooting down the branches to the tips.

Autumn. Kelly's second favorite season, summer being the first, of course. There was something poignant about autumn that resonated more vibrantly than the rebirth that was spring's calling card. She loved the smell of fall in the air.

A slight breeze rustled the gold above her head and ruffled her dark hair. She'd need a sweatshirt tonight for the softball game. The team had already begun playing under the lights. If the snow held off, they could finish out the fall season by Thanksgiving. But in Colorado, weather was always a gamble. It could be sixty degrees and sunny one day, then a foot of snow the next. Rocky Mountain High.

She was almost at the back steps when she spotted Burt.

"Hey, Burt," she called, watching him approach along the brick pathway. "Join me for a cup of coffee?"

"Matter of fact, I will, Kelly," he said, pausing at a table. "But I'd rather stay out here, okay?"

Kelly signaled to the waitress then joined him. Pete's staff knew her so well, they were on automatic. Coffee appeared magically. "Gorgeous day, isn't it?" she said as she settled into a chair. "I've been super efficient today and am actually caught up. So I figured I deserved a knitting break."

"Sounds good, Kelly. Actually I'm on the way to teach a spinning class, but I thought I'd share something with you. Something of interest."

Kelly waited for the waitress to deposit Eduardo's nectar before she leaned over the table towards Burt. He must have talked to his former detective partner. "Have the police learned something new about Allison's death?"

"In a manner of speaking, yes," Burt said, hunching over the wrought iron table. He clasped his big bear-paw hands together. It amazed Kelly that Burt could maneuver those spindles and bobbins as well as he did. "My contact says that there's some new information in the case, and consequently, Morrison is taking another look. Allison's death may not have been a suicide after all."

"What kind of new information?" she probed, suppressing a desire to say "I told you so!"

"Investigators learned that Allison had a boyfriend who was threatening her, according to the downstairs neighbor. Apparently Allison threw the guy out of the apartment when he didn't pay the rent, and he came back twice and forced his way in. Either he was drunk or high. The woman claims he's got a drug problem that was getting worse. The woman wanted to call the police, but Allison begged her not to. She didn't want to get him madder than he already was. It seems that Allison had sold his expensive sound system to pay the rent. When the guy came over and found it was gone, he was furious. Demanded Allison pay him for the system. The neighbor heard him yelling that he'd get paid 'one way or another.'"

Kelly stared into her coffee, letting Curt's news settle in. Everything he said meshed with what Kelly had read in Allison's diary. "Are the police thinking he might have killed Allison?" she ventured.

Burt shrugged in his usual way when he didn't want to commit to an answer. "Let's just say they're looking at him real close. Especially when the neighbor told them that Allison confessed to her she was an insomniac and used sleeping pills regularly. And guess who supplied her when the doctors wouldn't?"

Kelly already knew the answer. She'd read about Allison's dependence on pills in the diary. "Her boyfriend, Ray."

"How'd you know his name? Did Allison mention him to you?"

"She told Megan and me she'd kicked him out of the apartment because he hadn't paid the rent in six months. What she neglected to tell us was all the other stuff. About his threatening her and trying to break in. Megan and I found that out from her diary."

Burt straightened. "Where'd you find her diary, Kelly?"

"Megan found it in the trunk of her car in some things Allison had left behind." Kelly reached into her knitting bag and withdrew the black leather volume with gold clasp and laid it on the café table. "Megan read it and found all sorts of entries about Ray Baker and how scared Allison was of him. Megan asked me to read the entries to see if she was imagining things. I agreed with her. There're lots of details in there we think the police should know. I promised her I'd give it to you today." She gave him a reassuring smile. "Everything you told me a moment ago echoes what Megan and I read in the diary. Read it for yourself and decide."

Burt fingered the small book. "I'll let the detectives in

charge decide. Thanks, Kelly. And thank Megan, too. I'll
get this downtown first thing tomorrow." Checking his
watch, Burt rose to leave. "Better get inside before my class
starts. Thanks, again, Kelly." He waved the diary as he
headed for the back of the shop.

"Anything to help," Kelly replied, then drained her cup
of coffee. Calling after him, she added, "Hey, Burt, did you
remember to ask about those beads?"

Burt halted on the brick pathway alongside the shop.
"Matter of fact I did, Kelly. But no one found anything resembling beads. It appears the floor was swept clean. Nothing hiding in the corners, either. Sorry about that. Maybe
Mimi can create a weaving of her own for Allison."

"Maybe so," Kelly said, concealing her disappointment.
"Thanks, anyway, Burt." Burt strode off with a wave.

Checking her own watch, she started a mental countdown
in her head, measuring out the minutes available for relaxing
before a quick dinner and off to ball practice at the city park.
She grabbed her bag and scurried along the same pathway,
determined to treat herself to a few moments of relaxation.

The familiar jangle of her cell phone sounded, and Kelly
slipped it from her pocket. "Kelly Flynn," she announced.

"Well, good afternoon, Kelly," attorney Lawrence
Chambers's voice sounded in her ear. "How are you?"

"Overworked and underpaid," Kelly joked. "How are
you, Mr. Chambers? The last time you called in the late afternoon like this, you told me I had alpaca along with the
cattle and sheep. Don't tell me you bought some ostriches
at that auction."

Chambers's chuckle rumbled into her ear. "No, my dear.
I'm afraid those cattlemen don't deal in ostriches. Just cattle. No, no, I've got some other news."

Kelly's stomach involuntarily clutched. "Oh, boy.
Whenever you say 'news' I get nervous, Mr. Chambers.
What is it this time?"

"This is good news, Kelly. Nothing to be nervous about. In fact, it can do a lot to help that second condition you mentioned when you answered the phone."

Condition? "Uh, I'm afraid you've lost me, Mr. Chambers."

He chuckled again. "I believe you said you were overworked and underpaid. Well, we've got some news that could greatly change that situation. The oil and gas exploration company that contacted me about your Wyoming property has completed its seismic testing, and they are definitely interested in developing your land. This is really good news, Kelly."

Her nervous stomach clutched again. That could mean only one thing. "They found oil?" she ventured.

"Not oil. They found gas deposits. And from what the gentleman indicated over the phone, there may be a fair amount. Because of the results of the seismic tests, they want to offer you a lease agreement."

Kelly stopped walking and stood, holding the phone to her ear, letting his words sink in. Whoa. Talk about news. Lawrence Chambers didn't exaggerate.

"Kelly? Are you there?"

"I'm here, Mr. Chambers, I'm . . . I'm letting it sink in," she said softly. "This is going to take a while to process, you know. It's a whole new world, and I don't know anything about it."

"I understand, Kelly," his gentle voice reassured. "Don't you worry. You've got good people there who can help you understand what's involved. I've already heard from Curt Stackhouse this week, and he's checking into things. Curt's got a lot of experience in these matters. He'll guide you."

Kelly felt her insides unclench. Chambers was right. Curt was there. She already knew that. There was no need to panic. She had consultants. Ranch consultants, Curt called them. That memory sent a warm feeling, which chased away the vestiges of worry. "You're right, as always, Mr. Chambers. I've got lots of help, and it's a good thing, because I'll need it," she said with a laugh.

"That's what we're here for, Kelly. Remember, you're not alone."

A slight breeze whispered through the trees of Fort Connor's Old Town plaza, and Kelly was glad she'd worn her sweatshirt tonight. She hadn't needed it earlier when she was chasing down balls and running bases, but she welcomed it now. She glanced about the outdoor cafes emptying onto the plaza, tables not as packed as they would be on a balmy summer's night. All it took was the hint of chill in the air to chase some people inside. But softball players were a hardy lot. They had to be.

She looked around the packed table at her teammates. Most were from the summer league, but others had joined when the seasons changed. Across the plaza, she noticed Steve wave goodbye to his teammates at another table and head their way.

"How'd you guys do?" Steve asked, pulling up a chair across the table.

"Beat 'em, twelve to two," Megan crowed, lifting her glass with a big grin.

Kelly hadn't had a chance to share Burt's news with Megan yet. Tomorrow at the shop would be better, she decided, as she sipped her favorite local microbrew. The delicious amber ale with the funny name was now being shipped out of state. It was hard to keep something this good a secret.

"Good job," Steve decreed, leaning back in his chair. "We annihilated the other guys, too. In fact, the score was getting so bad, we eased up."

"No way, Steve," Kelly scoffed. "You guys never slack off."

"Not against you guys," he countered.

"Flattery, flattery," Lisa joked.

"That sounds like my entrance," Jennifer announced, suddenly appearing beside Kelly.

"Did the party get boring or are you just slumming?" Kelly teased as Jennifer balanced her frosted margarita and pulled up a chair.

"Naw, we're taking a break between sets. Trish, say 'hi' to the nice softball jocks. They won't bite." Jennifer gestured to the voluptuous blonde girl who was approaching.

"Hey," Trish chirped, with a dazzling smile and a little wave. Like Jennifer, she held an extra-large strawberry-colored drink.

Kelly and the others called out greetings as Trish pulled out a chair beside Steve and joined the conversation, confessing in a breathy voice that she'd played "lots of softball" back in high school.

"You look like you're doing better. Megan, too," Jennifer observed. "Good thing. Having two of you down at the same time was scary." Jennifer glanced over her shoulder towards some of the couples spilling from the club she'd left.

"Yeah, we're doing okay," Kelly said, not wanting to share the information she and Megan had discovered.

The high-pitched sound of girlish laughter across the table captured her attention. Kelly watched Trish lean closer to Steve, turning up the wattage of her smile and flirting like crazy. Glancing at Steve, Kelly noticed his reaction was that of any normal red-blooded male who had a voluptuous blonde hanging onto his every word. Clearly, Steve was enjoying himself. Kelly watched the exchange for a full minute before she turned away. Okaaaaay, she thought, then noticed Jennifer staring across the square. Brother, she couldn't hold anyone's attention tonight.

"Choosing your dance partner?" Kelly tweaked.

"Oh, I've already chosen him. And I hope it's for more than dancing," Jennifer replied with a wicked smile.

"Who's the lucky guy?"

"The one wearing the silver shirt. Jet black hair. Extra hot. Best dancer out there."

Kelly scanned the crowd. It didn't take long to find Jennifer's target. Whoa, Kelly thought, surveying Mr. Extra Hot. Talk about tall, dark, and handsome. Unfortunately, Extra Hot also had a girl in each arm.

"He's hot, all right," Kelly agreed. "But he's also got two girls with him."

Jennifer gave a dismissive wave and took a big sip of her drink. "That's nothing. Wait till we dance. They'll be history."

Observing Extra Hot nuzzle one girl while sliding his hand provocatively down the other's back, Kelly shook her head. "I dunno, Jen. He looks like trouble to me."

"Oh, I certainly hope so," Jennifer said with a wink as she rose from her chair. "See you guys back at the shop. It's 'showtime.'"

Kelly watched Jennifer meander across the plaza, drawing lots of male attention as she walked. Kelly hoped her friend knew what she was doing. Extra Hot looked a little exotic even for Jennifer's tastes.

Scanning the table, Kelly saw that several of her teammates had already left. Only Lisa and two others remained, and, of course, Trish still held Steve enraptured in her voluptuous spell.

Time to go, Kelly decided, and drained her beer. Rising from the table, she gave a quick goodbye wave to everyone and scurried across the plaza toward her parked car. She'd tell Steve about the Wyoming news another time.

Seven

Kelly paused at the patio right outside the front door to the knitting shop, trying to balance her knitting bag, coffee mug, and cell phone. Curt Stackhouse's voice came on the line.

"Hey, Kelly, what can I do for you?" he asked.

"Well, Curt, I certainly hope you were serious about needing a challenge, because I've got one for you. The oil and gas company contacted Lawrence Chambers. It looks like their seismic tests found gas deposits, and they want to develop the land."

"I'm not surprised, Kelly. That entire area up there is dotted with wells."

"They sent Chambers a lease agreement for me to consider. I've read it over and over, Curt, and I think I understand what's involved. However, I'd feel better if you looked it over and translated for me."

"Don't worry, Kelly. That's what I'm here for. Do you have it with you?"

"Oh, yeah," she said, feeling the extra weight of her knitting bag. "I'll be over here at Lambspun for an hour or so. But don't make a special trip. We can arrange another time."

"No problem, Kelly," Curt assured her. "I'll see you in a little bit."

Kelly sighed audibly. "Bless you, Curt," she said before clicking off.

She'd spent more hours than she'd wanted to last night, pouring over the lease agreement Chambers had delivered to her door. Pages and pages of contractual obligations. Kelly was used to deciphering complex accounting situations for corporations and had some experience with royalties and copyrights. Unfortunately, she didn't have extensive experience with mineral rights and royalties. Those were a whole new ballgame. Only the thought that she had experienced Curt Stackhouse ready and willing to help her allowed Kelly to finally fall asleep after three A.M.

Stifling another yawn, Kelly entered the shop, deposited her bag on the library table, and headed straight for the cafe and coffee. She had to get more sleep. This was getting ridiculous. Spying Jennifer, she held out her empty mug. "Unless you want to see me dissolve in a puddle on the floor, fill this up now. Please!"

"How late did you stay out last night?" Jennifer teased, as she swiftly followed Kelly's instructions.

"I didn't stay out late. I stayed *in* late," Kelly explained wearily, sniffing the provocative aroma. "Can't you move any faster?"

Jennifer laughed. "Brother, you are in bad shape. What on earth were you doing at home that kept you up so late?" She held the mug just out of Kelly's reach.

"Gimme that," Kelly demanded, snatching it away to take a deep drink. Maybe she'd live after all. Another drink would tell.

"I swear, if you did dissolve, all the police would find is a puddle of caffeine. What kept you up?"

"An exploration company leasing agreement. They found gas deposits." Another long drink.

"Whoa."

"That's what I said. Curt's coming over to get it. I poured over it when I got back last night, but I need someone to translate that stuff for me. I'm up to my neck translating accounting stuff."

"That definitely changes the Wyoming picture, Kelly, as you well know. You're going to have more options than you've ever imagined."

"I know, that's what's so confusing. Every option is complicated. That's why I need Curt."

Jennifer reached over and gave Kelly a pat on the arm. "It'll be okay, Kelly. Curt's the expert on that stuff. He'll advise you." Glancing over her shoulder, she added, "Gotta check on my section. See you later."

Kelly nodded and returned to her coffee. She was approaching a semi-alert state. Now, if she could sit quietly and knit until Curt appeared, she might have a chance to wake up completely. When she returned to the library table, however, she noticed Megan at her usual spot. Upending her mug, Kelly drained the last of the coffee. This conversation required caffeine. She didn't want to forget anything Burt had told her.

"Hey, Megan, I'm glad you're here," Kelly said as she settled into her chair. "Burt talked to me yesterday, and I gave him the diary. He also had some news."

Megan looked up expectantly. "The police found something, didn't they?"

Kelly picked up her circular knitting where she left off, and glanced over her shoulder to make sure they were still alone. "Police interviewed Allison's downstairs neighbor, and the woman told them about Ray Baker. How furious he was when Allison threw him out, especially when he found she'd sold his sound system. And he was threatening Allison about the money. She also told them about the drugs. How Ray was supplying Allison with her pills."

"A witness! She's a witness!" Megan croaked in an excited whisper. "I *knew* it! I knew Allison didn't kill herself. That creep, Ray Baker, poisoned her, and that woman can prove it."

"Whoa, slow down, Megan," Kelly counseled. "This woman didn't witness anything, otherwise Ray Baker would be arrested. She simply gave police the reason to take a closer look at Allison's death." Fingers relaxed into the rhythm of the knitting. Row after row of garter stitch, round and round, magically transforming into stockinette stitch without purling once.

Crestfallen, Megan scowled at the drab blue sweater she was creating. It looked halfway finished to Kelly. "Well, it sounds like the police are taking her seriously, at least. Boy, I hope they grill that Ray Baker good."

An image appeared of Megan in a bright red devil's outfit skewering Ray Baker on a pitchfork as she held him over a bonfire. "I'm sure the police will interrogate him, Megan. Maybe not as, uh, enthusiastically as you would," Kelly said with a grin. "But Morrison can be fairly intimidating. And this Ray sounds like he's pretty squirrelly, with the drugs and all. I'll bet if Morrison squeezes him, Ray Baker will talk."

"He'll lie. I'm sure he will," Megan said, fingers picking up speed. At that rate, the sweater would be finished by tonight.

"And the police will catch him in that lie. That's their job. Don't worry, Megan. Morrison and his guys are doing exactly what we wanted them to do. Thanks to that neighbor. Brother, talk about good luck. Not every neighbor would be so forthcoming. Some people shut up when police start asking questions."

Megan let out a sigh, shoulders dropping from their tensed pose. "You're right, Kelly. The police will handle it. Just make sure Burt knows he has to keep us updated, okay?"

"I'm sure he will. Burt's good about keeping us in the loop. I also asked him to check if any beads were found in the apartment, and he said that nothing like that was found. No beads of any kind. He mentioned the floor was swept clean, which I figured was your doing."

Megan's disappointment was visible. Her face clouded. "Damn," she whispered. It was the first time Kelly had ever heard Megan swear. "I so wanted Mimi to be able to use them in her weaving for Allison."

"Do you think they might be in one of those boxes Allison's parents took with them?" Kelly ventured.

"No, I'm certain," Megan replied firmly. "There was only one open box on the floor that morning, and only a few papers were in the bottom. I know, because you told me to walk around and look at everything, and I did. The other three boxes were the ones that I had packed and sealed myself."

Seeing how much this meant to Megan, Kelly suggested, "Do you remember where Allison got the beads? We could order some and give them to Mimi."

Megan shook her head. "That's all right, Kelly. Mimi will come up with an idea."

"All right, we'll leave it to Mother Mimi."

Watching the rows of neat stockinette appear, Kelly smiled. This would be a beautiful sweater, luscious rose and rainbow colors winding together. Size six needles, too, she thought proudly. Kelly had never used such small needles before. Of course, sock knitters would scoff at the idea of size six as small.

"Thought I'd find you here," Curt Stackhouse's voice sounded as he appeared beside her.

"Wow, Curt, you are speedy this morning." She observed that Curt was looking more and more like his old self every time she saw him.

"Hi, there, Megan," he said as he straddled a chair. "Are you keeping Kelly out of trouble?"

Megan stared back, clearly astonished at the thought. "Who, me? I couldn't do that if I tried."

"Believe me, Curt, I'm too tired to get into trouble. I was up till three, going over that leasing agreement."

"This sounds like business," Megan said, gathering her knitting as she rose. "Which reminds me I've neglected mine for too long. Gotta get back on the computer and drum up some work. Talk to you guys later."

"That's the scary thing about consulting," Kelly said with a goodbye wave. "It's not regular."

"Some of it is, Kelly, but we'll get to that another time," Curt countered. "Right now, I want to take a look at that lease agreement."

Kelly dug into her knitting bag and drew out the legal size portfolio. "Here you go, Curt. Again, I can't thank you enough for helping me wade through all this stuff."

"Actually, Kelly, I'm looking forward to sinking my teeth into this," he said as he took the package. "It's been a few years since I had any land holdings with mineral deposits, but I've kept up. It'll be a chance to renew some old acquaintances as well." He smiled, more and more of the old Curt reappearing.

"I'll be curious to see how much gas they found. The lease didn't say."

"The lease didn't say, because they're not sure, Kelly. That's why they want to drill a wildcat. When an exploration company drills a well on a piece of land, they're taking a big risk. They don't know exactly how much gas is down there in the bubble. Just that it's there. If there's really good pressure, it can mean a lot of gas. But there are no guarantees."

Kelly stared at the portfolio. "Any idea how much income this lease could yield, Curt?"

He grinned and swung himself out of the chair. "Not until I see how much they're offering you, Kelly. But you may be in for a surprise."

"Boy, I could use a good surprise."

"I'll even work up some examples of the royalties from my old properties, years ago. That way, you can see some possible income options."

"Great. I love options," she said with a grin.

"There's also another option," Curt said as he headed for the door. "You could do absolutely nothing, like Martha and her husband did for all those years. It'll be your choice, Kelly."

Kelly shifted the plastic grocery bags and tried to dig her car keys from her pocket at the same time. A tricky maneuver, especially since she was also balancing a plastic-wrapped bouquet of flowers. Wrestling the car door open, she dumped all the purchases in the passenger seat and delicately placed the floral bundle on top.

The idea of taking flowers to Allison's neighbor came to Kelly suddenly. It was a way of saying "thank you" for providing crucial information that the police might never have discovered. Flowers were a universal way of expressing thoughts that words alone could not.

Turning her car toward the streets on the western edge of town, Kelly headed for Allison's apartment complex and parked near the corner. She hesitated a few moments beside the mailboxes, trying to decipher the name of the resident directly below Allison. The name appeared to be "Diane Linstrom."

Kelly took a calming breath and knocked on the apartment door. Nothing at first, then she heard the metallic sound of a peephole sliding, then the door itself opened a few inches. A young woman peered out at Kelly, her face as pale as her short blonde hair.

"Diane Linstrom?" Kelly offered. "I checked your name on the mailbox. I'm a friend . . . I was a friend of Allison Dubois." Sensing Diane's apprehension, Kelly quickly added, "Megan and I went with Allison to Santa Fe last week. We all met at the knitting shop, Lambspun."

Diane's expression changed dramatically. "Oh, yes, yes. Allison told me about you," she said, relief evident in her voice. Glancing around the open stairwell, she gestured. "Why don't you come in. It's more private."

"I hope I didn't disturb you," Kelly said as she entered, noticing the aroma of lemon permeating the air.

"No, no, I'm a web designer, so I can juggle my hours any way I need. Please sit down. Would you like some coffee?"

When didn't she like coffee? Kelly thought as she watched Diane head for the open apartment kitchen. She noticed Diane wore the same comfortable uniform that Kelly chose for at home computer work—sweats and a tee shirt. Even under the sweats, however, Kelly could tell that Diane was rail thin. The pronounced bone structure of her face, neck, and hands revealed more than the bulky clothes hid.

"That would be great," Kelly said, then held out the flowers. "I brought these. It may sound weird, but I wanted to say thank you for talking to the police. Some neighbors wouldn't, you know."

Diane stared at Kelly from the kitchen, her surprise evi-

dent. "Who told you I talked to the police?" she asked, the
fearful tone creeping back into her voice.

Adopting the most reassuring manner she possessed,
Kelly tried to explain. "One of my friends is a retired police
detective. Megan and I told him our concerns about Allison's death when it happened. We couldn't believe she'd
kill herself. So, he made some inquiries for us and discovered that thanks to you, the police are taking another look."

"I just told the police everything I know," Diane answered quietly, pouring coffee into two colorful ceramic
mugs.

Kelly surveyed Diane Linstrom's apartment while the
tantalizing coffee aroma drifted from the kitchen. An all-
white sofa and black glass end tables lent a stark quality,
while bold splashes of color hung from the wall on posters,
paintings on canvas and wood, carved wooden heads, and a
geometric black and white weaving which hung over a corner desk, which Kelly surmised was Diane's work area.

"Thanks," Kelly said as she took the proffered mug.
"Ummm, smells good. I can tell you like your coffee
strong."

"The only civilized way to drink it." Diane said as she
took the flowers back to the kitchen. "Thanks for the flowers, Kelly." She grabbed her coffee mug and settled on the
matching white loveseat.

"You're welcome. I wanted to say thank you and, I guess
I also wanted the chance to talk about Allison," Kelly admitted. "It's hard to believe she's dead. I mean, she was so
vibrant and alive."

Diane drew her legs beneath her on the sofa and cradled
the mug in both hands. "I know. She was a fabulous and
gifted artist. And a good friend. We were very close and
could talk about anything." Her voice drifted away. Pointing to the weaving, she added, "That's her work."

"I guessed as much," Kelly said. "You know, I'm glad

she had you to talk to, Diane, because Allison never told Megan and me much about her boyfriend. Except that he hadn't paid the rent and she had to throw him out."

"That was awful," Diane said with a shudder. "Allison had to wait until he was out overnight playing with some band in Denver. Then she put all his stuff in boxes in the breezeway." She pointed outside. "She stayed over here that night with me. When Ray came over the next morning, he saw everything outside, and he just lost it. Started yelling for Allison and banging on her door. She had to threaten to call the cops to get him to leave." Diane's pale face had grown paler with the telling. "I begged Allison to let me call the cops anyway, but she made me promise not to. She still felt sorry for him." She screwed up her face in obvious disgust.

"What did he do when he discovered she sold his sound system?" Kelly pried, resting the mug on her knee.

Diane rolled her eyes. "Then it got worse. He started showing up and sitting outside in his car, waiting for her to come home. Then, he'd waylay Allison and start yelling. 'That was mine! You didn't have the right to sell it! You owe me that money!' Stuff like that. Over and over." She shivered again. "Then he'd leave ugly notes on her door, threatening her. Saying she'd better pay him the money or else."

Kelly leaned forward. "Or else what? What do you think he meant?"

"That's what always scared me about Ray. You didn't know what he'd do. He'd get this look in his eyes that was part druggie and part shrewd. I tried to convince Allison that he was dangerous, but she refused to believe me. She was convinced that Ray had simply gotten in with the wrong crowd. He was really a nice guy." She gave a disgusted snort. "Maybe he was nice once, but I never saw it. He gave me a bad feeling the first time I met him last year, and he was only doing half the drugs he is now."

"Really heavy user?"

"Oh, yeah." Diane nodded.

"Sounds like his whole personality changed."

"Well, I didn't think he had much personality to begin with, but Allison must have seen something in him." Diane stared into her cup.

Kelly pondered her next question. "Do you think Ray could have killed Allison?"

Diane looked her straight in the eye. "Absolutely. There was a calculating streak in Ray that Allison never saw. He'd do little things to sabotage her, like spill soft drinks on a yarn she was using for a project or leave her car with no gas when she had to get to work. Crappy stuff like that."

"Sounds like a weasel to me."

"Yeah, and he was getting worse. He trashed Allison's car two weeks ago. She'd had to park down the street near the playground where no one was around. Ray smashed the windows, slashed the tires, and totally trashed the interior. It's a total wreck. Didn't she tell you?"

"No, she never said a thing." However, Kelly did remember a diary reference to Ray messing up her car. "I can't believe Allison wouldn't tell us. Are you sure it was Ray?"

Diane nodded. "Oh, yeah. He knew Allison wouldn't report him, so he even left a note in the car, telling her to 'watch out.'" She enunciated the words dramatically.

"Whoa," Kelly said, a more menacing image of Ray Baker forming in her mind. "That is scary. I can't believe Allison wouldn't take the threat seriously."

"I always got the feeling that if Ray ever did explode, it would be bad. Real bad."

Kelly leaned back in the soft sofa and pondered her next question. "Did Ray come over that night? Did you hear anything?"

Diane nodded. "I sure did. He came stomping up the stairs. I checked and saw his beat-up Toyota outside so I knew it was him. Plus, when you live below people for a while, you learn to recognize their footsteps. It was him in the apartment that night."

"Did he yell and threaten Allison?"

She shook her head. "No. That's what surprised me. I didn't hear any raised voices at all. And I have to say, that made me suspicious."

"What do you mean?" Kelly pried.

Diane stared out into her immaculate living room. Kelly got the feeling that everything was in precisely the right place. There was no way she'd ever be able to have a room like this. Not with big, scruffy old Carl galumphing about, rubbing his head against the sofa. Multi-colored, heavy-duty upholstery worked best for big dogs.

"I think Ray came back with those sleeping pills and coffee. And I told the police that, too. I mean, Ray was the one who supplied Allison with sleeping pills. The doctors stopped prescribing for her long ago. And he knew she loved those special coffees, too. You know, the sweet caramel ones." Diane gave a dismissive wave.

Kelly's ears perked up. "Really? Megan and I noticed there was a takeout coffee cup lying on the floor."

"Ray must have brought it with him, because Allison didn't leave the apartment after she returned from the university dinner."

"Maybe she bought the coffee herself on the way home."

Diane shook her head. "Nope. She came right to my place to say goodbye. The only things she had in her hands were her purse and a small trophy from some local weavers."

"Hmmmm," Kelly said, deliberately pondering out loud so Diane would join in.

"So, you see? Ray had to be the one."

"And you're sure that Allison never left the apartment after she returned?"

"Positive." Diane gave an emphatic nod. "That's why she came to say goodbye, because she was going to be up late packing, and she didn't want to miss me in the morning. She knows I work late at night and sleep in."

Another question suddenly walked in the back door of Kelly's brain. "Did anyone else visit Allison that night?"

Diane sipped her coffee then nodded. "Yes, a tall brunette came over about an hour after I heard Ray leave. I was on the stairs taking the trash out, when this girl comes hurrying past me on the steps and knocks on Allison's door. And she was wasn't carrying anything in her hands at all. Not even a purse."

"Did you recognize her as one of Allison's friends?"

"Nope. Not at all, but Allison knew her because she called her by name. She sounded kind of surprised, too."

"How so?"

"Well, it was the tone of Allison's voice when she said, 'Kimberly.' Like she wasn't expecting her."

Kimberly Gorman. It had to be. Considering the competitive relationship that existed between the two designers, Kelly wondered what could have brought Kimberly Gorman to Allison's door the night before she was to leave for New York.

"Did you hear anything else that was said?" Kelly probed.

"No, they went inside. I didn't hear any loud voices, if that's what you mean. They didn't even walk around much. She only stayed a few minutes, too, because I heard the door close and footsteps coming down the stairs."

"Did you hear Allison walking around afterwards?"

"Oh, yeah. Like I said, she still had lots of sorting to do. She was making trips back and forth to the Dumpster all evening, throwing out trash." Diane settled back into her alabaster sofa and brushed a stray lock of pale hair off her forehead.

Diane's hair was so blonde, it was nearly white, accentuating her never-seen-the-sun-complexion. With all her years of running and outside sports, Kelly figured she must be wrinkled already but simply hadn't had the time to notice yet. She'd once heard that wrinkles hide until forty, then they pop out all at once.

Something Diane said niggled at her. "You know, that makes me wonder," Kelly mused out loud. "If Ray Baker had poisoned Allison earlier, then how could she be running back and forth to the Dumpster? Wouldn't those sleeping pills have put her out?"

Diane shrugged. "Who knows? Allison had abused those pills for so long, maybe she'd built up a tolerance or something. Maybe it took longer for them to kick in."

Maybe, Kelly thought. And maybe it wasn't Ray who put the pills in her coffee. Could Kimberly have hated Allison so much she'd poison her right before Allison was about to get her big break?

That thought lasted about ten seconds before it nosedived into the image of a drug-laced caramel coffee. It was highly unlikely that Kimberly Gorman would be running around Fort Connor with a pocketful of sleeping pills and murderous intent. Just because she was insanely jealous of Allison's success, didn't mean Kimberly was insane.

"How long would you guess you heard Allison moving around upstairs after Kimberly left?"

"Oh, at least another couple of hours or so. I was working and remember hearing her upstairs."

Kelly hunched over her coffee. "You know, that doesn't make sense, Diane. Those pills surely would have kicked in after a while. If someone drank coffee that was loaded with barbiturates, they wouldn't be able to run up and down the stairs for very long."

Diane stared out into the living room. "Unless someone came back," she said quietly. "I heard another set of footsteps on the stairs later that night. And I heard Allison's door opening and closing, too. I looked outside and saw a dark car parked across the street. I'd never seen that car parked around here before, and I know all my neighbors' cars."

Kelly looked up. "You think she had a late night visitor?"

Diane nodded and kept staring at the floor. "I couldn't hear any voices, but I heard different footsteps walking around as well as Allison's."

"But no voices?"

"No, just walking for a while, then nothing."

Kelly felt the hair on the back of her neck rise. "Nothing?" she repeated. "When did the person leave?"

"That's the strange thing. I never heard anyone leave. In fact, when I finally went to bed after midnight, I looked outside because I was curious. That dark car was still parked on the other side of the street, and it was still there at three fifteen in the morning. I'd gotten up for a drink of water and looked outside. There it was." She gave Kelly a sober look.

"Did you tell the police all of this?"

"You bet I did," she said with conviction. "And I told them who I thought it was, too."

That took Kelly by surprise. "Who?"

"Ray Baker. I think he sneaked back here and slipped the pills in Allison's coffee when it was late at night. He probably borrowed someone's car, too, so no one would know it was him."

Kelly stared at Diane. Clearly, Diane Linstrom had already convicted Ray Baker in her mind. But was the weasely Ray capable of such conniving details and actions? Or was he out getting high with his friends? Kelly rather suspected the latter, judging from Ray Baker's past behavior.

"Do you really think Ray was capable of being that

stealthy and clever? He sounds like he's destroyed too many of his brain cells to be that conniving."

"Ohhhh, no," Diane fixed Kelly with a laser-like stare. "Ray was shrewd and clever when he wanted to be. And I told the police that, too."

"But why would he come back a second time?"

Diane's eyes narrowed. "I think he came the first time to get money from Allison. When she didn't give him any, he came back later. And that's when he brought the coffee. Out of revenge." She enunciated the last word.

Kelly let everything Diane said settle in. Diane's obvious bias against Ray Baker aside, the scene she'd painted was entirely plausible. It certainly made much more sense. According to Diane, the noise upstairs stopped about midnight after the late night visitor.

Had Ray Baker really come back that night in a borrowed car to kill his former girlfriend who'd spurned him? Others had killed for less, Kelly knew sadly. It had gotten so she hated to listen to the news. Some people found it far too easy to rationalize murder. A slight chill rippled through her, and Kelly rubbed her arm.

"Brother, that's one horrible picture you've painted, Diane. You told the police all of this, I hope."

"You bet. I want that bastard to go to jail for what he did. Allison was worth a thousand Ray Bakers, and he just snuffed her out like a cigarette."

Kelly shivered, whether from the image of Ray Baker's cruelty or Diane Linstrom's hatred of him. "Thank goodness, you were here, Diane," she said as she rose to leave. "If not for you, the police would have nothing to go on to investigate this guy."

"Believe me, Kelly, I was happy to help," Diane said as she accompanied Kelly to the door.

Pausing on the threshold, Kelly sent Diane a grateful smile. "You've been really thoughtful to share so much with me, Diane. I'll make sure and tell Megan. She'll feel much better knowing the police have a solid lead."

"It actually felt good to get that off my chest, Kelly," Diane admitted. "Stay in touch, would you? I'd particularly like to know if the police learn anything new, okay?"

"Will do. Take care, Diane, and thanks again," Kelly said and gave a quick wave as she hastened to her car.

Eight

Kelly checked her watch, then tried to relax in the morning sunshine's warmth that was streaming through the knitting shop's windows. She'd called Megan as soon as she arrived and gave her a summarized version of her meeting with Diane Linstrom yesterday. Unfortunately, the call had been cut short with the arrival of a knitting class.

Taking a deep drink of coffee, Kelly endeavored to settle into the knitting rhythm once more. She could use some meditative moments right now. The neat rows of stockinette had grown and grown, inches upon inches of colorful stitches. Were those really her stitches? They looked so neat. Maybe she was getting better like everyone said. Mimi always told her she was too hard on herself, and here was the proof. A sweater-in-the-round coming to life on her needles. Who would have thought?

A tinkling doorbell and the sound of hurrying feet brought Megan rushing into the room. She collapsed on the chair beside Kelly, not even bothering to take out her knitting. "Okay, pick up the story where you left off," she demanded, leaning closer, although they were the only ones at the long library table.

"Did I tell you that Kimberly Gorman visited that night?" Kelly began.

"Yes!" Megan hissed dramatically. "But she didn't stay long, and that's where you left off."

"After that visit, Diane said Allison was still moving around upstairs packing and running up and down the stairs with loads of trash. That made me suspicious. How could Allison be running around if Ray Baker had slipped enough pills in her coffee to kill her?"

Megan drew back. "Oh-my-gosh! You're right. Do you think Kimberly did it? Allison said Kimberly was crazy jealous of her."

Kelly shook her head. "According to Diane, Kimberly didn't have anything in her hands when she arrived at Allison's. Diane was outside and saw her on the steps."

"So it *was* Ray Baker," Megan said ominously.

"Well, Diane Linstrom is sure he's guilty, and she told the police, too. She's convinced Ray came back later because she heard footsteps on the outside steps and in Allison's apartment. And she saw an unfamiliar car parked outside, too. Diane thinks Ray brought the coffee later that night, because Allison stopped moving around after that."

"Bastard," Megan whispered, her pretty face darkening.

"I have to admit, Diane's version of events makes more sense," Kelly said. "But, there's something that still bothers me, and I can't put my finger on it."

"You don't believe her?"

"Oh, no, I think she's a powerful witness to what she saw and heard, it's—"

"It's what?"

Kelly shrugged. "I can't explain it. But that suspicious little lobe of my brain keeps jabbing. I dunno."

"I heard that," Lisa announced as she strolled into the room, looking workout- trainer-physical-therapist healthy.

Kelly figured if she could get more sleep at night, she might look better, too. This morning she was certain she had seen dark shadows under her eyes. Work was making her old before her time. At this rate, those wrinkles wouldn't even wait until forty. They'd pop out at thirty-five. Kelly hadn't told anyone her birth date, hoping to keep it a secret, but the Big Three-0 was due the end of October.

"Boy, don't you look cheerful," Kelly teased, ignoring Lisa's comment.

Lisa was hard to ignore. "What're you up to now, Kelly?" she asked as she settled across the table and resumed knitting the bluish-gray wool that was forming into a nearly-finished shawl.

"Who, me? Nothing," Kelly declared in wide-eyed innocence.

Lisa glanced from Kelly to Megan. "Liar. Megan's face tells me you're up to something."

Sure enough, Megan's reddened face and downcast gaze spoke volumes. "Boy, you're a lot of help," Kelly teased her friend. "Your face is a dead giveaway. You could never keep a secret if you tried."

"Sorry, can't help it," Megan said with a laugh as she pulled out her knitting. Kelly noticed the navy-blue sweater was almost finished. Worry worked wonders with yarn.

"Seriously, Kelly, what were you and Megan whispering about when I came in?" Lisa asked.

"Nothing secret, really. We'd learned that the police are now looking into Allison's death as a homicide rather than a suicide."

"Really?" Lisa's swift fingers actually stilled. "Do they have any idea who might have done it? I didn't know Allison, but you guys always said how great she was. Who would want to kill her?"

Kelly glanced at Megan and let her do the honors.

"Allison had a really bad-news boyfriend who was hanging around, living off her, doing lots of drugs, until she threw him out," Megan replied. "We heard that police are checking him out now. Apparently a neighbor of Allison's saw him over there that night."

"Wow, that doesn't sound good."

Kelly picked up her own needles and let the rhythmic motions work their magic. Settling, calming. No one spoke as all three knitted silently.

Kelly needed some quiet time before returning to her accounts. Yesterday's visit to Diane Linstrom had dominated her thoughts ever since. Talking with Megan helped a little, but her mind was still full of little niggling thoughts, buzzing like insects inside her head.

What was it about Diane's recitation of that night's events that bothered her? Diane was certainly a credible witness. Intense to the extreme, yes, but still credible. Kelly wound the deep rose yarn around the needles again and again. Stockinette stitches combining row after row. Diane's version definitely made sense. If what she was saying was true, Ray Baker had a violent and destructive streak. Did that spill over into murder?

The neat rows continued to grow, nearly ten inches so far. How many rows did she need? Wasn't there an armhole she was supposed to watch for? Kelly examined the circular sweater. The pattern was back at the cottage. She hadn't looked at it since she began the sweater months ago. She'd better be careful or she'd be knitting a gloriously colorful tube instead of a sweater.

Deciding she had a ways to go yet before the armhole appeared, Kelly let her mind return to the puzzling thoughts. The insects were still buzzing. But every now and then, one would alight long enough for her to swat it.

There was one way to check if Diane was exaggerating

or not. The other neighbors surely must have heard Ray Baker's noisy behavior. Maybe Burt could find out if the investigators confirmed Diane Linstrom's account. She'd ask Burt.

No sooner had Kelly swatted that insect when another one buzzed in her face. Kimberly Gorman. Why in the world did she come to Allison's apartment that night? Given their past history, Kelly doubted Kimberly came to wish her well. Or, had she?

That thought continued to annoy her through an entire row of stockinette. Finally, Kelly gave up and shoved her knitting into its bag and rose to leave. She needed some answers and she knew exactly where to get them: Allison's friends at the university. Fellow designers, all, they surely were well aware of Allison's relationship with Kimberly. Plus, many of them had probably attended the same banquet that evening. If Kimberly was acting strangely, surely someone would have noticed.

"See you later, guys. Got some errands to run," she said with a wave as she headed for the door, hoping to leave without too many questions.

"I smell sleuthing," Lisa said, without even looking up.

"And don't forget practice tonight," Megan called out behind her.

"I'll be there," Kelly promised and hurried out the door, wondering how her friends could read her mind.

Strolling along the winding pathway between the university's Fine Arts building and adjacent parking lot, Kelly weighed the next question she wanted to ask the young woman walking beside her. Earlier, Allison's major professor mentioned that Shannon Deaver was Allison's design-workshop partner, and they'd shared many classes together. Kelly waited for Shannon between classes, hoping she knew something that could add a missing piece to this puzzle. There were too many missing pieces.

"So, you and Allison shared a table at the banquet?" Kelly ventured.

Shannon nodded, slipping her long dark hair behind one ear. "And she acted perfectly normal, too. There was no indication that she was . . . you know, depressed or anything like that."

Kelly jumped on that opening and gave a big sigh. "That's what frustrates me, Shannon," she exclaimed. "Allison was excited, not depressed. My friend, Megan, was helping her pack that day, and she said there was no sign. It makes no sense."

"None of it makes sense," Shannon agreed, adjusting the backpack on her shoulder. "I can't even think about it too much. It hurts. She was such a sweetheart."

"Did anything happen at the banquet? Anything at all unusual? Did anyone say something to Allison that upset her, maybe?"

Shannon stopped short in the middle of the path, her eyes wide. "Oh, my God, yes!" she said. "I forgot until now. Kimberly Gorman was at the banquet that night, too, and she started an argument with Allison right outside in the hall afterwards."

Swat. Kelly smashed the annoying insect flat. "Really? What was that about?"

"I didn't hear all of it, but enough. Kimberly was being her bitchy self, saying how she wished Allison success in New York, and she expected to see Allison's designs on the cover of *Vogue.* Yeah, right." Shannon's face revealed her opinion of Kimberly. "Kimberly was a jealous bitch. She was always finishing second to Allison, and she couldn't accept it. She'd complain to the professors of favoritism when the truth was, Allison was a better designer. She was a genius with fibers and textures. She could put the craziest

things together and come up with something entirely new."
Shannon looked Kelly in the eye. "Kimberly never could
accept that."

"What did Allison say?"

"She stood there and didn't say a word until Kimberly
took a breath, then Allison told Kimberly she should go
home and sleep it off—that Kimberly had had too much to
drink. Then she turned around and walked back into the
dining room." Shannon grinned. "Allison was a class act."

"What did Kimberly do?"

"She stood there, swaying on her feet, looking like a
fool." She shrugged. "She probably *had* been drinking.
Someone told me they'd seen Kimberly at some Denver
bars in LoDo with friends. She'd never go out with any of
us here at school. It was like we weren't good enough for
her. Snooty bitch," Shannon said with an ill-disguised
sneer.

"Is she still taking classes here?" Kelly probed. The idea
of talking to Kimberly was forming, like an itch that needed
scratching.

Shannon shook her head. "No, she finished her master's
last spring the same time Allison did. I heard she's been
working at some gallery in Denver since then. That's where
she came from, so I'm not surprised she went back there."

"Sounds like she'd much rather be in New York." Kelly
deliberately fed the fire, to see if Shannon's dislike of Kimberly would jostle loose any more memories.

"Yeah, like that's gonna happen," Shannon sneered as
she checked her watch. "Whoa, I'd better go. Don't want to
be late for class." She shifted the backpack on her shoulder.

"Thanks, Shannon. It's been good talking to you," Kelly
said, watching her head down the pathway.

"You, too, Kelly. Bye." Shannon waved and picked up
her pace.

Watching her speed away through the arching cottonwood trees brought a brief memory of Kelly's own college days at the University of Virginia, years ago. Racing between classes, backpack over her shoulder, trying to ignore the gorgeous autumn display around her as she hurried from building to building.

Taking time now to enjoy the brilliant yellows and greens rustling overhead, Kelly strolled slowly toward the parking lot, pausing every now and then to drink in a particularly vivid display. The university gardeners had planted young maples that positively shouted "Look how beautiful we are!" Rich reds mixed with verdant greens of every hue and pattern—scarlet, burgundy, bloodred, fire-engine red. Kelly stopped and drank all of it in.

"Beautiful, aren't they?" a man's voice said behind her.

She turned to see the professor she'd spoken with earlier approaching, briefcase in hand. "Gorgeous. I swear these young trees must be a new strain or whatever," she replied, glancing toward the trees again. "I've never seen such vivid combinations of colors here in Colorado. Back East, where I used to live, sure. But not here, until now."

"I think you're right. They're a new variety," he agreed with a genial smile. "Did you get a chance to speak with Shannon?"

"Yes, I did. Thanks, again, Professor Jaeger, for your help," Kelly added, matching his stride towards the parking lot. "It was good to talk with her. There was another former student I wanted to talk to as well. Kimberly Gorman. Shannon said she works at a gallery in Denver. Would you happen to know which one?"

"Uh, yes, yes, I do," Professor Jaeger hesitated, clearly surprised at Kelly's request. He glanced appraisingly at her.

Kelly assumed a guileless expression. It was her most convincing, but unfortunately, it only worked on strangers. Anyone who knew her, laughed out loud when they saw it.

"Kimberly is with Santa Fe Artists. It's on Santa Fe Drive in Denver. I'm afraid I can't remember the address."

Kelly gave him her brightest smile as she backed away, planning to escape before he had the chance to ask a question of his own. "Thank you, professor." Then, from the back of her mind, another question appeared. "By the way, has anyone contacted the designer, Sophia Emeraud, in New York? Has she called about Allison?"

"Yes, she called here to the university when she couldn't reach Allison," Professor Jaeger said sadly, his genial expression clouded now. "I had to tell her what had happened. She was shocked, to say the least." He shook his head. "So tragic, so tragic."

Kelly nodded and didn't say a word. The truth about Allison's death would come out in time. Professor Jaeger and Allison's university friends would hear it then. Meanwhile, Kelly decided that Sophia Emeraud should know the truth now, out of respect for Allison if nothing else.

"Enjoy the afternoon, professor," Kelly said with a goodbye wave and headed for her car.

Once inside, she dug out her cell phone and dialed Megan's number as she drove from the parking lot.

"Megan, do you still have those bags of Allison's leftover stuff in your car, or have you mailed them already?" she asked when Megan came on the line.

"I boxed up everything and sent it to her parents the other day, why?"

"Did you put Allison's cell phone in there, or were you sending that separately?" Kelly held her breath, hoping.

There was a pause on the line followed by the sharp intake of breath. "Oh-my-gosh! Her cell phone! I completely forgot about it. Where did I put it? Oh-my-gosh, oh-my-gosh," Megan squealed, panic in her voice.

"It's okay, Megan," Kelly said, trying to calm her friend. "It's not like her parents are waiting for it or anything."

"I know, but I feel so stupid for forgetting. Wait a minute—" A sudden clunk told Kelly that Megan had dropped the phone. Sure enough, Megan returned to the line, relief pouring out. "I found it! Thank goodness," she exclaimed. "It was in the pocket of the jacket I wore that morning. I hadn't worn it since then."

Grateful for Megan's uncharacteristic bout of forgetfulness, Kelly said, "Actually, I'm glad you forgot, Megan, because we need to check her directory for phone numbers."

"You've learned something new, haven't you? What is it?"

"Well, I confirmed that Kimberly Gorman was in Fort Connor that night, because one of Allison's university friends saw her at the banquet. So, Diane Linstrom must have been right about her coming over to the apartment."

"Are you checking out everything Diane said or something?"

"No, I'm just checking a few things. I left a message for Burt to see if Diane's story checked out with the neighbors. But I did learn something else, and we have to take care of it."

"We?" Megan squeaked.

"Don't panic, it's just a phone call," Kelly reassured. "Allison's professor told me that the designer from New York, Sophia Emeraud, called the university when she didn't hear from Allison, and he told her what happened. I asked him because it occurred to me that no one had contacted her. I think we should call and tell her Allison didn't commit suicide. The police are investigating it as a homicide now. Allison would want us to tell her."

A long pause lapsed before Megan spoke in a tentative voice. "I guess you're right, but you call her, okay? I don't think I can."

"Don't worry. I'll do it. But I need you to check Allison's cell phone directory. She must have that designer's

name and number there. Matter of fact, go through the entire directory and take down all the names and numbers.
That could be important. And, check the messages."

"Anything else, Sherlock?" Megan joked.

"Oh, darn! I forgot. You don't know her password. You
won't be able to get in." Kelly scowled in frustration.

"Don't be so sure," Megan countered. "You're not the
only clever one."

"All right. We're back in business then," Kelly exulted,
turning toward the street that ran adjacent to the golf
course.

"See you later, and don't forget practice tonight."

"Absolutely," Kelly said, clicking off. She already had.

Nine

"You'll never catch him, Carl," Kelly advised her dog as he raced toward the corner of the shady, fenced backyard. A squirrel had made the mistake of abandoning the treetops to investigate some flowerpots on the concrete patio. Planning to hide a cache of nuts, Kelly figured. However, all winter storage concerns were abandoned the moment Carl came charging out the patio door. The squirrel was as fleet of foot as usual and reached the fence seconds before Carl came crashing behind. Kelly was secretly glad the little creature was as speedy as he was. Little guys needed an advantage.

Grabbing her knitting bag and coffee mug, she headed for the door—until she spotted her reflection in the antique mirror beside the front entry.

Kelly stopped and stared. God, she looked awful. Undeniably awful. Dark shadows had deepened beneath her eyes. Lack of sleep and an unrelenting workload had clearly taken a heavy toll. She was aging before her time. Right here in the mirror was proof. At this rate, she wouldn't even make it to forty. And the wrinkles weren't even waiting for thirty-five, she noticed, peering more closely into the mirror. She could see them now. She was sure of it.

Something had to be done about her work schedule. For the fourth week in a row, the number of account files coming from her corporate CPA office had increased. And every night Kelly was working into the wee hours of the early morn. Sleep was becoming shorter. And there was no letup on weekends. She'd been working straight through. The only breaks she had were the stolen moments with friends in the knitting shop or on the softball field. She'd even cancelled a dinner with Steve this week to sit in front of the computer.

Kelly scowled at her rapidly deteriorating reflection. This was ridiculous. She was going to have to have a talk with her boss. If he was trying to force her out by making the telecommuting workload so overwhelming that it was unworkable, then she needed to know. Either they could come to an agreement on her workload, or . . . or . . .

Or what? That cold feeling of uncertainty reached into her gut and squeezed. All the fearful thoughts crept out of hiding, whispering in the dark. *Are you crazy? You can't quit your job. How would you support yourself?* And, of course, the scariest thought of all: *What would your dad think? He worked until he dropped dead.* Almost. Cancer stopped him first.

Usually that thought alone was enough to keep Kelly in place, nose to the grindstone, or rather, eyes glued to the computer screen. She'd never knowingly disappoint her father. But now, she noticed those old thoughts didn't carry the same sting they used to. Strange, Kelly thought, as she closed the cottage door behind her. Something had changed, and she wasn't exactly sure what.

Heading across the driveway, Kelly was surprised to see Megan coming toward her. "Hey, did you have any luck with the cell phone?" she asked.

"Yes, I did, and we need to talk. Privately," Megan announced then glanced over her shoulder. "Why don't we sit outside and have coffee. There's an empty table away from the others."

"Whoa, what was on those phone messages?" Kelly joked, almost amused at Megan's secretive behavior.

Megan didn't respond, just gave Kelly a solemn look as she walked toward the outside patio of Pete's cafe. Signaling a waitress, Megan didn't even wait for Kelly to settle in her chair before ordering. "She'll have a huge mug of black coffee, and I'll have some Earl Grey with cream, please."

Kelly leaned back in the black wrought iron chair and watched the young waitress scurry off. "I take it you were able to get into Allison's cell phone."

"Piece of cake," Megan said with a dismissive wave. "She was still using the factory password code. You'd be surprised how many people do that."

"Do you break into many phones?" Kelly couldn't resist teasing.

Megan ignored her as she withdrew a printed page of numbers. "Here are all the numbers in her phone directory. There's Sophia, the designer from New York. See, there's Ray Baker. You and me, her parents, and lots of others. She must have had over fifty names."

Kelly glanced over the sheet. "I'll give this to Burt. He'll get it to his police partner. What about the messages? Were there many?"

"Oh, yeah. Several from the designer, right after Allison was killed, wondering why Allison hadn't contacted her or shown up." Megan shook her head. "Be sure and explain everything, okay? I don't want that woman thinking poorly about Allison."

"I promise. Now tell me what's got you all spooked?" Kelly probed. "Something's bothering you."

Megan waited until the waitress had deposited coffee

and tea before she leaned over the table. "Notice this name way down here," she said, pointing farther down the paper. "Brian. It's a Denver number. There's a message from him I want you to hear. It gave me goose bumps to listen. Everybody else's messages were normal, but his . . ." She shivered before she dug into the knitting bag and withdrew Allison's cell phone.

Kelly paged through the phone's message directory until she came to the one marked "Brian." It was dated two days before Allison's death. Kelly clicked on the message and listened.

A man's voice came across the line, a low baritone speaking just above a whisper, in angry tight tones. "I spoke with Sophia Emeraud today and asked when to ship my pieces for her show. Imagine my surprise when she didn't know what I was talking about. In fact, she didn't even know who I *was*," he hissed the last word. Kelly's skin crawled at the sound.

"You never told her about me, did you?" the ominous voice dropped lower. "You lied to me, Allison. To *me*, of all people. I'm the one who got you started, you ungrateful little bitch. And you couldn't even grant me that one favor, could you? Oh, no. You wanted all the attention for yourself, didn't you? Well, do you know what your selfishness cost me? My career, that's what! You've ruined me, damn you! Do you know that? I'd made promises to a gallery in New York that I'd be in Sophia's next show, and they set up a showing of their own. They'd even printed brochures. I had to call that smarmy little bastard today and cancel. He was livid and hung up before I finished apologizing. He'll never hire me now, Allison. I'm finished in New York. No one will hire me after this."

Kelly heard the slightest catch of despair in the man's voice, and there was a pause before he spoke again. Despair was gone and the ice had returned, along with an edge that made the hair on Kelly's neck stand on end. "I expected better from you, Allison. You knew how much this meant to me. To have you stab me in the back like this . . . I never thought you capable of such cruelty."

There was another pause, then the line went dead. Kelly switched the phone off and glanced at Megan. "I see what you mean. He sounded pretty scary. Who is this guy?"

"He's listed as 'Brian' with no last name," Megan offered from behind an oversized teacup.

"This has got to be the 'Brian' that Allison mentions in her diary. I wish we knew who he was."

"I checked the number to see if a name or address came up, but it isn't listed. All we know is he called from the Denver area code region, but who knows where he lives."

Kelly stared at the little phone as if it could speak. "The police should know about him." She held her oversized coffee cup closer, absorbing its warmth, before she took a sip.

"Perfect timing," Megan said, glancing toward the driveway. "There's Burt. Hey, Burt! Over here," she called, waving at their friend in the parking lot.

Burt returned her wave and strode toward the cafe patio. "Hey, I was coming to find you two," he said with a friendly grin. "Okay if I join you?"

"Don't even ask, Burt," Kelly chided. "We were just talking about you."

"Well, I've got some news that the two of you will find pretty interesting, I'll bet," he said as he sat. Leaning his arms on the table, he hunched forward in what Kelly called his "confidential" pose. "My partner, Dan Jacobsen, told me that Ray Baker is definitely arousing a lot of interest in the department. They've corroborated all of the downstairs neighbor's statements, and Baker is getting bigger and bigger on the radar screen. Particularly after a couple of other neighbors confirmed Baker's threatening behavior after Allison threw him out."

Kelly felt a tightened muscle in her chest let go. Thank goodness it wasn't all Diane Linstrom's overactive imagination. "Including his trashing Allison's car?"

Burt nodded. "Yep. We checked the mechanic where she had the car towed. He had pictures, and the insurance guy confirmed as well. It was totally torn apart inside. And that neighbor swore Baker left another threatening note in the car." He shook his head, as if still amazed at another human being's violent behavior. "Since everything else of hers checked out, the department believes her on this, too, even though they never found a note."

"The diary mentions it, though," Megan pointed out, eyes wide as saucers.

"You're right, Megan," Burt said with a smile. "Good sleuthing. You been taking lessons from Kelly?" He winked across the table.

Megan blushed. "No, I'm not as brave as Kelly, she's—"

"Was there anything else in the diary that helped?" Kelly deliberately interrupted before Megan could reveal their latest investigatory efforts.

"All of it helped," he replied. "It definitely showed that Allison was scared of Ray Baker. Of course, it could never be used as evidence or anything, but it steered the guys in the right direction."

"And it looks like that's Ray Baker," Kelly prompted.

Burt nodded. "What with his drug problem, which they've confirmed, and his being the source for Allison's pills, which was also confirmed. They found the guy who was supplying Baker and squeezed. Baker got a regular order of the same sleeping pills that were found in Allison's coffee." He settled back into the chair now and waved away the approaching waitress. "Plus, the neighbor told us Allison had a weakness for those real sweet specialty coffees. And if she knew that, then Baker surely did. After all, he lived with Allison."

"So, the police think Baker came over that night with a poisoned coffee? Boy, if I'd been Allison, I wouldn't have opened the door. Judging from what she wrote in her diary about him, I mean. He was always yelling and threatening." Kelly purposely sketched in a scenario to see how Burt would respond.

"You know, Kelly, I was thinking the same thing after I read those diary entries, but my partner thinks Baker actually went over to the apartment twice. And they think he brought the coffee on the second visit."

Kelly had to clamp her mouth shut to keep from saying "Yes!" Instead, she affected surprise, noticing Megan was studiously staring into her teacup as if a bug were swimming in it. "Really? Why do you think that?"

"Because the neighbor remembers seeing him earlier in the evening, but he didn't stay long. And she swears she heard Allison banging around upstairs packing afterward, which would be hard to do if she was poisoned. Then, the neighbor swears she heard footsteps sneaking up the stairs later that night and walking around in Allison's apartment. After that, nothing. No noise."

Burt's voice had dropped dramatically with the now familiar recitation of events, Kelly noticed, but she continued to play along. "Well, that certainly sounds suspicious."

"The department thought so, too, especially when she said she noticed an unfamiliar dark car parked across the street."

"You think Baker came in a different car with the coffee?" she prodded.

"It's a possibility, Kelly," Burt affirmed. "Of course, the investigation is still in progress. If Baker is brought in for questioning, I'll let you know."

Kelly took a long sip of her coffee, pondering Burt's news. Apparently the police had confirmed everything that Diane Linstrom told them. So, Kelly's first instincts about

Diane were right. She did make a powerful, credible witness. Why then, was this annoying little insect still buzzing in the back of her brain?

She picked up Allison's cell phone from the table. "Take this to your old partner, Burt. It's Allison's cell phone. She gave it to Megan to buy a new battery when they were packing up her apartment. Megan understandably forgot it was in her pocket the morning of the murder. She was going to mail it to Allison's parents, but fortunately she listened to the messages first." Kelly looked Burt in the eye. "There's a pretty scary message on the voice mail. You need to hear it, Burt. It's from some guy in the Denver area named 'Brian.'" She handed him the phone.

"Where was this again, Megan?" he asked, eyebrows furrowed.

"In the pocket of the jacket I was wearing the morning we walked in and . . . and found Allison," Megan explained breathlessly, face flushed. "I totally forgot about it until yesterday. I swear!"

Burt stared at the phone, then shot a glance at Kelly. "I have a feeling it wasn't your idea to listen to the messages, was it, Megan?"

Kelly raised her hand. "I confess. I made her do it. We wanted to know if that New York designer had called Allison when she didn't arrive. We wanted her number so we could call and tell her what happened." She smiled innocently, which she was able to pull off because everything she said was the truth. That is exactly why they'd searched the phone. The fact that they'd also uncovered a mysterious message was purely by accident. "Here's the list of numbers in the cell directory that Megan made. I was going to give this to you today. Honest." She grinned as she handed him the list.

"Let me write down Sophia's number first," Megan interjected, digging out a pen and paper.

"Which message disturbed you?" he asked, thumbing through the directory. "Brian?"

Kelly and Megan nodded dutifully and sat without a word, watching Burt listen to the menacing message from Denver. Burt's face remained impassive as he clicked off.

"Megan and I both thought that guy sounds pretty darn scary," Kelly offered.

Burt pursed his mouth in a way Kelly noticed he did when he didn't want to commit himself. "Well, I agree he sounds mad as hell, but I wouldn't say scary."

"He sure scared me, Burt," Megan swore earnestly.

Kelly could tell Burt was trying to hide his smile. "I'll be sure to give the phone and the list to my partner. He'll give it a thorough once-over. Thanks again, Megan. You did a good job bringing this to me." Burt's voice reached over and verbally patted Megan on the head as he stood up to leave. "I'd better get inside before Mimi starts teaching my class. See you gals later."

"Thanks, Burt," Kelly called after him as he hastened down the flagstone path toward the shop's entry.

"What do you think?" Megan asked. "Burt didn't sound too impressed with that phone call. Are we so close to this stuff we can't judge anymore?"

"Maybe so, Megan," Kelly agreed. "But I'm with you. That Brian certainly wasn't calling to wish Allison good luck in her new career. Heck, no." She shook her head. "Let's wait and see what Burt's old partner thinks about this guy."

"Hey, you two," Lisa called from the parking lot.

Kelly beckoned her over to join them. Megan had already taken out her knitting and was working the neck edges of the somber navy-blue sweater. Kelly followed her lead and picked up where she'd left off on her circular sweater.

"Great idea," Lisa announced as she pulled out a chair.

"Let's take advantage of the great fall weather while we still have it. Winter will be upon us next month, probably."

"Whoa," Kelly said. "You're right. It's been over a year since I've been here in wintertime, and it was usually only for the holidays. I may have to buy a real winter coat."

Lisa grinned across the table as she worked the blue-gray yarn into lacy knots. "That means you're seriously thinking about staying here and not going back East?"

Kelly blinked. Had she really meant that? Had her real intention slipped out? All of her friends knew she wanted to stay here. But she hadn't made a decision yet. Had she? "Welllll," she hedged. "I'm not sure my boss will let me stay much longer, so I don't know for sure."

"C'mon, Kelly. You've been saying that for months now, yet you're still here," Lisa countered in her infuriatingly observant way. "Either you still want to stay here, or your boss wants you to stay here. Which is it?"

"That's easy," Kelly admitted with a laugh. "I want to stay here. All I have to do is find a way."

"I thought Curt was working on that now," Lisa continued.

The Lambspun network was up to the minute with the latest information, Kelly acknowledged. Amazing. Faster than the Web at times. Maybe it was telepathy. All her friends seemed to read her mind. Brother, she never would be able to keep a secret.

"Yes, he is. But it all depends on how much income that Wyoming land would produce," Kelly said, feeling the peaceful sensation settle as the rows of stockinette appeared.

"I thought I spied you guys." Jennifer strode up to the table and joined them. "It's so gorgeous out here, I think I'll trade sections with Sara so I can be outside today," she said, pulling out a vivid sapphire-blue yarn and extra large needles.

Kelly noticed Megan sit up and take notice, clearly attracted to Jennifer's new project. That was a good sign, Kelly decided. Megan was coming out of her self-imposed mourning.

"What're you making?" Megan asked, peering at the bright yarn.

"I'm thinking of adding some sequined yarn and making a loose-weave shawl like the one Lisa is finishing," Jennifer said, casting loopy stitches onto a large needle. Glancing toward Pete, who was crossing the patio, Jennifer called out, "Pete, is it okay if I take my break outside today? Everybody's here."

"Are you kidding, Jen? Your friends make up a quarter of my business. Sit wherever you want," Pete joked, without breaking stride as he led two construction workers around the building.

"Thanks, Pete, you're a sweetheart."

"That's what all the girls tell me," Pete retorted.

"Was Burt giving you an update or something?" Jennifer asked Kelly. "I saw him talking with you."

"He just told us that Allison's old boyfriend is looking kind of suspicious, given his violent behavior," Kelly said, deliberately not giving too many details.

"Everything Allison said in her diary was backed up by that neighbor," Megan volunteered earnestly, concentrating on the neckline once again.

"You read her diary?" Jennifer sounded appalled.

"Well, I found it in a bag of her things, and . . . and I thought it might have some information," Megan said defensively.

Jennifer shook her head. "Boy, I wouldn't want you reading my diary. Or anyone else, either."

"Megan wouldn't be able to read yours, Jennifer," Kelly shot back, hoping to mute Megan's embarrassment. "It's X-rated. Megan only reads PG or R diaries."

Her comment was greeted by good-natured laughter that bounced around the table as each of them joined in ribbing Jennifer.

"Hey, at least I have a sex life," Jennifer retorted. "Not like someone I know who's knitting a rose-colored sweater-in-the-round right beside me. Not to mention names, of course."

"Excuse me?" Kelly countered, not sure she liked the tables being turned.

"See? It's been so long, she doesn't even know what we're talking about," Jennifer addressed the others. "Someone's going to have to explain the process before she goes out again."

"Oh, and speaking of going out, look who's coming," Lisa teased, glancing over her shoulder.

Kelly looked up and saw Steve coming their way, engaging grin in place. She felt her cheeks get hotter. If it wouldn't be so obvious, she'd give Jennifer a swift kick under the table. Unfortunately, Jennifer would announce it to everyone, and Kelly would wind up even more embarrassed. She couldn't win. When Jennifer was in a teasing mood, it was no-holds-barred. Kelly took a deep breath.

"Did Mimi pay you guys to sit out here and knit?" Steve quipped as he strolled up to the table. "It's a great advertisement for the shop."

"We're enjoying this gorgeous weather before it disappears," Lisa said with a smile. "You're welcome to join us. We'll even measure you for a sweater."

Steve laughed. "That's okay. I promised Mimi I'd run a couple of errands for her."

"Hey, it'll only take a second," Lisa teased, leaving her chair. "Gimme that sweater, Megan. You'll never wear that color, and you know it." Lisa snatched the sober navy-blue garment out of Megan's hands.

"Hey!" Megan protested, laughing at the same time. "I will wear it, honest."

"No, you won't. You want this color, admit it," Jennifer taunted, waving the vibrant sapphire-blue shawl coming to life on her needles.

"What the heck . . . ?" Steve said, laughing as Lisa held the drab navy sweater up to his chest.

"Good job, Megan. You made this extra large. It almost fits Steve," Lisa said, stretching a sleeve down his arm.

"That's Megan's worry sweater," Kelly ventured into the fun. "The more she worries, the longer it gets."

"Better take it now, Lisa," Jennifer advised. "Before it gets any bigger."

"That's okay, guys. I'm not really the cardigan type," Steve said with a laugh as he backed away from Lisa and her measurements. Heading down the stone path, he glanced back at Kelly. "Hey, Kelly, you missed some great jazz last Saturday. Let's reschedule that dinner when you come up for air, okay? Let me know."

Busted. Kelly braced herself. Steve just blew her cover.

An enormous cloud of Absolute Silence descended over the cafe table. Kelly kept her rapt attention focused on the neat rows of stockinette continuing to form, but gone was the peaceful knitting feeling. She felt her face growing warmer. Maybe if she ignored them, maybe . . .

Not a chance. She slowly lifted her gaze from the yarn to the faces of her friends. Lisa was smirking at her, Megan was grinning ear-to-ear. Only Jennifer wasn't smiling. She was staring at Kelly as if she'd sprouted another head.

When in doubt, play dumb. Kelly stared innocently. "What?"

"That's great, Kelly!" Megan exclaimed, her face as flushed as Kelly's felt.

"Don't pull that innocent look with us, Kelly. We know

you," Lisa taunted. "All I can say is it's about time. When did you start seeing Steve?"

"Start? Well, uhhhhh . . ." Kelly stalled.

"*Start?* She hasn't started anything!" Jennifer broke in, staring at Kelly incredulously. "You heard Steve. He just said she backed out of their dinner date. I cannot believe you'd do that, Kelly. You stood him up. Steve, of all people."

"Hey, I didn't stand him up," Kelly protested, decidedly on the defensive now. "I told him I was swamped with accounts. He understood."

"You're nuts, you know that?" Jennifer declared. "To dump a great guy like Steve who really likes you is—"

"Crazy," Lisa decreed as she settled back into her chair. "I have to agree with Jennifer on this one. All that corporate accounting has drained your brain cells. You are running on empty, girl."

"Hey—"

Megan shook her head, looking at Kelly sadly. "They're right, Kelly. You've got to get a life."

Kelly stared blankly at Megan. Super geek, stay-at-home, too-shy-to-date Megan had just decreed that Kelly had no life. Something was wrong with this picture. Or, was there?

"Wait a minute," Kelly defended herself. "I can't help my workload, I—"

"Kelly, that's an excuse, and you know it." Lisa eyed her sternly. "You need to clear your head. Why don't you join Greg and me next weekend on a hike? Come up with us into the mountains and breathe that fresh air. It'll clear out those cobwebs."

"Are you kidding? I'd probably pass out from the lack of oxygen at that altitude," Kelly attempted to joke.

"I rest my case," Lisa replied. "All you do is sit at that computer most of the day, visit with us for a few minutes, and play a little ball. Then, you head back to the computer. You're out of shape for a Colorado girl."

Kelly opened her mouth, but closed it again. She had no response. Lisa was dead on. Damnably infuriating, analytical Lisa had done it again. Hit a bullseye. She would have made a good accountant.

"No, I don't think that's the right place," Jennifer said, observing Kelly. "She needs more than a hike in the mountains. She needs a retreat. There's a great convent up north of here. Since you've obviously taken the vows, you'll fit right in, Kelly."

Kelly stared at Jennifer. Convent? Vows? What the heck? "Wait a minute, what do you know about convents?"

"Hey, just because I'm lapsed doesn't mean I'm no longer Catholic. I keep up. Besides, I went up there on a retreat myself once. Really peaceful."

Jennifer on a retreat at a convent? That image would take more imagination than Kelly possessed.

"Of course, it's a comtemplative order, so the nuns don't talk much," Jennifer continued blithely. "I know that'll be a problem for you, but it's only a weekend."

"*Me?* I have a problem with talking?" Kelly cried, amazed at Jennifer's pronouncement.

"You can take your knitting, too. I did. Matter of fact, the nuns do some knitting of their own, but it's a little different," Jennifer chattered away, seemingly oblivious to the laughter of her friends. "They have a farm with livestock and crops, so they knit together a web of rope to keep the silage from blowing. It's really fun to watch them. They use broomsticks for needles."

Kelly shook her head. Entirely too many conflicting images were fighting for space. Jennifer retreating to a convent. Knitting nuns. Broomstick needles. Farm, livestock, silage. What the heck was silage anyway?

She held up her hand. "Enough. I'm on overload. Cannot process any more input."

"That is precisely your problem," Jennifer fixed her with a wicked grin. "And Steve is decidedly new input. Or, he wants to be."

Lisa sniggered at that comment, and Megan blushed. Kelly pondered. Did she miss something? Was there a joke in there somewhere? Brother, Lisa was right. She really was losing brain cells. Which would it be, the mountains or the nunnery?

Kelly didn't get a chance to think about it too long, because a high-pitched female voice called out from the parking lot. "Jennifer! I've brought your sweater."

She turned and recognized Jennifer's friend Trish approaching, a forest-green sweater in hand.

"Hey, thanks, Trish," Jennifer said, reaching out for the sweater. "I appreciate it. Are you working afternoon shifts now?"

Trish gave a girlish wave. "Naw, I don't go on till five. Besides, the restaurant would never let me get away with jeans." She gestured to her clothes.

Kelly looked her over and decided the jeans were not the problem, even though they looked painted on, they were so tight. It was Trish's low-cut scoop-neck shirt that might raise a few eyebrows and cause more than a few spilled drinks. Maybe a choking incident or two. Trish's voluptuous figure was definitely on display. Kelly hoped the restaurant's staff was up-to-date with CPR.

"You remember these guys from the other night in Old Town, right?" Jennifer gestured toward them.

"Yeah, the softball team, right?" Trish said with her high wattage smile. "Do you guys sit out here and knit a lot?"

Kelly stifled a laugh, letting Lisa answer. It was clear from Trish's question that she pictured them sitting in rockers like premature grannies.

"Sometimes, we do," Lisa answered sweetly. "It's so nice out here and—"

"Whoa!" Trish interrupted, her gaze fixed on the parking lot. "There's that cute guy again. This time I'm getting his number. See ya, Jen." Trish was already walking away, leaving a trail of words floating after her.

Kelly glanced at the parking lot and spotted Steve approaching his truck. Trish clearly had him in her sights and was closing in fast. Oh, brother! Kelly flinched inside. Now, she'd really be in for it. Just when she thought the teasing had died down.

Steve greeted Trish with his engaging smile, Kelly noticed before she deliberately turned away. She didn't want to watch this. Trish was probably leaning over his truck in full flirt.

"Well, well, well," Jennifer said, shooting a devilish grin at Kelly. "Looks like our buddy, Steve, is going to get a little action."

"Jennifer!" Megan cried, clearly shocked.

"Well, Kelly doesn't want him," Jennifer said with a nonchalant gesture. "Besides, she's taken the vows. But I guarantee Trish hasn't. She'll show him a good time."

Lisa ducked her head and laughed softly, but Megan lifted her nose and said, "Trish is not Steve's type."

"Are you kidding?" Jennifer cackled. "Trish is *every* man's type. I have yet to see a man resist her full frontal assault."

Lisa burst out laughing at that, and Kelly had to join in. She couldn't resist, even though she knew she was the intended recipient of all this teasing.

"Frontal is right," Lisa agreed.

"I'm serious. There's not a man alive that could resist her. Heck, she'd even thaw out that old guy who's always on television talking about interest rates, you know , ."

Kelly stared at Jennifer in disbelief. The image of Trish

seducing the elderly chairman of the Federal Reserve definitely would not come into focus. Thank goodness.

"He's eighty years old, Jennifer. Think what havoc that would cause with the financial markets," Kelly teased. "Better sic her on somebody else."

"Well, Steve is young, healthy, and strong. I'm sure he'll survive," Jennifer added, picking up the sapphire shawl again.

As if on cue, Kelly heard the sound of a truck engine. She couldn't help herself. She looked. Sure enough, Steve was pulling out of the parking lot with Trish in the passenger seat. Kelly braced herself for the next wave.

It didn't come. Not at first. They all sat quietly for a couple of minutes, only the knitting needles moving. Then, Megan spoke up softly. "You've known Steve the longest, Lisa. Didn't he have a girlfriend a few years ago?"

Lisa nodded. "Yep. Sandra. Nice girl. She was a lawyer with the EPA in Denver. I guess the distance really took its toll on the relationship, though. They stopped seeing each other about three years ago. About the time Steve was building up his construction business."

"All work and no play . . ." Jennifer left the rest of it dangling.

Lisa grinned. "Yeah, he's been with several different women since then."

"Playing the field. Smart strategy. I highly recommend it," Jennifer decreed in a professional tone.

"Centerfield, actually," Megan interjected with a giggle.

Kelly had to laugh out loud at last. "You guys are outrageous. You know that? You've made your point, okay? I work too much. I don't play enough. I live like a nun. And I have no life." Kelly cried out, "I give up. You win. You guys can stop now."

"But we were having so much fun," Lisa said.

"*You* were."

Jennifer started to shove her knitting away. "Fun's over. Got to get back to work. Oh, by the way, Kelly, whenever you get some spare time and are not glued to the computer, I can tell you about one of my clients who donated a portion of his farmland. There's more than one way to set it up. I figured you might be interested."

"You bet I would," Kelly replied, as an idea that had been stirring at the back of her mind moved to the front. "Matter of fact, do you have a day this week you could spare? I thought I'd go to Denver. You can come along and fill me in on land donation while we drive."

"You can get away to Denver, but you can't have dinner with Steve," Lisa barbed.

"I can plan ahead and work around it," Kelly countered, studiously ignoring Lisa's jibe. "How about you, Jen? You up for it?"

"Yeah, I think I can swing it," Jennifer said as she drew away. "We can do a little shopping, then go by some clubs. Sounds good. Talk to you later."

Clubs? Kelly hadn't planned on club-hopping, but it was too late to back out now.

"Good luck getting home before dawn," Lisa warned.

Megan looked at Kelly with a little smile. "I think I know why you're going to Denver. You're going to see Kimberly, aren't you?"

"Who's Kimberly?" Lisa asked, needles busily creating the open-weave design.

"Kimberly Gorman is another designer that went to school with Allison," Megan explained. "And I'll bet Kelly's going to ask questions. Am I right, Kelly?"

Kelly grinned. "Boy, I have got to do something about you guys reading my mind. This is getting scary."

Lisa shook her head. "Sleuthing again. You take a whole day to play Sherlock, but you can't even spare one night for dinner with Steve. I don't know, Kelly."

At that, Kelly gave in and threw up her hands in total surrender, joining the good-natured laughter that bubbled around the table. Even though she was the butt of the joke, somehow she didn't mind at all.

Ten

"Where are we heading first?" Jennifer asked as Kelly changed lanes on the fast-moving interstate.

Denver's skyline rose straight ahead, glass and steel and angular designs competing with turn-of-the-century brick. Kelly noticed the number of skyscrapers had increased over the last fifteen years as Denver's population grew. Suburbs sprawled endlessly from the hub of the city, devouring farmland to the east and north and foothills to the west and south. Traffic, of course, had become correspondingly awful. Mid-morning, however, was endurable if not pleasant.

"We're going over to Santa Fe Drive first. Professor Jaeger said the gallery where Kimberly works is located there. Plus I remember Megan mentioning several other galleries along that stretch. I don't know about the shopping. You may have to hang with me for a while, Jen. I promise we'll head into LoDo later."

Kelly was secretly hoping Jennifer would exhaust herself with all the trendy boutiques in Denver's redeveloped

Lower Downtown area. The once shabby streets formerly
housed warehouses and abandoned buildings. Now the area
was completely renovated, buildings restored or rebuilt
with turn-of-the-century architectural charm intact. The
formerly dead streets pulsed with a new energy as people
poured in, drawn by specialty shops, bookstores, coffeehouses, and restaurants of every persuasion. And, of course,
there were the clubs. Lots of clubs. Kelly wasn't sure if
even shopping could keep Jennifer from the clubs.

"That's okay. I enjoy a gallery stroll every now and
then," Jennifer said. "Don't worry. I won't cramp your
sleuthing style. I'll pick another gallery farther down the
street. What kind of information are you trying to pry out of
this Kimberly, anyway?"

Kelly grinned. "Actually, I'm not sure. I plan to start
talking about Allison and see what happens. See how she
reacts, see what she says. I'll play it by ear, I guess."

"Gutsy," Jennifer replied. "But that's your style. By the
way, Megan said you called that designer in New York. I'll
bet she was surprised to hear about Allison."

"Yes, she was," Kelly said, guiding her car onto the
Santa Fe Drive exit ramp. "She was as shocked as we were.
I could tell she really cared about Allison from the sound of
her voice. It was clear that she thought of Allison as this
budding star, and she wanted to help develop her talent. Of
course, she couldn't understand how anyone would kill her,
and she made me promise to keep her posted with how the
police investigation develops."

"Is she still going to use some of Allison's designs in her
show? Or did that idea die along with Allison?"

"You know, I took a chance and asked her that, too. She
told me she was definitely including them in the show. Sort
of a tribute to Allison, so to speak."

"Hey, that would make a great road trip, wouldn't it?"
Jennifer suggested. "We could all go to New York for a

fashion show. I'm up for it. Maybe you and Steve could drive us. How about it?"

Kelly chuckled. "A four-thousand-mile road trip? I don't think so, Jen. I'm not sure Steve could get away either. I sure can't," she added as she drove along Santa Fe Drive.

"Oh, incidentally, he and Trish never got together," Jennifer mentioned as she stared out the window. "Trish said she'd call him again. She's relentless, you know."

"Don't distract me, Jennifer, I'm looking for a parking place," Kelly admonished. "Wait . . . I think I see one." She turned swiftly and slid into an empty curb space.

"Perfect," Jennifer said as she climbed out and slammed the car door.

Kelly glanced along both sides of the street as she clicked the car lock. "I think that's Kimberly's gallery up the street. Santa Fe Artists."

Jennifer surveyed the streets with a professional shopper's eye. "I see lots of shops to keep me occupied. I'll cruise along both sides and find you later. You can't get lost in a gallery, can you?"

"I'll try not to," Kelly promised with a grin.

Several other galleries beckoned to Kelly as she walked along, artwork reaching through the windows, tempting her to stop. She'd succumb later. Right now, Kelly wanted to meet the much-maligned Kimberly Gorman, wondering if she was really as unpleasant in person as others had said. Crossing a side street, Kelly approached the first of two wide front windows proclaiming SANTA FE ARTISTS. She paused briefly at the color beckoning from inside before entering.

This building must have been some sort of warehouse, Kelly decided as she stepped into a large open room with white-painted walls that rose to join a high ceiling. Now, the white walls were adorned with canvases of oil and acrylic, weavings of all manner of fibers, pottery masks,

stonework and metal carvings. Glass display cases were
arranged in cozy browsing sections around the worn oak
floor, holding ceramics of every description, jewelry of
gemstones and hand-painted china, and intricate carved
wooden figures.

Kelly stood quietly and drank in the color and texture of
it all, exactly as she did whenever she entered a shop filled
with luscious yarns. She let the sensual wave wash over her.

A slender man appeared from a corner doorway and
smiled at her. "How delightful. An art lover who appreci-
ates morning light. Browse at will, my dear," he called out
in a friendly tone before he disappeared into what Kelly assumed was an office.

Kelly did just that. She started at the front of the gallery
and wandered through all the displays, absorbing the colors
and textures even though she couldn't reach out and touch.

"Is this your first visit?" a tall brunette asked as she approached.

"Yes, it is," Kelly answered, observing the woman.

She wore her dark hair swept up and fastened with a
gold clasp, which heightened her elegant long neck, high
cheekbones, and olive complexion. Her eyes were hazel
and observed Kelly coolly. This had to be Kimberly, Kelly
figured. The aloof expression and statuesque poise probably got beneath the skin of some of the less composed design students.

"You have a marvelous variety of artwork displayed,"
Kelly remarked. "How many artists exhibit in your
gallery?"

"Oh, it varies. We can have anywhere from ten to twenty
or so exhibiting at the same time. It all depends on which
pieces they want displayed." The aloof expression warmed.
"There's only so much wall and floor space. And, of course,
we all continually change our exhibit pieces, too."

Kelly paused in her deliberate stroll and focused on the

young woman. She'd heard the opening she needed. "We? Is there a particular group that exhibits here?"

"Yes, indeed." She gestured to a back doorway. "We all rent studio space here and contribute to the maintenance of the gallery. It's sort of like a cooperative of artists, you might say. Eugene Tolliver actually owns the building and manages the displays."

"Do you have any pieces here?" Kelly asked.

"That's my weaving over there." She pointed to a wall. Kelly surveyed the red, black, and white fabric draped above a grouping of charcoal portraits. The fabric's design was striking. Devoid of a discernible pattern, it resembled an abstract painting. The weaving was drastically different from anything she'd seen other weavers make, including Allison.

"Wow, that's striking," Kelly observed out loud. "It's so bold and . . . and . . ."

"And out there," the brunette agreed, a real smile claiming her face this time.

"You must be the weaver that Professor Jaeger mentioned," Kelly ventured. "Is your name Kimberly?"

"Yes, I'm Kimberly Gorman. What did Professor Jaeger say about me?" Kimberly's smile had vanished quickly, replaced by a wary expression.

"He mentioned that you worked at this gallery," Kelly explained in an off-hand manner. "I was asking him about some of his design students."

"Why? Are you interested in studying design? If so, I can highly recommend Professor Jaeger's classes. He's a gifted designer himself and is very supportive of his students."

Kelly deliberately resumed her slow stroll so she could process what she'd heard. Kimberly had kind words about her former teacher, not snide comments or lukewarm praise. Could it be that the other students' versions of Kimberly's behavior were colored by their jealousy of her obvious talent? Not to mention the discomfort some of them no doubt felt in her presence. Kimberly's laser-like stare was definitely formidable, even for a veteran of corporate skirmishing like Kelly.

"Well, that's good to hear," Kelly replied. "He certainly has some talented students. I saw their work when I visited him the other day."

"Why were you visiting, again?" Kimberly pressed. "Are you an artist?"

Kelly had to laugh at that. "No, not at all. I can barely draw a straight line. Maybe that's why I admire those who can create all this." She gestured to the walls and glass displays.

"I visited the professor to ask some questions about Allison Dubois."

The change in Kimberly's expression was immediate. Her eyes widened, and Kelly detected a touch of apprehension there. But Kimberly said nothing, so Kelly continued in the same matter-of-fact tone.

"He did tell you about Allison's death, didn't he?"

"Ah, yes, yes, he did," Kimberly answered in a softer voice. "That . . . that was awful. I was shocked to hear it."

Kelly nodded in somber agreement. "All of her friends were. I hadn't known Allison as long as some others, but I couldn't believe she'd take her own life. That's why we went to the police with our concerns. The police investigated further and discovered that Kimberly's death was not a suicide at all. She was murdered."

Cool and aloof no longer, Kimberly's mouth dropped open, clearly astonished by what she'd heard. Her face paled as well.

"Murdered?" Kimberly whispered. "Who . . . who . . ." Her voice trailed off.

"The police are still investigating," Kelly replied. "Apparently Allison had a boyfriend with some violent history. Neighbors said he was over at her apartment that night."

This time, Kimberly's olive complexion paled to alabaster, and Kelly swore she detected a slight backward step, as if Kimberly wanted to run away from what she was hearing but couldn't.

Kimberly wrapped both arms around herself as if she was cold, even though the brilliant morning sunshine warmed the gallery's open space. "Do . . . do they think he killed her?" she whispered.

Kelly shrugged noncommitally. "They're investigating him and anyone else who might have seen her that night. My friend Megan spent the whole day helping Allison pack, so the police questioned her thoroughly. I know, because I was there. I'm Kelly Flynn, another friend of Allison's" Kelly shook her head. "You see, Megan and I were the ones who found Allison that morning. We went to pick her up for the airport."

"Oh, God . . . that's awful . . ."

Kelly nodded, then fixed Kimberly with a laser stare of her own. "Didn't the police call you with questions?"

This time, Kimberly actually took a backward step. "*Me?* Why . . . why would they call me?" she asked, clearly horrified at the thought.

"Because the downstairs neighbor said she saw one of Allison's friends visit her that night. She remembered Allison called out the name 'Kimberly' when she opened the door." Kelly kept her voice friendly. "I assumed that was you. You were the only Kimberly Professor Jaeger mentioned."

Kimberly swayed on her feet ever so slightly. Kelly wasn't sure if her terrified reaction was caused by a guilty conscience or by shock. She stared at Kelly, speechless. Gone was the composure. Kelly sensed a curious vulnerability emanating from Kimberly now.

"To be honest, that's why I came here today, Kimberly. I was hoping you might remember seeing someone or something when you visited Allison that night?" Kelly deliberately phrased her question as a matter-of-fact statement. Kimberly was seen at Allison's apartment, so there was absolutely no wiggle room for denial.

Kimberly's mouth opened once, twice, as if she was trying to speak but couldn't. If her reaction was a contrived performance, then she was one talented actress as well as artist, Kelly decided. Her horror at the discovery of her visit was real. So was her fear. Kelly could practically see the fevered memories that must be running through Kimberly's mind right now—former jealousies, arguments, frustrations boiling over into anger. All magnified and blown out of proportion when related by fellow students who harbored no good will.

"I . . . I . . . I didn't stay long," she admitted in a contrite tone. "And I didn't see anyone else hanging around, either. Honest. I was only in there a few moments. *Really!*"

Part of Kelly wanted to stop her interrogation. Kimberly's voice held a childlike plaintive quality to it. Looking for approval and not finding it. But there was one question left, and Kelly had to ask it.

"I'm curious, Kimberly. Why'd you go over there anyway? I heard you and Allison had an argument after the banquet that night. Did you go over to make peace or something?"

Kimberly stared back at Kelly as if an Inquisitioner's robe had suddenly materialized. Her face was chalk white with fear. Kelly could practically smell it. But this fear was different. It had nothing to do with Allison or petty jealousies or even art, itself. Kelly sensed this fear came from somewhere else, some private place within, a deep wound.

Tears welled up in Kimberly's frightened eyes and spilled silently down her cheeks. She didn't make a sound.

Instead, she clutched herself tighter and closed her eyes as her voice choked. "That's why . . . that's why I went. I wanted to apologize for everything I'd said after dinner. I'd had some drinks . . . and I made a fool of myself in front of everyone." She bit her lip. "Stupid, stupid, it was all so stupid. I was just so tired of being second. Always second to Allison. Always pushing it down, trying not to let it show, but it spilled out anyway." She shook her head.

Kelly watched Kimberly berate herself for her behavior and felt the unmistakable resonance of truth in her words. Kelly'd been there, herself, a time or two. Berating herself for a hasty word or action. She had an advanced degree in kicking herself. Kelly dug into her over-the-shoulder purse and grabbed a handful of tissues.

"Here, use these, and stop being so hard on yourself," she said, handing them to Kimberly.

Kimberly's eyes blinked open and she stared out at Kelly with a wet gaze of total surprise. Without saying anything, she took the tissues and wiped her face thoroughly. She even managed to blow her nose daintily, something Kelly had never quite mastered.

"I can't imagine how hard that must have been," Kelly said gently. "Artists have to be so brave to even create, let alone put it out there for others to judge. I admire you for persevering. And, it looks like you've attracted some attention." She gestured toward Kimberly's dramatic woven exhibit.

"Thank you," Kimberly said between ladylike snuffles. "You're very kind to say that."

"I'm not being kind," Kelly retorted, looking Kimberly in the eye. "I'm being totally honest. That piece is really dramatic. Do you have any more here on display? I'd love to see them." She smiled warmly.

Kimberly responded like a chastised puppy whose owner suddenly patted its head. Gratitude spilled over into

her voice. "Oh, yes, yes. Why don't we go back to my studio space? I've got more back there." She eagerly beckoned
Kelly towards the door in the rear of the gallery. "Eugene,
could you watch the floor for a few moments?" she called
to the man Kelly'd seen earlier.

Apparently he'd been silently arranging a display case
while they talked. Kelly wondered how much the gallery
owner had overheard and proceeded to kick herself mentally for not noticing.

"Take as long as you need, my dear," Eugene replied in
a kind voice.

The rear doorway opened to a long hallway which was
bordered on both sides by workrooms. Most doors were
wide open even if the artist wasn't present. This afforded
Kelly an unobscured look into the creative processes of several artists.

Kimberly strolled slowly through the hallway, pointing
out metal sculptures, potters at their wheels, modern stain-
less steel kilns with blinking red lights hulking in the corners. Watercolor artists, whose work was so delicate Kelly
thought it would float off the paper with the slightest
breeze. Canvases of oil and acrylic, bold colors and muted,
landscapes, geometric designs, nudes realistically rendered
and abstract, portraits of birth and decay.

Kelly followed Kimberly, absorbing the colors that
seemed to pulsate from each studio like music. "Thanks so
much, Kimberly," she said as they headed back toward the
gallery once more. "I've never had a chance to see art in the
making behind the scenes, except on film. It's so much
more vibrant in real life. And the weavings in your work-
room are as gorgeous as the one on display."

Kimberly beamed. "Thank you, Kelly. It was my pleasure to show you around." Glancing at her watch, she
added, "I'm afraid I have to leave for an appointment now.
Please stay and browse as long as you like."

"Thank you. My friend should be meeting me here in a few minutes." She gave Kimberly her warmest smile. "And thank you for being so tolerant. I hope I didn't upset you too much with my nosy questions. Sometimes I get carried away when I'm poking around. Sleuthing, my friends call it."

"Actually, Kelly, it was good to talk with you about Allison," Kimberly said, staring off into the sunlit gallery. "I've been carrying that stuff around for so long, it was feeling really heavy inside. I can't explain it, but I feel, I don't know, lighter, somehow." She gave a crooked little smile. "Thanks, Kelly. Stay in touch, okay? I want to know what you find out."

"It's a promise."

Kimberly headed for the back hallway. "Eugene, I'm leaving for that appointment now, okay? Edward should be here soon."

"That's fine, Kimberly. Good luck with the interview," Eugene called after her as he strolled toward Kelly.

Kelly checked her watch and resumed her leisurely walk through the gallery once more. It was after twelve noon, so hunger would surely bring Jennifer to the gallery's door any minute. Meanwhile, she'd have to deflect the gallery owner's curiosity. Eugene Tolliver was homing in on her like a heat-seeking missile.

"My, my, I've never seen our Ice Princess melt in the six months she's been here. Whatever did you say to Kimberly? She looked positively petrified," Eugene asked as he drew beside Kelly.

Kelly stared fixedly at a rich mahogany carving of the nude torso of a girl emerging from a huge wave. Was it a mermaid? She deliberately kept staring in hopes this Eugene would stop asking questions and drift away.

"I'm afraid I was the bearer of sad news about one of her

artist friends in Fort Connor," Kelly replied in a perfunctory tone.

"Murdered, I believe you said. That's shocking."

Kelly decided this guy had been blatantly eavesdropping and was obviously hoping for more details. Well, too bad. She lifted her coldest corporate gaze to his. It had taken years to develop that stare. It could drop a man at fifty paces. Unfortunately, Eugene Tolliver met it with a genial smile and laughter in his eyes.

"My, that's a seriously scary stare. I'll bet it's very effective."

Kelly stared at him. Was he laughing at her? Tolliver was tanned and handsome in a distinguished way, sandy brown hair with a trace of silver and styled fashionably, his clothes casually elegant and expensive. She decided he could be anywhere from forty to sixty years old. His face was smooth and relatively unwrinkled, yet Kelly sensed the humor she saw in his eyes came from a life richly lived and many years of observing people.

"Usually it's quite effective, but apparently it doesn't work on you," Kelly countered.

Eugene grinned. "I'm impervious, my dear. Judgmental reactions roll right off, like water on a duck's back."

"You're also an eavesdropper, I might add," Kelly jibed. "That was a private conversation with Kimberly and not meant for common gossip."

"Ouch," Eugene flinched dramatically, even though Kelly sensed that her jibe rolled off like water. "A barbed tongue as well. Your defenses are formidable, indeed. I'll bet not many eager young lads venture too close, do they? If the stare didn't drop them, that tongue would finish them off."

Kelly pretended to scowl, which seemed to amuse Eugene even more. Clearly, she needed to practice her scowls. They seemed to be losing their effectiveness. Steve laughed out loud when he saw them, and now this stranger was teasing her.

"Besides, I wasn't intentionally eavesdropping," he continued amiably. "It's simply the acoustics of this wonderful old building. You can whisper across the room and still be heard over here." He gave a sly wink. "No one can keep a secret."

"Not with you around," Kelly retorted, trying not to be swayed by his good nature. She'd tried to insult him but Eugene refused to be insulted. "Are you the gallery owner?" she probed.

"Technically, yes. I own the building and rent the space, but we like to think of this as an artists' cooperative. In a way, we all own the gallery." He gestured around him. "But, let's get back to your conversation with Kimberly. Despite the glorious acoustics there were certain crucial parts I missed."

Kelly lifted her nose. "Serves you right for being a snoop."

"I have a feeling that's like the pot calling the kettle black," he retorted.

Touche. Eugene hit center on that one. "I'm only trying to help a friend," Kelly replied, smarting a bit, as she resumed her stroll through the gallery. "Besides, it's none of your business anyway."

"Not so, my dear. I happen to be quite fond of Kimberly. She's a uniquely talented artist, and as gallery manager I'm fiercely protective of my artists."

Kelly didn't reply, simply kept strolling and surveying the artwork. Maybe if she ignored him, he'd go away. No such luck.

"You can't ignore me," Eugene said, as if he'd read her mind. "I'm nothing if not tenacious. Relentless, actually."

She believed it, and despite herself, Kelly was beginning to like Eugene. She sensed he really was protective of his emerging artists, even though he attempted to disguise it with a dry wit. Kelly glanced over her shoulder and scowled at him playfully. "Yes, you are. Do you plan to follow me out into the street?"

Eugene laughed. "If necessary."

"Relentless is right. I'm surprised you have any customers if you treat them like this."

"I prefer clients, my dear, and to my knowledge, they've never harassed the gallery staff."

"I wasn't harassing Kimberly, I was merely asking questions," Kelly protested.

"Questions? You were interrogating the poor girl. It was *Chinatown* all over again. Just like Jack Nicholson. A veritable pit bull. It was scary to watch." Eugene shivered dramatically.

Oh, brother, Kelly thought. Not only was she aging before her time, sleep-deprived, and out-of-shape, but her sleuthing had changed her into a pit bull. Now she really wouldn't have a social life.

"Please don't tell me I look like Jack Nicholson," she said with a crooked smile.

Eugene grinned. "Of course not, my dear. I simply meant you *resembled* him. When you were browbeating poor Kimberly, that is."

Kelly threw in the towel. Eugene really was relentless. "I give up," she surrendered, rolling her eyes. "I'm sorry if my questioning came across that way. I really didn't mean to be so intense. I was just trying to find out if Kimberly had any information that would help in solving my friend's death back in Fort Conner. That's all."

Eugene drew back, clearly surprised. "Good Lord, don't tell me you're with the police? This really is like the movie."

"No, no, no," Kelly said with a dismissive wave. "I'm just a friend who's trying to help."

"Ahhhh, an amateur sleuth." Eugene relaxed visibly. "Now, that I can believe. You're much too blunt to be in law enforcement."

Kelly had to laugh, picturing her take-no-prisoners attitude when it came to fact-finding. She'd never last on that job. Her mouth would get her fired fast. "I have to agree with you, Eugene. I'd insult someone for sure."

"More than one, I'm fairly certain. Multitudes, probably." His eyes danced merrily.

She couldn't believe it. Everyone teased her. Her friends, Steve, and now strangers. What was it about her that was so irresistibly teasable? She couldn't figure it out. "Okay, okay. You can stop now," she retorted.

"But it's so much fun," Eugene tweaked. "All right, Nancy Drew, let's get back to your investigation. I take it your friend was someone Kimberly knew, correct? Despite the acoustics, I was only able to hear tantalizing bits and pieces, but no names."

"She was a fellow student of Kimberly's at the university and a very talented artist in her own right. In fact, her work had even attracted a fashion designer who wanted to bring her to New York."

Eugene's smile faded. "You don't mean Allison Dubois, do you?"

Kelly noted his reaction with interest. "Yes, did you know her?"

"Yes, I met her when she worked and exhibited here in town a couple of years ago." He shook his head. "Such a tragedy to lose a young talent. And by her own hand."

After a pause Kelly spoke up. "But it wasn't. Police investigated and now believe that Allison was murdered."

Eugene paled beneath his tan. "Good Lord! You're not serious? Who would kill Allison? She was a sweet girl. I cannot believe . . ." He stared at Kelly, aghast. "Surely you don't suspect Kimberly, do you? Is that why you came?"

Kelly fixed Eugene with a no-nonsense stare. "I came here for answers because I'd heard that Kimberly and Allison were rivals and there was 'bad blood' between them, so to speak."

"You've been talking to those little gossips at the university, haven't you?" Eugene said with a sniff. "They were simply jealous of Kimberly because she wasn't like them. Lesser talents are always threatened by those with more, you know that."

"That may be true, but one of Allison's neighbors also saw Kimberly visit Allison the night she was killed. So, you can understand how suspicious that looks."

Eugene pursed his lips but made no reply, obviously considering what she'd said.

"Now that I've met Kimberly and spoken with her, I agree with you, Eugene," Kelly continued. "Kimberly didn't go over to harm Allison. She went there to apologize and wish Allison well."

"That sounds like Kimberly. Dramatic and hotheaded, but reason always returns."

"Unfortunately, she didn't see anyone else lurking about, either, so my *Chinatown* investigation has been in vain, I guess." She gave him a sly wink, noticing the sound of the front door opening behind her.

"Not at all, my dear," Eugene said, genial good humor returning. "Remember, I met Allison several times over the years. I'll be glad to dredge up any memories for the cause. You may pump me for information if you'd like."

"Don't be too hasty," Jennifer spoke up clearly from across the gallery. Good acoustics, indeed. "She's brutal, you know. Truly brutal. A pit bull when she wants to be."

Kelly observed Jennifer strolling towards them, a familiar mischievous smile in place. Oh, brother. Now, there'd be two of them giving her a hard time. Great. Stereo teasing.

"I figured the moment your stomach growled, you'd find me," Kelly said.

"A kindred spirit. Wonderful," Eugene declared. "A friend of yours, I take it?"

"That depends on how annoying she is," Kelly replied. "Jennifer, this is the gallery manager, Eugene Tolliver. Eugene, Jennifer Stroud."

"Ignore her," Jennifer scoffed with a gesture. "She gets fussy when I tell her the truth, that's all."

"Absolutely charmed," Eugene said with a wicked grin as he reached for Jennifer's hand. "Now, I'll have two delightful lunch companions."

"Oooooo, I did come at the right time."

"That's very kind of you, Eugene," Kelly demurred. "But you don't have to—"

"I don't have to, but I want to, my dear," he said, taking Kelly's arm, then Jennifer's. "Besides, it's the only way I'll divulge everything I know about Allison Dubois. You tell all about this murder investigation, and I'll tell about Allison and Brian Silverstone. She worked and exhibited at Sanderson Gallery with Brian for two years."

"Wonderful," Jennifer enthused, falling into step with Eugene. "Dish and dine. My favorite meal."

"Oh, I like you already, Jennifer. Maybe you can help loosen up Kelly. She's a bit intense, I've noticed."

"Eugene, you don't know how much I've tried," Jennifer declared with a dramatic sweep of her hand to an unseen audience. "It's a Herculean task. And she fights me every step of the way."

"Edward, I'm leaving for lunch and I have absolutely no idea when I'll return," Eugene called to the older man who had emerged from the studio hallway. "Jennifer is definitely good for you, Kelly," Eugene repeated, glancing her way as he continued to the door.

Kelly nodded. "Sometimes."

Her mild response caught Eugene's attention immediately, and he peered at her. "Oh, my, oh my. I can see that little computer in your brain whirring away. Something I said, I hope?"

"Yes. Brian Silverstone," Kelly admitted, as the name resonated within. Was this the Brian of the diary entries and the angry, ugly cell phone message?

"I can tell from your response that you've heard his name before," Eugene said, opening the door for Kelly and Jennifer.

"Wellllll," Kelly hesitated.

"Ah, hesitation. That seals it," Eugene decreed. "Let's grab your car and head for the Pavillions. I don't think I can wait for more than a few blocks."

"Eugene, you're my kind of gossip," Jennifer offered.

"Nonsense, my dear," he said with a righteous toss of his head. "We're not gossiping. We're sleuthing."

Eleven

Kelly toyed with the rim of her water goblet. "You're certain they were having an affair?" she asked.

"Positively," Eugene said, settling into the fashionable restaurant's thick upholstered chair. "One can always tell." He winked.

"Always," Jennifer agreed sagely, before taking another bite of her chocolate mousse.

Kelly stared at the same tempting chocolate decadence that sat on her plate, untouched. Eugene really knew how to pick a restaurant.

"But she was still taking courses for her master's back then. How'd she manage a long-distance love affair and study?" Kelly wondered out loud. "Boy, that's a lot of driving."

Eugene laughed softly. "Obviously, my dear, you've never been head-over-heels in love. Distance heightens desire. Especially for a hopeless romantic like Allison. She was truly swept away."

"Kelly wouldn't know about that," Jennifer observed. "She's a workaholic accountant. They don't sweep."

Kelly made a face at Jennifer before sampling her chocolate mousse. Silky smooth and luscious. "I was swept away once. At least I thought I was. My mistake."

"He was just the wrong guy, that's all," Jennifer said, leaning toward Eugene. "But there's another guy in the wings now, and he's definitely a winner."

"Oooo, tell," encouraged Eugene.

"Excuse me? We were discussing Allison's love life not mine."

"You don't have one. What's to discuss?"

Deliberately ignoring Jennifer, Kelly zeroed in on Eugene again. He was laughing, obviously enjoying their repartee. "A-hem. Let's get back to Allison and Brian Silverstone. You said she was in love, but what about this Brian?"

Eugene gave an elegant shrug. "I suppose Brian's always in love with his young conquests at first. He fancies himself an all-knowing mentor who helps them unleash their talent. Of course, the unleashing comes at a high price. He manages to convince them that their most innovative ideas are actually inspired by his work."

"Sounds manipulative," Kelly said before savoring the last spoonful of creamy chocolate.

"Very," he said with a frown. "I've seen some very promising young women lose their creative spark after being with Brian. That's why I was actually glad Allison left before he could ruin her, too."

"She left him? Good for her," Jennifer added with a righteous nod as she licked her spoon.

"How'd that happen?" Kelly probed. "Was there an argument or something? You said Allison's work was attracting attention and awards. I'll bet he was jealous."

"First, coffee." Eugene beckoned the waiter over. "I'll

have a double espresso, and she will have regular coffee. Black," he ordered, indicating Kelly. Glancing to Jennifer, he grinned. "And she will have one of your wicked white chocolate mochas."

"Eugene, you read my mind," Jennifer said with a smile.

"Actually, you read mine, too," Kelly admitted.

"I sleep with a psychic," Eugene said with a wave. "It rubs off."

Kelly wasn't about to follow that line, even though she could tell Jennifer was dying to. Instead, she asked, "Surely you're not going to make us wait until the coffee before you tell us what happened? Why'd Allison leave? Did she finally recognize what was happening?"

"Well, I don't know for sure, but rumor has it that Brian was trying to use Allison to weasel his way back into the Santa Fe art scene. Allison started attracting attention with her weavings in some of the shows there, and Brian probably thought he could ride her coattails, so to speak."

"Why would he need her? You said earlier that he was an accomplished artist with exhibits of his own."

"He is a very talented painter, and his collages are particularly impressive. Brian's done very well here in Denver," Eugene observed. "But he wanted what he once had. He wanted New York again. And he knew he needed something dramatic to grab attention. After all, he'd ruined himself there."

"How'd he do that?"

Eugene sighed. "With that barbed tongue of his. Brian is extremely talented, yes. But he's also extremely critical of other artists' work. Dismissive, almost. And he never misses an opportunity to express his opinion. That's what happened in New York. He made the crucial mistake of eviscerating an up and-coming artist at a studio show and was overheard by the artist's patron. Well, the patron was particularly well-connected, and Brian found himself 'artist-non-grata' at the most prestigious galleries. He was devastated, from what I've heard. And abruptly moved to Santa Fe, probably thinking he'd sweep the local art scene off its feet." Eugene wagged his head knowingly. "Unfortunately, Brian had neglected to do his homework thoroughly. Santa Fe is a magnet for some of the finest artists in this country as well as the world. Needless to say, Santa Fe was not 'swept away' by Brian Silverstone. He was simply another talented artist. And, that wasn't enough for Brian. He skulked away from the desert and landed here several years ago."

"It sounds like you artists have one heckuva grapevine," Jennifer said, as the waiter served their coffees.

"Oh, it is formidable, indeed," Eugene said with a smile.

"Well, he must have done well here if he owns a gallery," Kelly observed, lifting her cup and inhaling the provocative aroma of rich coffee.

"Actually, he doesn't own it, even though he acts as if he does. He manages the gallery for a consortium of owners. That's why he holds such sway over his young protÇgÇes, as he calls them. Brian decides what artwork is displayed. If you displease Brian, your work disappears. Literally."

"So did Allison finally wake up to all this manipulation? Did she refuse to take his work to Santa Fe?"

"You know, I'm not sure exactly," Eugene replied, sipping his espresso. "I spoke with her at an exhibit right before she moved back to Fort Connor, and while she didn't come out and say it, I sensed she was leaving because of Brian's behavior. She was looking at him with new eyes. Also, she did let it slip that Brian believed her weaving designs were totally inspired by his collages. I could tell that angered Allison. She was an extremely creative person, and had grown up in southwestern Colorado with all that richness of Native American art and cliff dwellings. Allison's imagination provided all the inspiration she needed." Eugene stared into his coffee for a moment before draining the tiny cup.

"It sounds like they didn't part on the best of terms," Kelly probed.

"Well, I cannot attest to that. They appeared civil to one another at the exhibit. Of course, that was over a year ago."

Kelly pondered what he'd said. Had Brian Silverstone held a grudge against Allison because she refused to let him use her when they lived together? If so, the episode with the New York designer would have been another slap in the face. And much more devastating, according to the cell phone message.

"Have you ever seen Brian and Allison together since then?" she asked. "At some art show or something?"

Eugene stared off into the restaurant's posh interior, bold rich colors dominating the decor. "Not at any exhibitions in Denver, but now that you mention it, I could have sworn I saw him at the university's awards banquet a few weeks ago."

That surprised Kelly. "Was that the same banquet Kimberly and Allison went to?"

"Yes, it was. But I did not witness any unpleasantness between the two of them," he added. "Professor Jaeger had invited me, and I was at the faculty table. I remember glancing toward a side doorway of the ballroom, and I was certain I spotted Brian standing there. I assumed he'd been invited as well, but when I looked around the room again, I didn't see him."

Kelly's buzzer went off inside. Brian Silverstone was at the banquet. Brian of the ugly menacing phone message. That was the same night Allison was killed.

"Maybe he came to make peace and wish Allison well," Jennifer offered, swishing her white chocolate mocha.

"Maybe," Kelly offered, noncommittally.

"But that's not what she's thinking," Eugene observed as

he slipped a credit card from his billfold into a leather folder and handed it to the waiter—all in one fluid movement. "I can see those little wheels turning in your head right now, Kelly. You're thinking about Brian Silverstone as a possible murder suspect, aren't you?"

Kelly pretended to frown at him. "You know, this mind-reading thing has got to stop."

Eugene grinned. "Can't help it. It's a reflex now. But seriously, Brian Silverstone couldn't harm Allison. He's emotional and temperamental, of course. He's an artist! But he's all bluster. Talk is Brian's weapon of choice, not something as brutal as murder."

"Yeah, Kelly. Why are you even looking at this Brian guy? Megan says Allison's old boyfriend, Ray Baker, is the one with the violent history," Jennifer observed before she drained her cup.

Kelly sipped her coffee, choosing her words. Then, in her usual fashion, threw caution to the wind. "It wasn't a violent crime, remember? Allison was poisoned. Too many sleeping pills in her coffee." She shrugged. "I'm simply trying to look into every possibility, that's all. And it sounds like this Brian guy held a grudge against Allison."

She purposely didn't say any more. Eugene had already wormed out most of the details of Allison's death throughout their delicious soup-and-salad luncheon. Eugene was truly tenacious. Nearly as bad as she was, Kelly had to admit.

"Grudge or no grudge, Brian Silverstone is simply not the type to . . ." Eugene gestured as if searching for the word.

"Get his hands dirty?" Kelly supplied with a wry smile.

"In a manner of speaking, yes," Eugene agreed. "I think your local police have found their man with this Ray Baker."

"Maybe so, but since I'm already in Denver, and have

enjoyed an absolutely delicious lunch at a fabulous posh restaurant that I could never afford, I might as well pay a visit to Brian Silverstone's gallery." Kelly winked at Eugene's expression. "Thank you, Eugene. This has been a delightful treat."

"I'll say," Jennifer concurred. "I've always wanted to come here, but champagne-tastes and soft-drink-budget about sums it up. Thank you, Eugene. You're a doll." She leaned over and kissed Eugene on the cheek.

"My pleasure, ladies, I assure you," he said, slipping a cell phone from his coat pocket and punching in a number. "But you're not escaping yet. Since we're so close to his salon, I want you to meet Ronnie. He's right here in the Pavillions."

"Who, pray tell, is Ronnie?" Jennifer pried.

"He's the psychic," Eugene said with a sly grin. "You must meet him Kelly. He may pick up something that can help with your invest—" Eugene interrupted himself. "Natasha, it's Eugene. Is Ronnie available? What? Don't tell me she did that again? Where is that woman's head? Oh well, at least she compensates him outrageously for wrecking his schedule. Put him on, would you, please?"

Kelly shook her head. A psychic, that's all she needed. Eugene was bad enough, reading her thoughts without her permission. If this Ronnie was any good, she certainly didn't want him peering inside her head. It was chaotic enough in there as it was. Even she didn't know what was happening sometimes. Meanwhile, Jennifer was grinning like the Cheshire cat, she noticed, obviously relishing meeting Ronnie the psychic.

"Ronnie, Natasha just told me. How you remain so calm with all that undue aggravation is beyond me. Anyway, I just finished lunching with two delightful young women from Fort Connor, and I'd simply love to introduce you to them now if you have a moment? You would? Wonderful! We'll be right over."

Kelly rolled her eyes. "Eugene, I think I'll pass on the psychic evaluation if you don't mind. I want to check out Brian Silverstone. Who knows? He might not be in and I'll have to wait."

Eugene gave a dismissive wave as he rose from the table. "Don't worry. He's always there in the afternoon. Besides, this is simply too good an opportunity to miss."

"Hey, I'm game," Jennifer said as she pushed back her chair and rose. "Sounds like fun. Besides, maybe Ronnie can give me some ideas. I'm in the mood for a new hair-style."

"Well, you're about to meet the master," Eugene said, gesturing for Kelly to proceed him. "By the way, Kelly, have you ever tried removing that lovely gold clasp from your hair and seeing what happens?"

Kelly gave him a sardonic look over her shoulder as they left the restaurant. "Yes, I have. All the hair falls in my face and annoys the living daylights out of me. That's what hap-pens."

"So there." Jennifer laughed.

Eugene raised both hands in surrender. "Simply trying to suggest new things, that's all."

"Well, I'm game for a total redo," Jennifer announced, taking Eugene's arm as they strolled past the boutique shops. "And Ronnie can 'psych' me as much as he likes."

Kelly followed behind them and sneaked a quick peek at her watch. She figured she could spare a few minutes to meet Ronnie the psychic, but no more. The sleuthing lobe of her brain was buzzing and would not be denied. Besides, she didn't want to stay too long around this Ronnie. No telling what he might pick up. She had enough trouble as it was trying to keep secrets.

• • • •

Kelly flicked the car door lock and headed across the street. Brian Silverstone's gallery was farther down, but she wanted to appear like any other visitor, strolling from gallery to gallery in the newly-revitalized art district.

She'd managed to escape from Ronnie's exotic spa-salon unmoussed and unchanged, her practical-but-boring hairstyle untouched. The fashionable salon was filled with ultra-chic women—sleek, tanned, and gorgeous. Ronnie was as low-key as Eugene was high-octane. Soft-spoken and pensive, she'd noticed a twinkle in his eye when Eugene related her lack of interest in changes. Jennifer's enthusiasm, of course, made up for Kelly's reluctance as she plopped herself into Ronnie's leather chair with the irresistible invitation: "Ronnie, I'm yours. Show me what you've got." Kelly was able to exit gracefully to the sound of laughter.

Wide windows beckoned ahead as Kelly approached Sanderson Gallery. She purposely paused before the windows and stared inside, ostensibly studying the large paintings that adorned the walls. In reality, Kelly was searching for anything that looked like an office. There, in the far right corner, she spied a modern swoop of metal that curved into a desklike platform. A tall man stood behind it, staring at a computer screen.

Kelly took a deep breath and entered the gallery, then began a leisurely stroll about the strategically placed displays. Most of the canvases were oil or acrylic abstracts, some so lined and detailed they looked like they'd been created by draftsmen. Another wall, however, held a cascade of color-bright collages and painted silks, lacy woven fibers with light-reflecting glass beads woven throughout. The collages were bold and layered with color and texture, and she wondered if they were Brian Silverstone's.

Glancing toward the man at the corner desk, Kelly

pasted her friendliest smile in place and strolled his way. "What a fascinating variety of work you have on display," she remarked as she approached.

The man looked up with a professional's smile. He was tanned and handsome, with dark brown hair, silver streaks at the temples, and eyes as black as ebony. "Why, thank you. We do try to keep our exhibits changing with fresh work."

"Are you the gallery owner?" Kelly asked.

"I'm the manager, Brian Silverstone." He lifted his finely-chiseled chin a bit. "This is your first visit, I take it."

"Yes, I'm from out of town, Washington, D.C.," Kelly said, deliberately reaching into her purse to withdraw a notepad and pen. "Actually, I'm a freelance writer, and I'm doing a story for *ARTWorld DC* magazine. I don't know if you've heard of it or not," she continued, using the name of a local art periodical she remembered from the Washington area. "The editors wanted an update on some of the developing art communities out west."

Brian Silverstone's expression changed dramatically, Kelly noticed. He appeared taller somehow, and his smile was truly radiant. Brian positively glowed. "Why, of course I've heard of it. *ARTWorld* is a wonderful magazine. I read it religiously, as I do all the art journals from the East. That's where I began my career, you see." His chin lifted again.

"Oh, really?" Kelly observed with great interest as she began to scribble on her pad. "And is some of your work exhibited here as well?"

"Yes, indeed. Those two collages are mine," Brian said, gesturing to the wall display that Kelly had admired. "Each piece took prizes at the Southwestern Festival last year."

"Congratulations," Kelly exclaimed, and then heaped more praise. "Those are simply wonderful, Mr. Silverstone. I noticed them right away. Truly bold work." She scribbled some more. "Have you always done collages? Do you work in another medium as well?"

"Oh, yes, of course," he gave a dismissive gesture as he smiled. "But the collage is my favorite, I must admit. And it has won me most of my acclaim." This time, Brian's aquiline nose lifted.

"Do you have any brochures or catalogues that list your work and some of your fellow artists? Maybe with photos? My camera skills are definitely amateur, and my editors would really like professional quality photos. They were pretty disappointed with my last photo efforts."

Brian beamed. "Why, of course. I have some brochures in the back." He started toward a back doorway then beckoned for Kelly to follow. "Come along. I'll show you some of my other work."

Kelly eagerly scurried after him, reporter's pad and pencil at the ready, as he walked through the doorway and into an adjoining studio. There, indeed, were several more striking works of art—bright collages with layers of contrasting textures and colors, draped fabric which looked like silk painted with abstract floral designs, and pen-and-ink drawings everywhere, lining the shelves, scattered about the worktables, stacked on counters. Brian Silverstone was a talented artist, indeed, Kelly decided and wondered if Eugene's opinion of him was perhaps colored by professional jealousy.

"Artist at work," Brian offered jokingly with a nonchalant gesture about the room as he approached a file cabinet. "Those brochures are in here."

Kelly surveyed the room, drinking in the color and texture just as she had earlier that morning in Eugene Tolliver's gallery workshops. As her gaze roamed, one pen-and-ink drawing stood out from the rest. Kelly studied the work. It looked familiar and resembled a fashion design, for the model had no features. All the drawing's detail was con tained in the garment the model wore. A shawl-like top was drawn in at the waist, almost like . . . almost like . . .

She stared at the drawing, recognizing it immediately. This was one of Allison's drawings, Kelly was sure of it. She'd seen several of those drawings when Allison was showing them her portfolio. There was an unmistakable style to them. Had Allison given one to Brian as a parting gift or something?

"Here, we go. These are our latest brochures with gallery notes and photos on all our exhibiting artists," he said, handing Kelly a glossy, thick brochure.

"Thank you, Mr. Silverstone. My editors will really appreciate this."

"Please call me Brian," he said with a sly smile as he gestured toward the doorway once again.

"I must say, your work is absolutely stunning," Kelly said in a fawning voice as she followed Brian into the gallery.

"You are too kind. When did you say that issue would come out?"

She didn't. "Well, I'm not sure, Brian. I'm merely the writer. The editors decide all that," she said with a genial gesture. It was time to slide into the next subject.

Concentrating on her scribbling, Kelly ventured in an offhand tone, "If I'm lucky, this article may expand into a cover piece. One of the other gallery owners here told me about this great local story. Apparently some young Colorado artist was about to break into the bigtime. Seems her work was winning awards and caught the eye of some New York fashion designer who offered her a job."

Kelly let her eyes grow wide with the telling of the tale. "Well," she said in a dramatic hush. "Here this artist is about to start the career of her dreams, and she kills herself! Unbelievable. I'm going to call the editors today to see if they'll go for a bigger spread." She gestured. "Tragic early death of a brilliant young designer. I think they may go for it," she said, watching Brian Silverstone carefully.

The change in Brian's expression was minimal but still noticeable. His eyes narrowed slightly and his smile faded. "Yes, it was tragic, indeed," he said in a sad voice. "Allison Dubois was a talented artist. In fact, she was one of my brightest protégés. She studied with me for two years, working on her designs, practicing. She was particularly taken with my collage work and modeled most of her designs on their patterns. I was happy to help her develop her talent, of course. That's one of the reasons I'm here and no longer in the East. I can help so many struggling young artists along the path." He gave an eloquent sigh and stared out into the gallery.

With great effort, Kelly kept her wide-eyed reportorial expression of wonder. Son of a gun, she thought. Eugene wasn't exaggerating one bit. Brian Silverstone had just taken credit for all of Allison Dubois's creative inspiration.

"Oh, my, how generous of you," Kelly gushed, then turned to scribble before her stomach heaved. "Do you have any of her work here? I'd love to see it."

A pained expression crossed Brian's aristocratic features. "No, I'm afraid we don't. Allison took all of her work with her when she left last year. You might try the state university in Fort Connor. Apparently she exhibited a lot in their galleries."

"Why, thank you, Brian. You're so helpful," Kelly said, then deliberately checked her watch. "In that case, I'd better get moving. I've got several more galleries to visit, and now I'll have to drive up to Fort Connor." Waving the brochure, she added, "Does this have your email address, Brian? I'd like to stay in touch."

"Yes, it does, but why don't you give me your card, too, Miss, Miss . . ."

"Kelly Flynn," she said with her brightest smile as she

reached for Brian's hand. "You've been a goldmine of information, Brian. A veritable goldmine. I guarantee that I'll
be in touch with you," she promised. "Unfortunately, I'm
all out of cards. I'm kind of new at this reporting business.
But I'll be emailing you, okay? Let's see what the editors
say. Maybe we'll get a cover story."

"I'll keep my fingers crossed," Brian said with a high-
wattage smile as Kelly headed for the door.

Kelly checked her watch as she approached the Santa Fe
Artists gallery. She'd deliberately spent over an hour and a
half browsing through other galleries on Santa Fe Drive in
hopes that Jennifer would have returned. Maybe Jen would
be so happy with the "renovations" that she'd forget all
about hitting the clubs tonight. The image of her bulging
email inbox kept popping into Kelly's mind all afternoon.
What she really needed to do was go home and work. The
likelihood of Jennifer agreeing to an early departure, however, was slim to nonexistent, she had to admit.

Spying Jennifer and Eugene at the back of the gallery,
Kelly called out, "How'd it go?" as she stepped inside.

"Judge for yourself," Eugene gestured to Jennifer.
"Doesn't she look fabulous?"

"How's it look, Kelly? Cool, huh?" Jennifer asked as she
slowly turned in a circle.

Kelly blinked. "Wow, Jen, you *do* look fabulous. That's
a great look on you," she exclaimed, admiring the new cut.

Psychic Ronnie had cut Jennifer's rich auburn hair at a
dramatic angle, tapering from long in front to shorter at the
nape of the neck. Suddenly Jennifer's beautiful eyes and
cheekbones were even more striking than usual.

"You're not just saying that, are you?" Jennifer quirked
a brow at her.

"Heck, no!" Kelly swore. "You look fantastic. Boy, I'm really impressed with Ronnie the psychic hairstylist."

"Impressed enough to try something new yourself?" Eugene tempted.

"I'm not as adventurous with hair as Jennifer," Kelly backtracked with a grin. "Hey, isn't that a new outfit? Did you go shopping?"

Jennifer danced around again, clearly delighted. "Yes, isn't it great? There was a shop right across from the salon, and they had a sale! Soft-drink budget just scaled back to water."

Kelly had to laugh, watching Jennifer's shopping celebration. "What do you say we get on the road before rush hour traffic starts? We can round up some of the others at home and show off your new look," she suggested.

"It's too late, Kelly," Eugene interjected. "Rush hour is already upon us. It'll be gridlock for the next couple of hours. You're better off celebrating in Denver. And I have just the spot."

Jennifer positively danced in place. "Yesss! I'm ready for the clubs."

Kelly groaned inwardly. Lisa was right. She'd be lucky to get home before two A.M. Forget about catching up on account files. "Jen, I'm not up for a whole night of clubbing, to be honest. How about just one, okay?"

Jennifer feigned a pout until Eugene stepped in with a suggestion. "Ladies, I told you I have just the spot, and I'll guarantee it's much more appropriate for Jennifer's new look. Those other clubs . . ." He made a disparaging gesture. "It would be like casting pearls before swine to take you there."

"Welllll," Jennifer drawled, hand on her hip.

"I promise you won't be disappointed," Eugene teased with a sly grin. "They've got hot jazz and great martinis. Five different chocolate ones to be exact."

Jennifer grinned. "Eugene, you are truly evil."

"I know."

"What about men? Cute guys?"

"The cutest," he said, chuckling, clearly enjoying Jennifer's interrogation.

"Dancing? I really want to dance."

"My dear, I'm sure the jazz trio will be so captivated by you, they'll let you dance atop the piano."

"Don't encourage her, please," Kelly admonished.

"All right, Eugene. You've been on target all afternoon, so we'll give your club a chance. But those martinis better be yummy, and the guys better be hotter than the jazz."

Kelly rolled her eyes while Eugene laughed out loud this time. "Hey, speaking as the designated driver on this trip, I vote for Eugene's cool club then head home. Okay?"

"Okay, Miss Workaholic. I've got clients tomorrow morning anyway. And speaking of clients, I'd better give them a call," Jennifer said, withdrawing a cell phone from her pocket.

Watching Jennifer step away for her conversation, Kelly caught Eugene's attention. "Eugene, this evening will be my treat. Besides, I'll need to have dinner. I can't live on fumes alone like Jen."

"Don't worry, Kelly. This place has great tapas and a wonderful menu." He glanced over at Jennifer then looked back with a sardonic smile. "She's a force of nature, isn't she?"

"Oh, yeah. My words exactly."

Eugene's smile disappeared. "Take care of her, Kelly. When you get back to Fort Connor, I mean."

"*Me?* Take care of Jennifer? You've got to be kidding!" Kelly joked. Noticing his expression, she added, "Did Ronnie pick up on something?"

Eugene glanced away. "Nothing specific. Just keep an eye on her, okay?"

"Easier said than done, Eugene. Besides, you may have noticed that Jennifer has a mind of her own."

"Would you like to know what Ronnie picked up from you?" Eugene asked, smile returning.

Putting her fingers in her ears, Kelly closed her eyes. "I'm not listening," she chanted playfully.

"Apparently you're going to have good news soon, which will help solve this problem you've been wrestling with."

Kelly heard that, despite herself. She stared at Eugene, watched his amused smile spread. "You two are seriously scary. I'd better head back to Fort Connor while I've got a shred of privacy left."

"You and Jennifer will definitely have to stay in touch. This has been too much fun."

A bright idea popped into Kelly's mind, and she blurted without thinking. "You bet we will. Plus, I'll even knit you a scarf for the holidays. I've been dying to try out that luscious alpaca wool."

"How wonderful. A handmade knitted scarf. Will it be warm enough to wear skiing?"

"Absolutely," Kelly promised. "Alpaca's the warmest according to Jen."

"You both knit?" Eugene's eyes widened. "I'm amazed. You two continue to surprise me."

"Shall we?" Jennifer invited as she joined them, slipping her arm around Eugene's. "I'm ready for the hot men and cool jazz. Or was it the other way around?"

Twelve

Sniffing the delectable aroma wafting from her mug, Kelly took a sip. "Ummmmm, you're a lifesaver, Eduardo," she said to the smiling cook. "I couldn't have gotten through today without your coffee."

Kelly was about to turn toward the doorway into the knitting shop, when Jennifer suddenly raced into the cafe kitchen. "Eduardo, has Pete come back yet? I need to talk to him."

"I haven't seen him since this morning. I think he's at the bank or with the builders," Eduardo answered.

"How's it going with your clients, Jen?" Kelly asked.

"Pretty good. I've been showing them houses all day, and they've got a short list already."

Kelly made a thumbs-up sign. "Sounds good, Jen. Incidentally, I still can't get over how wonderful that hairstyle looks. Have you shown it to the others?" She gestured toward the shop.

"I haven't had the time. Been with these clients all day." Jennifer checked her watch. "I've gotta get back to them.

Darn, I really wanted to talk with Pete. Hey, here he is," she said as Pete walked into the kitchen. "Great timing, Pete. I've got clients in the car."

"Hi, folks, how're . . ." Pete started then stopped. He stared at Jennifer. "Whoa, Jen, you look . . . you look great! I mean . . . wow . . ."

Jennifer gave him a big grin. "Thanks, Pete. I had a psychic hairdresser work me over yesterday in Denver. Anyway, I wanted to know if it would be okay if Bev substitutes for me again tomorrow morning. These clients are ready to buy, and I've gotta be with them. Strike while the iron is hot, you know."

Kelly watched Pete stare while Jennifer continued. He looked like he'd been hit on the head. In fact, he didn't answer right away when Jennifer paused, just kept staring.

"Pete? You okay?" Jennifer prodded. "Did the builder take you up on the roof or something?"

"Uh, no, no," Pete hesitated, snapping out of it. "Yeah, it's okay if Bev works. Yeah, sure."

"Thanks, Pete. You're a sweetie. Maybe you'd better stay out of the sun today," she teased as she headed for the door.

"Hey, Jen," Pete called after her, his genial smile back in place, Kelly noticed. "When the addition's finished and we're open, you might want to work some dinner shifts. You'd have them lining up to sit in your section, I swear."

Jennifer grinned and waved goodbye. "See you guys later."

"Well, I'd better get back to my allocated knitting break," Kelly said as she turned toward the shop doorway once again. "I've been in front of that computer all day."

"You've got to get outside more," Pete teased. "That computer will turn you green, you know."

"Hey, remember what Jen said about staying out of the sun," Kelly joked as she headed for the shop.

Trailing her fingers across several bundles of new fall yarns, Kelly squeezed and stroked her way toward the main room.

"Well, it's about time you dragged yourself in here," Lisa announced as Kelly dropped her knitting bag onto the library table. "How was yesterday? Did Jen keep you out all night?"

Kelly stretched her bare legs under the table. Thanks to the sunny weather, tee shirts and shorts were still the order of the work day. Boy, she liked telecommuting. "Actually, no. We got home before midnight."

"You're kidding? What happened? The clubs were closed?"

Kelly laughed. "That gallery owner, Eugene Tolliver, suggested to Jennifer that she skip her old clubs and try something new. He took us to this cool club. Great food, yummy martinis, and fantastic jazz. Of course, Jennifer, being Jennifer, flirted outrageously with the trio. I swear, if she could sing, she'd be touring with them now."

Lisa laughed as she worked the finished edge of the delicate blue-gray wool shawl. "Thank God, she can't sing a note, or we'd have lost her years ago."

"I never thought anything could tempt Jennifer from salsa, but she's acquired a whole new appreciation for jazz."

"More like an appreciation for jazz musicians," Lisa said with a sly smile.

"And, she's got a new hairstyle, too, which looks fabulous on her. Wait'll you see it. She's out with clients today."

"How about you? Was the sleuthing successful?"

Pulling the circular sweater from her bag, Kelly picked up where she left off. The deep rose silk and cotton cooperated, as if grateful to escape from the bag's imprisonment. Despite the beautiful color in her lap, Kelly found herself glancing surreptitiously at the lacy creation on Lisa's needles.

"Matter of fact, it was," she answered. "I got to interview this guy who worked at the same gallery Allison did a few years ago. Very interesting."

"Interview?" Lisa joked.

"Well, I told him I was a freelance writer for an art magazine I remembered from DC. I needed a cover story to be asking all those questions about Allison and all."

"Shameless, truly shameless." Lisa wagged her head.

"I had to be. Eugene told me Allison had an affair with this guy, and they did not part on the best of terms, either."

Lisa looked up, surprised. "Hey, I thought you said that Allison's old boyfriend was the leading suspect."

"Well, he is. I was just making sure we didn't leave any stone unturned, so to speak," Kelly said with a shrug.

"Hey, how were the clubs?" Steve's voice sounded. "I heard you took Jennifer to Denver. You're even braver than I thought, Kelly." He appeared beside Kelly and pulled out a chair.

"You guys ready for us tomorrow night?" Lisa challenged.

"Oh, yeah. Be ready to eat dirt." Steve leaned back and laughed.

Kelly slapped her forehead. "Oh-my-gosh. We've got practice tonight. And I was hoping to catch up with my workload."

"All work and no play," chanted Lisa, shoving her knitting into the bag as she rose from her chair. "And speaking of work, I've got a client. See you guys later."

"Later is right," Kelly mumbled.

"Hey, if Jennifer kept you out all night, you ought to skip practice and stay home. Better yet, skip tomorrow's game, too. They can use a sub on your base," Steve tempted with a sly grin.

"Riiiiight," Kelly retorted. "You guys would love that,

wouldn't you? No way. Besides, I need to get my blood moving. I've been on that blasted computer all day."

Steve turned serious. "Any word from Curt on that drilling lease?"

"Not yet," Kelly was about to reply when she heard a familiar voice behind her.

"Well, well, glad I found the two of you together. Saves time explaining," Curt announced as he strode into the late afternoon sunshine streaming through the windows and bathing the bookshelves.

Kelly looked up with a grin and put down her knitting. "Hey, Curt. Steve just asked me about the Wyoming property." She noticed Curt had the leather portfolio from the exploration company in his hand.

Curt glanced about the room, empty except for them, and pulled out a chair across from Kelly and Steve. He laid the portfolio on the table and looked across at Kelly with a smile. One of his old familiar smiles, Kelly noticed with delight. She hadn't seen Curt smile like that since . . . well, since before Ruth died. He was coming back. And if her Wyoming land was the reason, all the better.

"Kelly girl, I told you several months ago, that with some luck, your financial troubles might be over. Now that I've gone over this leasing agreement and talked to one of my friends in the business, I can say that prediction is looking pretty good."

"Really?" she ventured, trying not to get too excited even though she could feel her pulse speeding up already. The blood was moving even without ball practice.

Curt nodded, a smile dancing in his eyes now. "I summarized everything the exploration company is offering you. Dollars and cents. How much and for how long. Then, I drew up some examples of how a lease agreement works. That'll help you understand. I used numbers from my old properties to show how the money flows."

He opened the portfolio and turned it toward Kelly and Steve, then proceeded to explain page by page.

Kelly read through each page carefully, noticing how Curt had highlighted key financial information. The accounting lobe of her brain began to sort through the details, making sense of it all. He had taken the jargon of the lease agreement and transformed into a format where the financial possibilities could be analyzed.

Kelly stared at the summary pages again. "So, the exploration company will pay me up front for the exclusive right to drill on my land for the next three years. What happens if they don't drill?"

"You keep the up-front money, but there won't be any royalty income unless they drill and the gas starts flowing."

"That's when the 70/30 split comes in, right?" Kelly glanced at the examples Curt had provided. "Those are good numbers, Curt. Any chance my property would yield like that?"

Curt grinned. "You won't know until they drill and find out. Lots of Wyoming gas bubbles are pretty deep. Others are shallow. The deeper the well, the more expensive to drill. That's why it's risky. The company eats all the expenses, and some wells take longer to pay out than others. Some run dry early. It's a gamble."

Kelly shook her head. "Sounds like it."

"But not for you," Curt added. "You're not paying the bills. The drilling company is. And if the well starts paying out, you'll get a regular stream of income as long as it lasts."

"How long would that be?"

Curt shrugged. "Depends on how much gas is there. An average field can last thirty years."

Kelly looked at Curt's income examples again and allowed the reality of the numbers to settle in. Possibilities began to dance inside her head, and a little ripple of excitement ran through her.

"But if they don't drill, there's no money coming in," she said. "That's the part that's scary."

"It's a three-year lease, Kelly," Curt added. "I figure they'll start within a year. Mostly because the wells are producing on your neighbor's property. They'll want to get yours into production, too."

"If they drill, does that mean I can't donate the land?" she probed.

Curt shook his head. "Nope. You own the land. In fact they'll pay you an extra amount for surface damages. You can run cattle, live on it, or donate it. But I have some ideas on that we'll save for another day."

Another day would be good, Kelly thought. Her head was already spinning with information and new possibilities. "Curt, I don't know what to say," she said, a wave of gratitude swelling within. "This is wonderful. It must have taken you, Good Lord, how long did it take?"

Curt leaned back in his chair and folded his arms as he smiled at her—just like he used to. "Believe me, when I tell you it was my pleasure, Kelly. I haven't had anything to sink my teeth into for months. Since Ruthie passed, actually. It was time for me to get busy again. Never could stand to be idle. I've been spinning my wheels for months now, it seems. Grieving for Ruthie, I guess. Sometimes it felt like I'd lost myself when I lost her."

He stared at the table for a moment. Kelly didn't say a word, surprised at Curt's open and insightful comments.

"Maybe I was looking for a challenge," Curt continued. "Something that would require all of my attention. I don't know. But, nothing seemed to capture my interest until you asked me to look at this project. I'm beginning to feel like my old self again. A little bit at a time. Plus, I got to re-connect with some old friends in the oil and gas business.

Hadn't seen them for ages. So this project helped me as much as it helped you, Kelly."

Kelly returned his warm smile. "I can't thank you enough, Curt. Now I can actually evaluate this project financially."

"Evaluate, huh?" Steve said. "That sounds suspiciously close to making a decision."

"Close," she admitted. "It's the first step. Decisions come later."

"How much later?" Steve teased. "Winter will be blowing over the mountains in a month or so. You may get snowed in."

"That's right, Kelly," Curt joined the fun. "You've forgotten Colorado winters, girl. You better knit some sleeves on that sweater." He pointed to the sleeveless shell trying to come to life in her lap.

Kelly ignored both men's laughter, delighted to hear Curt teasing her like before. He was healing. Slowly, as was to be expected, but healing. She remembered the process after her dad died. It took a while to truly release a loved one who'd passed.

"Seriously, Curt, you have to let me pay you for this report you've created. I insist," she said, deliberately changing the subject.

Curt made a face like he'd just stepped into a cowpie. "That's downright insulting, Kelly. I don't want to hear any talk about money," he said, leveling a stern gaze at her.

Kelly recognized that look. She wasn't going to get anywhere with that suggestion. Not to be deterred, she tried another tack. "Okay, okay, but if I decide to go with one of these options, then I'm going to need your advice and counsel on all of this. How about being a consultant?"

"Not if it involves money."

Kelly rolled her eyes and heaved a dramatic sigh.

"Sounds like you liked the look of some of those income examples," Steve said.

Kelly stared at the columns of figures. "Let's just say they're encouraging. They're making me think, which is exactly what Curt intended, I'm sure." She sent Curt a sly smile.

"You're a smart girl, Kelly. You know what those numbers mean."

"Yeah, they mean it's risky," she admitted in a moment of candor. "The low option is close, but still below my CPA income. The only way that would work would be if I had a sizable cushion in the bank to make up the difference. Unfortunately, that's not the case."

"The consulting is bound to pick up," Steve offered.

"Yeah, but until it does, I'm afraid I'll have to remain in bondage to the firm back East," she said with a rueful smile.

"What about the middle option, Kelly?" Curt probed.

"That one's doable. Definitely doable."

"Two out of three, that's not bad," Steve said, grinning.

"And we can always sell off more of the herd if you need cash in that cushion of yours. Then after a while, the gas royalties will start coming in. Not much at first, but they'll eventually grow," Curt added.

"It's the 'eventually' part that scares me, Curt. Carl and I have to eat. I may be able to cut down, but Carl would have serious objections to my rationing his doggie chow."

Curt chuckled. "Well, if I'm going to be a consultant, then let me worry about that, okay?"

"Only if you let me pay you," Kelly bargained with a sly grin. She figured she had him on this one.

"She's tenacious, Curt. You'd better let her pay you. Otherwise, she may offer to cook for you."

Kelly scowled playfully at Steve and was about to aim a kick at him, when Curt spoke up. "I have a better idea,

Kelly. We can exchange my consulting services for your ram's services. You remember Monty, don't you?"

"Monty?" she stared blankly.

Curt grinned. "You do remember you've got sheep and alpaca on that ranch, don't you?"

"Ohhhhhh, yeah," Kelly played along to the men's laughter. "But who's Monty?"

"He's that prizewinning ram you've got up there. I'll be glad to exchange you service for service. How about it?"

Kelly tried to wrap her mind around that. Consulting services in exchange for a sheep's amorous activities. It served her right for working so much, she guessed. Her sheep had more of a social life than she did. Now, she had to keep track of their dating habits. Insult to injury.

She was about to agree when the accounting lobe of her brain buzzed vehemently. Suddenly Kelly remembered a rather significant detail.

"Boy, that's tempting, Curt," she admitted with a dramatic sigh. "But, I'm afraid the IRS has some very strict regulations regarding bartering income. I don't even want to think about the paperwork."

Both Curt and Steve laughed out loud at that. Curt pushed back his chair and rose. "Lord, Kelly, you really know how to clear a room, don't you?"

"One of her finer traits," Steve added as he rose as well. "I'd better get going. I told Mimi I'd move some furniture for her, and I want to grab some of Eduardo's coffee first."

"Hey, you'll be able to lift a whole sofa after his coffee," Kelly promised as she lifted her mug.

"Well, in that case, I'll join you, Steve," Curt said, following after. "I need to say hello to Mimi, too. Talk to you later, Kelly."

Kelly picked up the portfolio, stared at the tempting columns of figures one more time, then shoved everything into her bag. Returning to the soothing knitting rhythms once again, Kelly let all the churning thoughts and ideas, plans and possibilities, swirl through her mind. Sorting them out and slowing them down. Soon the peaceful feeling that knitting induced would help her decide.

It was kind of like running, she'd discovered. Kelly always worked through problems when she ran. Somehow the rhythm of the run allowed her thoughts to order themselves more efficiently and new ideas to spring forward out of nowhere. Or, somewhere. Kelly'd never been able to figure it out. But, running had always worked that way.

What a surprise to discover the same thing happened when she knitted, even though the two activities were totally opposite. Running required total physical involvement. Knitting required sitting quietly and minimal physical motion. Kelly wasn't sure how such different activities could produce the same inner result, but she wasn't going to analyze it. She was just grateful for it.

"Well, well, how're you doing, stranger?" a familiar female voice startled Kelly out of her meditative state.

She looked up to see Jayleen Swinson stride into the room, pull out the chair beside her, and straddle it backwards. "Hey, Jayleen, I haven't seen you for a while. How's the alpaca business doing?"

"Lord, Kelly, I'm running ragged, I tell you," Jayleen leaned over the chair. "You know I bought most of Vickie's herd back in August, right?"

"Yep, Bob Claymore offered them to you first, you said."

Kelly noticed that despite the years spent outside and in the sun, Jayleen still didn't look her fifty-five-plus years. Maybe it was her exuberant youthful spirit. An ageless Colorado cowgirl, in boots and blue jeans.

"Yeah, he told me he wanted to sell everything off and leave Fort Connor. Too many bad memories after Vickie's murder."

Kelly could understand that. Bob had been the prime suspect for quite a while until, well, until Kelly and Jayleen had started poking around the facts. Sleuthing, again. "So, how many alpaca do you have now?"

Jayleen tossed her gray-streaked blonde curls over her shoulder. "Well, counting the thirty in my old herd and adding another thirty-two from Vickie's, I've got over sixty. And that doesn't count the babies that have arrived since then. Whew. I tell you, I thought I could handle it all, but I'm running so fast, I'm passing myself. Not enough hours in the day or night for that matter."

"Well, that's what you get for trying to be successful, Jayleen," Kelly teased. "Are you still doing the bookkeeping for those other ranchers, too?"

"Yeah, and that's what I wanted to talk to you about, Kelly. I'm gonna need your advice about something. I've got some ideas, and . . ." She glanced over her shoulder toward the wool room where Steve and Curt were standing and talking, coffee in hand. "Lord, is that Curt Stackhouse over there? He looks awful. I barely recognized him."

"Actually, he looks better than he did a couple of weeks ago when I first saw him," Kelly observed. "He's been grieving ever since Ruth died. Went into seclusion with his daughter and son. He was just coming out of it when I got the offer of a lease on the Wyoming property from an oil and gas company. I handed it off to Curt, and I swear, it's worked wonders. Today, he was starting to act like his old self."

Jayleen glanced over at the two men and shook her head. "Poor man. Ruth's passing must have hit him like a mule kick to the head. They were married a long time. None of my marriages lasted very long. So, I wouldn't even know what that kind of grief was like. But from here, it looks God-awful."

"Yeah, he still looks skinny, compared to before," Kelly observed, noticing Curt and Steve head their way.

"We need to fatten him up, and I know just the way to do it," Jayleen said, swinging her denim-clad leg effortlessly over the chair as she rose. "You up for a steak dinner this weekend?"

"You bet." Kelly said, salivating at the thought as she stood.

"Then follow my lead," Jayleen instructed and shoved her hands into her back pockets in her usual pose. "Good Lord, Steve, is that Curt Stackhouse walkin' beside you? You better reach out and hold him up. Anybody that skinny is bound to fall over any minute now."

Steve chuckled. "Hey, Jayleen."

Curt tried to scowl at Jayleen, Kelly noticed, but settled for a stern look. "Stop exaggerating, Jayleen. I've lost some weight, that's all."

"I'm not exaggerating. You're positively puny. A shadow of your former self." She wagged her head, scolding fashion. "I tell you, Curt, that's no way to honor a good woman's memory. Ruth must be having another heart attack up in heaven right now, watching you waste away down here."

Kelly had to stare at the floor in order to hide her smile. You had to hand it to Jayleen. She came straight to the point. Shock and awe. Kelly sneaked a peek at Curt's expression. It was a cross between amazement and aggravation. Steve was hiding his reaction behind his coffee.

"Blunt as ever, Jayleen," Curt growled and drained his coffee.

"Hell, no sense beatin' around the bush, man. We need to fatten you up. For Ruth's sake, if nothing else. What you need is a good steak dinner. In fact, why don't all of you come out to my place this Saturday? Kelly, you and Steve up for it?" She turned to Kelly.

"Hey, count me in," Kelly chimed obediently.

"Me, too," Steve agreed with a knowing smile.

"Kelly, why don't you invite your friends here at the shop, too? And tell Megan to make some of those biscuits of hers. That oughtta bring the menfolk," Jayleen said with a wink.

"It'll bring me, for sure," Steve said, then turned to Curt. "What do you say, Curt? Megan's biscuits and a good steak. Sounds good to me."

"Welllllll . . ."

"Hey, I've got a great idea!" Jayleen jumped in again. "Curt, did Ruth ever write down that blueberry pie recipe of hers? Kelly's told me how good it was?"

"You kidding? I still have dreams about it," Kelly joked, watching Steve nearly choke on his coffee.

Curt tried to scowl at Jayleen, but obviously couldn't bring it off. "My daughter's got her recipe book. I can ask."

"Good. I'll bet Megan could do justice to Ruth's pie," Jayleen continued. "What do you think, Kelly?"

"Absolutely," Kelly concurred, noticing that so far Curt had not refused to come. Maybe Jayleen's idea would work.

"Okay, folks, you can stop now," Curt grumbled. "We'll have a steak dinner on one condition. We have it at my place. I've got a freezer full of beef that needs to be used."

Jayleen opened her mouth, as if to protest, until Curt raised his hand.

"Those are my terms, take it or leave it, folks," he said.

Both Kelly and Steve readily agreed, while Jayleen frowned. Kelly sensed it was mostly for effect.

"Okay, your place, Curt. But I'm gonna bring my chili," Jayleen said. "And I don't think you're strong enough to eat it yet. You'll need two steak dinners first."

"That chili better be hot, or I won't even put it on the table."

Jayleen turned to Kelly with a grin. "That sounds like a threat to me. What do you think, Kelly?"

"It sounds like I'd better drag my chair right next to Curt's well, because I'm going to need lots of water," Kelly replied.

Thirteen

Watching Carl do his morning dog stretch, Kelly had to laugh. Perched across the yard, dried crab apple in his mouth, was Carl's arch nemesis—Sassy Squirrel. Carl was completely unaware of the squirrel's presence because he'd plopped down on the concrete patio to bathe in the sun, back turned. Squirrel went about his business of skirting across the grass and ignoring Carl. He probably knew Carl's schedule by heart, Kelly decided, as she slid the patio door closed. First order of the morning was sunbathing, not squirrel-chasing.

Kelly was about to reach for her coffee mug, when her cell phone rang. A vaguely familiar woman's voice came across.

"Kelly? This is Sophia Emeraud from New York. I hope it's not too early for you out there."

"No, no, your timing's perfect, Ms. Emeraud, I was about to settle into my home office. You've actually given me a few moments reprieve."

Sophia laughed lightly. "Please, call me Sophia. The reason I'm calling is I received an interesting express mail from an artist in Denver yesterday. Apparently he was close to Allison, and he's offered to create a wearable art design as a tribute to her. He even suggested doing it in her distinctive style. Apparently Allison studied with him when she was developing her early ideas."

Only one artist would have the nerve to try to advance himself at Allison's expense. Kelly felt righteous indignation rising, but deliberately suppressed it. "Oh, really? That is an interesting suggestion," she replied casually. "Who's the artist?"

"Brian Silverstone. Apparently he's well known for his collages. Do you know of him?"

"As a matter of fact, yes. I met him last week when I was in Denver doing a gallery tour. And, you're right, his collages are quite striking. Very dramatic."

"You know, Kelly, his suggestion surprised me at first, but it got me thinking. And I believe I've come up with an even better way to pay tribute to Allison. Rather than have one artist try to re-create her unique style, I thought I would hold a competition and open it to all the talented wearable artists I met in the area. That way, designers in Santa Fe and Denver and even at Allison's university can enter." Sophia's voice became softer. "I wanted the award to be a tribute to Allison. The Allison Dubois Award for Wearable Art."

Kelly was touched by the sincerity she felt coming from Sophia Emeraud. "Sophia, I think that is a wonderful idea and a beautiful tribute to Allison. What better way to recognize her blossoming talent than to give a chance to another young designer."

"I thought so, too. That's why the actual award only pays a small sum, but the winner would have a chance to come to my New York studio for six months. Who knows, Kelly? We may receive so many wonderful entries, we'll make the competition an annual event. I'm always on the lookout for new talent. That's how I found Allison."

An idea crept from the back of Kelly's mind, and she turned it over a few times before speaking. "I have an idea, Sophia. Why don't you give the design competition a tight deadline, say two weeks or so. That way it would be more realistic. After all, I imagine you designers often have to perform in pressured situations. I know I have to, and I'm a corporate accountant. We don't have to strut our financial reports on a runway."

Sophia laughed softly. "You know, Kelly, that's an ingenious suggestion. It would definitely rachet up the intensity and make the experience more real-world. In fact, it could be very useful for some artists to experience such pressure. They'll learn whether or not they can produce under those conditions. Not everyone can, you know."

"Would you be able to come to Fort Connor to present the award?" Kelly continued, another idea forming. "You know, I'll bet Allison's professor could organize an event like that at the university. They could have photos and maybe press coverage. Just think of all the good publicity that would be. For you as well as the university."

"Kelly, I'm going to put you on the payroll," Sophia said. "That's a fantastic idea. And you're right. Great public relations for all of us. Plus, it will stimulate more participation next year. Excellent!"

"Do you have Professor Jaeger's number? I'll bet he could help spread the word to the area artists, both here and in Santa Fe as well."

"Yes, I've got his number. Thanks, Kelly. You are simply a jewel. I can't wait to meet you," Sophia enthused.

"It'll be my pleasure. But you have to promise not to gag when you see my wardrobe," Kelly said with a laugh. "I'm strictly a casual Colorado girl who's happiest in shorts and tee shirts."

"Sounds good to me, Kelly. Believe it or not, I switch to

sweats when I finally get home. Comfort is number one," Sophia admitted.

"You'll be pleased to know that I'm presently knitting a beautiful silk and cotton sweater," Kelly added proudly. "So, maybe there's hope for me yet."

"Well, be sure to wear it to the presentation," Sophia suggested. "I think I'll tell Professor Jaeger that the deadline will be two weeks from this Friday. That will give time for us to get the word out. The art community has quite a grapevine. It'll spread like lightning through their Web groups. That way I'll have all weekend to judge the entries then fly to Colorado that week and present the award."

"Wow, two and a half weeks from now," Kelly said, checking her wall calendar. "I'd better start knitting faster."

Sophia laughed loudly at that. "Kelly, you're a delight. I'll stay in touch and let you know how everything's progressing."

"Thanks, Sophia." Kelly added, "And make sure you include Brian Silverstone in your list of invited artists. After all, he's talented, and his idea started all of this."

"I was planning to include him. He may not be a blossoming artist like the younger ones, but I'll be curious to see how he translates his collage designs to fabric."

So will I, Kelly thought, wondering if Brian would blatantly steal some of Allison's designs to submit as his. After all, he had one of her portfolio drawings sitting in his studio. He could copy that exactly and no one would ever know it wasn't his idea. No one except Megan and Kelly. They'd both seen Allison's portfolio many times.

"Yes, I'll be interested in seeing his designs as well," Kelly said, then added for good measure, "And, by the way, Sophia, I wouldn't put much credence on Silverstone's assertions that Allison developed her ideas under his tutelage, so to speak."

"Oh, really?" Sophia remarked, curiosity evident in her voice. "You sound as if you've heard something, Kelly."

"Let's just say I was privy to some 'uncommon gossip,'" Kelly replied. "I'll leave it at that for now."

Sophia laughed softly. "All right, Kelly. I'll be in touch. Thank you again." She clicked off.

Kelly shoved her phone into her pocket, grabbed her clean coffee mug, and headed for the door. Time for Eduardo's coffee, then back to the computer. A high-stakes softball game was scheduled for tonight, so she needed to make progress on her account files today. Skipping down the steps to her cottage, Kelly crossed the driveway, aiming for the flagstone pathway that wound through the gardens surrounding the back of the knitting shop and cafe. Meanwhile, Sophia's competition was still stirring in her mind, sending forth all sorts of ideas.

What if Ray Baker didn't kill Allison? What if it was someone who was jealous of her success? Someone like Brian Silverstone, for instance. He'd certainly tried to grab credit for Allison's ideas last week. And now, he blatantly uses Allison's death to put himself and his work in front of her mentor, Sophia Emeraud. The sound of Brian's ugly threatening voice on the cell phone still resonated inside Kelly's head.

Another voice intruded then. The calmer, persuasive voice of Eugene Tolliver insisting that Brian Silverstone couldn't possibly be the killer. Kelly let all of Eugene's objections run through her head again until they started colliding with the suspicions and everything fell into a disorganized heap.

She needed to knit on it, Kelly decided, glancing at the golden canopy above her head. Run on it or knit on it. Organize her thoughts . . .

"Kelly, I was looking for you," Megan called behind her.

Kelly turned to see Megan approaching through the garden. "Sorry, I only stayed at the shop a little while yesterday. It's hard trying to catch up on workload when you've missed a whole day."

"Don't I know it," Megan replied, then gestured to an outside table. "Why don't we take a moment before we put our noses back on the computer grindstone or whatever."

"Sounds good," Kelly said, settling into a wrought iron chair and signaling a waitress. "First, coffee. No serious conversation until caffeine kicks in."

"Okay," Megan agreed with a laugh as she pulled out a chair and plopped her knitting bag beside it. "Catch me up on Jennifer then. Lisa mentioned something about jazz musicians at practice last night."

"The usual, Bev," Kelly called out to the waitress. "For Megan, too." Then she proceeded to explain Jennifer's excursions into the Denver art scene, ultra high-end styling salon, and a trendy club that evening. Megan laughed through the whole account, wiping away tears at some of Kelly's descriptions.

Once Eduardo's nectar was in her mug, Kelly took a deep drink and changed the subject. "I got a call this morning from Sophia Emeraud. She's decided to have a design competition as a tribute to Allison. The Allison Dubois Award for Wearable Art. She wants to open it up to all the artists she met in Santa Fe and Denver as well as Allison's fellow design students at the university. I told her I thought that was a beautiful idea and a fitting tribute to Allison."

Megan's eyes misted, Kelly noticed. "That's . . . that's wonderful, Kelly. I'm so happy she's doing that for Allison. What sort of award will they receive?"

"That's the best part. She's going to give the winner a six month tryout with her studio in New York. Isn't that great? It's exactly what Allison dreamed of."

This time, the mist became tears and trickled down Megan's cheeks. "Damn, I thought I was over that," she said, swiping at them. Grabbing the napkin, she dabbed at her eyes.

Kelly tossed her napkin across the table. "Wait'll you hear who gave Sophia the idea. That'll dry up those tears."

Megan blinked wetly. "Who?"

Kelly smiled. "None other than Brian Silverstone. He called Sophia and offered to do a wearable art design in 'Allison's style,' he called it. Then went on to say how Allison had been studying with him years ago when she developed her design ideas."

Leaning back in her chair, Kelly sipped her dark brew and let the crisp October breeze ruffle her hair with its promise of winter. All the while, Megan's face went from blotchy crying to red with indignation. Righteous indignation.

"*What!*" Megan spouted. "That bastard! How dare he say that about Allison. Boy, I think I'll go to Denver and find this guy and tell him a thing or two. I'll . . ." She gestured vehemently, obviously picturing the tongue-lashing she'd administer to the offensive Brian Silverstone.

"Don't bother," Kelly suggested. "He'll be coming here in a couple of weeks for the award presentation. Sophia is inviting him to enter the competition. I told her I thought it was a good idea. After all, I've seen his work, and he's truly talented. He should have a shot."

"Kelly! What's the matter with you? This guy was threatening Allison, and now he's trying to steal her ideas. He doesn't deserve the chance to . . . to . . . advance himself on Allison's reputation."

"I feel the same way you do, Megan. It was all I could do not to gag the other day, listening to him talk about how he mentored Allison. But there's method in my madness. I want to see what kind of design he comes up with. I'm betting it'll be a blatant copy of Allison."

"He wouldn't dare," Megan said, eyes narrowing.

"I'm betting he will," Kelly countered. "He has one of

Allison's portfolio drawings in his studio. I saw it when he was giving me a tour. I can't be sure, of course, but I'd swear it was hers. The model is wearing a loose woven top that drapes like hers do. You know, with the contrasting woven belt. That's pure Allison."

Megan's anger colored her cheeks again. "That's her style, all right. Damn. That bastard is stealing her ideas. We ought to tell Sophia Emeraud."

Kelly smiled. "You're assuming Brian Silverstone would win the competition. He may not. But, you know, that gives me an idea. I remember seeing Allison's portfolio drawings spread out on the floor in her apartment the morning we found her. Do you know if Allison's parents took the drawings with them when they left a couple of weeks ago? I know you've been in touch with them."

"As a matter of fact, I had a call from her mother yesterday asking if I could mail the last of Allison's things to them in Durango. She said the police notified them that they took Allison's portfolio from the apartment when they were gathering items for investigation, and they were releasing it now. Apparently, they're keeping one drawing. She asked me if I could retrieve the portfolio and mail it to them." Megan shook her head sadly. "Poor thing, she still sounds so . . . so bereft."

Kelly stared into her coffee mug, pondering what Megan said. Allison's portfolio taken as possible evidence? What could be on the drawings? Why are they releasing all the drawings save one? It had to be fingerprints, Kelly decided. She needed to talk with Burt.

"Megan, do me a favor, will you? Hang on to the portfolio until after the competition," she suggested. "Maybe we can even have Allison's drawings at the ceremony. We'll let Sophia decide whether Brian Silverstone is stealing Allison's designs."

Megan nodded. "Okay, I'll tell her mom about the

award. Then it'll be easier to explain why we're keeping the drawings." She checked her watch. "I'd better grab that yarn Mimi's holding for me, then get back to work."

Work. Computer. Accounts. All waiting for her, too, Kelly thought with a grimace. "You're right. Time's up. I should go inside. I've spent my 'allocated knitting hour' for today." She gave a disgusted snort as she pushed away from the table.

"'Allocated knitting hour,'" Megan said with a chuckle as she grabbed her bag. "Boy, you've gotta get more time away, Kelly."

"That's the problem, Megan. I've been taking so much time away for other things like . . ."

"Sleuthing," Megan teased as they both strolled along the flagstone path.

"Yeah, that, mostly," Kelly admitted with a laugh. "Brother, I'm hopeless. I've got tons of work waiting for me, and yet I'm heading for the softball field tonight without looking back."

Megan gave her a knowing smile. "That's not hopeless, Kelly. That's healthy. See you tonight." And she raced up the steps to the knitting shop.

Kelly pondered Megan's comment as she headed toward her cottage. Healthy, not hopeless. Maybe Megan had a point. She'd think about it. But right now, she needed to dive into those corporate accounts and work straight through till dinner. After she'd placed a phone call to Burt, of course. Kelly had to laugh at herself as she slipped her cell phone from her pocket.

Kelly reached for her little phone with one hand while she steered her car around a corner with the other. "Kelly Flynn."

"Well, hello, Kelly Flynn. I've missed seeing you," Burt's friendly voice came across.

"Hey, Burt. How're you doing?"

"Great, actually. But we'll catch up tomorrow at Curt Stackhouse's cookout. Mimi told me we were all invited. Is he serious about having all of us at one time? That's a lot of big appetites."

"Well, Curt claims he's got a freezer full of beef, and he wants us to put a serious dent in it. I think we can manage that."

"Oh, yeah. Well, I'll pick up Mimi, and we'll both bring something. So, what else is on your mind, Kelly? I heard that tone in your voice in the message. What's up?"

Kelly chuckled. "You know me too well, Burt. Matter of fact, I do have some questions. How's that investigation into Allison's death going? Any new developments? Has Ray Baker talked or anything?" She slowed to a stop at an intersection.

Burt's deep laugh came over the phone. "Well, Ray Baker was questioned earlier on in the investigation. He swore he only went to the apartment once that night. But he didn't do too well under questioning, my partner said. Jittery as hell. Could be the drugs or a guilty conscience. Some people lie better than others. Some are lousy liars."

Kelly thought about that. Something told her she'd become an accomplished liar over the last few months, thanks to her sleuthing. Not exactly an admirable trait, she had to admit.

"Is he still looking like suspect number one?"

Burt paused. "Well, let's say the investigation's proceeding. They're waiting for some additional information to come in from the field."

"Boy, that's a lot of words telling me nothing," Kelly teased. "Tell me this, Burt. Why are the police holding on to one of Allison's portfolio drawings? Megan told me Allison's parents got a call from the department saying they could pick up the portfolio, minus one."

Silence on Burt's end of the line, told Kelly her suspicions were right, so she jumped back into the water.

"They found fingerprints, didn't they, Burt?" she probed, spying the softball field ahead in the distance.

Burt chuckled. "Boy, Kelly, you're relentless. You're also dead on. Yes, they found fingerprints on the drawings. Not only Allison's prints, but others as well. But more importantly, one of those fingerprints matched a print on the coffee cup."

That news sent Kelly's heart racing. She barely braked the car in time to turn into the softball field parking lot. The coffee cup. The cup with poison-laced specialty coffee.

"You mean there's another set of fingerprints on the coffee cup in addition to Allison's?"

"Yep. That's what the department is checking now. They're trying to find a match. So far, nothing. They're checking everything they can. All the databases available."

Kelly pulled her car into a parking space and shut off the engine. "I'm getting the feeling you have no record of Ray Baker's prints."

"Unfortunately, that's right. They're still checking, though. He may have strayed over the line in some little jurisdiction somewhere. He originally came from the East, apparently. That's a heckuva lot of territory between here and there."

"Boy, I thought everything was computerized," Kelly said as she gathered her hat and glove and slid out of the car.

"Well, it is and it isn't. Remember, there're a lot of little towns out there. And these changes take time. But, we're persistent. Don't worry. As squirrelly as Ray Baker is right now, he'll make a mistake. We've got our eye on him."

Kelly slammed the door and headed toward her team's side of the field. She could tell from Burt's voice that Ray Baker was still number one on Burt's list. "What did your partner say about those threatening cell phone messages from Denver? I discovered who the Brian guy is, incidentally?"

"Who?"

"He's an artist who had an affair with Allison a couple of years ago. Apparently they didn't part on good terms, either. Also, he tries to take credit for her work."

"I see. Well, that kind of fits in with my partner's read. Sounds like the guy was mad as hell. But, as you know, Kelly, it takes a lot more than that to drive a man to murder."

Kelly could almost picture Burt nodding, relegating Brian Silverstone's tirade to the "emotional artist" category. Totally harmless. "Well, maybe you're right, Burt. Megan and I thought you and your partner should listen to the message as part of the investigation. Just doing our civic duty as junior investigators," she added playfully as she waved her glove at Megan up ahead.

"Junior investigators, huh?"

"Yeah, I found the badge in my cereal box," she joked. "Listen, gotta get to my game, Burt. See you tomorrow."

"Take care, Kelly. See you then."

Kelly was shoving the phone in her pocket as the sound of running came from behind her. She whirled around just as Steve sped by. His hand snaked out and yanked her USS *Kitty Hawk* cap down over her face, and kept on running.

"Hey, just wait till you pass my base," Kelly threatened, straightening her cap.

"Yeah, yeah, yeah," Steve taunted over his shoulder.

The outdoor lights flashed overhead, blinking into fluorescent life as Kelly jogged toward her teammates. The chill of fall was crisp in the early evening air as the sun slid behind the Rockies, highlighting the foothills. Loosening her sweatshirt from around her waist, Kelly struggled into it. The breeze caught up a swirl of autumn scents—dried leaves, waiting snow. The smell of fall always sent her heart racing for some reason. Death of summer, maybe. Instincts taking over now, sleuthing slid to the back of her mind, as Kelly broke into a run. Time to play ball.

Fourteen

"Don't worry. Carl will be fine," Steve said as he steered his truck along the long gravel drive leading to Curt Stackhouse's ranch.

Despite the reassurance, Kelly glanced over her shoulder to check on Carl, who was riding in the back of Steve's Big Red Truck. Carl was clearly riveted by the passing scenery—pastures filled with cattle, sheep, and unknown creatures hiding in the grass.

"I don't know," Kelly worried, observing the cattle grazing in clusters across the long expanse of pasture from the county road to the barn and farmhouse. Off to the right, she spotted sheep covering the far pastureland like tufts of blown cotton caught in the grass. "Curt may regret inviting him. Carl finds ways to get into trouble," she fretted, watching Carl race from one side of the truck to the other, checking scenery in all directions.

"Carl will be so busy chasing quarry in the back pasture, you won't even see him until it's time to go home," Steve said, pulling the truck to a stop behind Curt's Big Black Monster. Serious trucks, both.

Kelly pushed open the door and leaped to the ground. Carl was already whining. "It's okay, Carl, we're here," she said as she loosened his leash.

Steve quickly lowered the tailgate, and Carl made a dash for freedom, jerking Kelly along with him.

"Whoa, Carl, slow down," Kelly commanded, reining in her dog as Curt approached. "I hope he doesn't start chasing your cattle or sheep, Curt. He's been going crazy all the way up the driveway."

"Curt will sic his sheep dog on Carl if he does," Steve joked as he lifted the beer-filled cooler.

"Welcome, folks," Curt greeted, Stetson low over his eyes in customary fashion. "Hey, Carl, don't get any ideas about those sheep, or I'll have to send Katy to keep you in line." He held out his hand for Carl to sniff. Carl obliged, then slurped Curt's entire palm with his long pink tongue. Curt chuckled and rubbed Carl's head. "You smell food, don't you? You've already forgotten about those sheep."

Kelly glanced toward the sprawling white frame farmhouse ahead. Lawn chairs and tables were spread across the grass, and a large grill sat beside a picnic table. Her friends had already arrived, she noticed. Megan was setting out packages of paper plates, Lisa and boyfriend, Greg, were carrying another cooler onto the grass, and Mimi and Burt were arranging soft drinks. The last outdoor picnic of the year, Kelly thought poignantly. Winter would be blowing over the mountains before she knew it. The last time she and Steve had been here, Ruth was still alive.

She let her gaze roam past Curt's expanse of pasture land out to where the foothills rose in the distance, protective and brooding, closer than in town. Pastures stretched in all directions, filled with creatures that would hopefully keep Carl occupied for hours.

"You were kind to let me bring him, Curt, but I hope we don't regret it," Kelly offered, watching Carl sniffing, nose-to-the-ground. "He's not real well-behaved, I'm afraid. It's all my fault for not taking him to doggie training when he was a puppy."

Curt gave a dismissive wave. "Stop your worrying, Kelly. Let me take him out into that far pasture and toss some sticks his way. He'll be up to his knees in rabbits and rodents once he gets into that tall grass." Carl perked up his head at that, almost as if he understood.

"Boy, I hope you're right," Kelly said, handing Curt the leash. "Carl, you be good, do you hear?"

"Those rabbits are gonna give him fits," Steve joked as they watched Curt stride off toward the high grass, Carl staining at the leash.

"He's been chasing squirrels all summer, now it's the rabbits' turn to run him ragged," Kelly said as they headed toward the farmhouse lawn.

"Well, well, I was wondering where you two were," Jayleen greeted as they approached. "We were about to put the steaks on."

"My fault," Steve said as he swung the cooler to the grass. "I had to stop by the Wellesley site on the way over." He withdrew two bottles from the ice, deftly opened both, and handed one to Kelly. "Jayleen, I won't make the mistake of offering you one. I'm learning." He gave her a wink then lifted the bottle.

"I appreciate that, Steve. It's been over ten years, but it's still one day at a time," Jayleen said as she sipped a cola. "Boy, this is one fine piece of property, isn't it? Curt says it's been in his family nearly a hundred years."

Kelly let her favorite amber ale with the mountain bike name slide down her throat, savoring. "Steve told me his family has been here longer than that. Didn't you say your great-great grandfather homesteaded out here in the 1800s?"

Steve shoved a hand into the back pocket of his jeans and nodded. "Yeah, he came out and started working the land and running cattle about 1886."

Jayleen wagged her head. "Brother, I'll be happy if my business lasts long enough to pass down to the next generation."

"Don't worry, Jayleen," Kelly reassured. "All small business owners feel that way. It's risky, especially when you want to grow."

"Oh, yeah," Jayleen nodded sagely. "I'm real acquainted with risk. In fact, I'm about to take on another huge chunk of it, and I'd kind of like your advice. You too, Steve. I'd really appreciate your opinions. Maybe later, we can—"

"Hey, Kelly, Steve!" Lisa called from across the lawn. "We need some more chairs. Curt's got them stored on the screen porch."

"We're on it," Steve yelled, upending his beer and heading toward the porch.

Kelly started after him, tossing a smile over her shoulder. "You've got lots of business owners here this afternoon, Jayleen. You're going to have more opinions than you want. Why don't we pick this up again after dinner?"

"Good idea, besides it's time to grill steaks. Boy, Curt wasn't kidding when he said he had a freezer full of meat." Jayleen headed toward the back porch steps.

Kelly and Steve reached the screened porch just as Jennifer was leaving, a huge glass bowl in her hands. "Hey, great timing," she greeted them. "You should see those steaks in the kitchen. They're huge. I already picked out one of those steers in the pasture, and Curt's promised to butcher him for me."

"Not today, I hope," Steve teased as he held the screen door open.

Kelly eyed the tempting mound of salad greens and vegetables nearly spilling from the bowl. "Did you make that?" she asked as she grabbed four lawn chairs from the porch.

"As a matter of fact, I did. I even followed a recipe," Jennifer called over her shoulder.

"Whoa, did you feel that?" Steve asked, scooping up the rest of the chairs. "The earth just shook."

"That's only a tremor," Kelly said with a laugh. "If you really want to feel the earth shake, wait till I try to cook something."

Lisa looked up from arranging bowls of chips and salsa and guacamole as Kelly and Steve approached. "What's so funny?"

"Kelly just threatened to cook something for the picnic, but I talked her out of it," Steve said, as he set out chairs.

"What did you bring?"

"Gourmet vanilla ice cream for Megan's pie. Curt's daughter gave her Ruth's recipe," Kelly replied. "Which reminds me, I'd better put that ice cream into the freezer right now."

"Hey, Kelly. Time to sit down and relax." Burt called to her as she sped to the cooler to retrieve the ice cream.

"In a minute," she promised, heading to the farmhouse back steps. Jayleen passed her on the way, carrying a platter that was piled high with steaks ready for the grill.

Kelly raced into the bright cheerful kitchen, slipped the ice cream into the freezer, and was about to race out again when she found herself pausing. She gazed about the open, inviting kitchen. Yellow and white trimmed the doors and windows, spice racks and shelves packed with cookbooks adorned the walls, along with family pictures. Homey was the word that came to Kelly's mind, along with memories of Ruth. Kind, gentle, sweet Ruth. Fantastic cook Ruth.

Ruth of the delicious blueberry pie that she and Steve gorged themselves on when they visited last summer.

So much had happened since then, Kelly thought as she pushed open the screen door. Standing on the screened porch, she looked out onto Curt Stackhouse's wide back-yard, which was still green since the snows had yet to arrive. They were coming, Kelly could tell. She could smell it in the early morning air when she took her run. The crisp fragrance of fall fast fading to winter hung in the air.

She hesitated on the top step, watching her friends gather together in the yard, laughing and talking, snacking already. Jayleen stood by the grill, long fork in one hand, cola in the other. Curt stood beside Lisa and Greg, talking. Megan had left her perch in the semicircle of chairs and was rearranging the abundance of food, homemade and store-bought. Steve had joined Mimi and Burt in conversation.

Would this be her last Colorado cookout? Would she be forced to return to the East and back into a routine that now seemed foreign? Or would she stay here and gamble that she could make it work? Glancing toward the protective ridges of the foothills, which rose in the distance, Kelly wondered if she could ever leave and be happy?

She shoved her hands in the back pockets of her jeans as she strolled over to rejoin her friends. Gazing off into the back pasture, Kelly thought she spotted Carl's black head pop up suddenly in the high grass. Then, just as suddenly, it disappeared again. Up to his knees in rabbits and rodents, she thought with a smile as she grabbed her forgotten beer and settled into a chair beside Lisa.

"Steve said you brought Carl. Where is he?" Lisa asked.

"Curt took him to the back pasture to chase game. With luck, he won't remember us until we've finished eating. Otherwise, we'll have to guard our plates."

Lisa leaned over the chair arm toward Kelly. "Greg said

he'd heard about that guy, you know, the one who trashed Allison's car."

"You mean Ray Baker?" Kelly asked, surprised.

Lisa gestured to Greg, seated beside her. "Remember the guy you told me about? Wasn't his name Ray Baker?"

Greg leaned forward, dangling his long-necked bottle between his knees. "Yep. That's the guy. He plays in the local bars, so I see him around. He's got a real bad temper. Starts fights all the time. If he's there, you'd better clear out by midnight, because he'll take a punch at anyone. Took a swing at my friend once." Greg ran his hands through his sandy blond hair. "It wouldn't surprise me if he had some-thing to do with your friend's murder. He's one violent dude."

Kelly stared into the foothills. There was that word again. Violent. "That's what everyone says about this guy. Brother. I cannot imagine what Allison saw in him."

"Some women just have bad taste in men," Lisa teased. "They're attracted to the wrong guys." She patted Greg's shoulder while they all laughed.

"I can surely testify to that," Jayleen remarked with a grin as she appeared beside them. "I've always had lousy taste in men, and even worse in husbands. They were all good for nothing. Except in bed." She winked.

Kelly threw back her head and laughed so hard, tears came to her eyes. Lisa and Greg nearly fell out of their chairs.

"Okay, now that I've got your attention, I need someone to watch over the steaks while I go put the last minute fix-ins' in my chili. Greg, you any good at grilling?" Jayleen jerked her thumb at him.

"Not unless it's salmon steak, Jayleen," he said with a chuckle. "I'm a vegetarian. So, you'd better not trust me with the meat."

Jayleen stared at him, clearly horrified at his blasphemy.

"Lord-a-mercy! What are you gonna eat, boy? All we've got is steak."

"Don't worry about me, Jayleen," Greg gave a reassuring wave. "There's plenty of good stuff here. Salad, chips, loads of guac, tons of cheese. I'll be fine."

Lisa sprang out of her chair. "I'll do grill duty, Jayleen. He hasn't converted me yet."

Jayleen handed over the grill fork, shaking her head sadly. "I don't know . . . a strappin' young man like you needs something more than rabbit food."

Kelly laughed softly, watching Jayleen head back to the kitchen. "She's something else, isn't she?"

"She's original, all right," Greg agreed with a grin. "I'm glad I met her at last. Lisa told me Jayleen has an alpaca ranch in Bellevue Canyon."

"Right at the mouth of the canyon," Kelly said, sneaking some of the chips Lisa had left on her plate. "But she's growing her herd so much, I'm not sure she's going to be able to manage on that small parcel much longer. She'll have to expand."

"Boy, what I wouldn't give for a piece of property up in Bellevue Canyon," Greg mused. "Those are still some of my favorite views. And I hike all over the Front Range."

"I have to agree with you, Greg," Steve said as he pulled up a chair across from Kelly. "Bellevue has a certain look and feel in the air. Greener. More alpine."

"Keeps the snow longer in the winter, but it's worth it." Greg agreed, upending his beer.

"Vickie Claymore had a beautiful piece of land up there. I wonder if her husband will sell it?" Kelly mused out loud. "Jayleen told me he sold off all of Vickie's alpaca herd after her death."

"Did I hear the word 'sell' in the same sentence with land?" Jennifer asked as she joined them.

"Boy, Jen, you've either got great instincts or great hearing," Steve teased.

"Both, actually." Jennifer grinned, sipping a cola. "Were you talking about the Claymore property? If so, the answer is 'yes.' Bob Claymore listed Vickie's ranch with our real estate office at the first of the month. We've only had a few showings, but that's because the market is slowing now. Boy, what I wouldn't give to sell that listing."

"I'll mention it to my dad," Steve said. "He may know someone who's been looking for a canyon ranch."

Curt strolled up beside Kelly. "Who's looking for a canyon ranch? How about you, Kelly? You could bring those alpaca down from Wyoming."

Kelly smiled. Curt was getting really good at reading her mind. She had to admit that every time she ventured into Bellevue Canyon, Kelly had pictured herself living there. With or without alpaca. Instead of admitting it, however, she replied, "Curt, I can barely make the cottage mortgage payments as it is. Now you want me to buy mountain property?"

"Kelly can't move," Mimi declared as she and Burt brought their chairs closer. "We won't let her. We like having her right across from the shop. Besides she can't sell for two years, right, Jennifer?"

Jennifer nodded sagely. "Not unless she wants to pay thousands of dollars in penalties to the mortgage lender."

"Kelly, you're not moving out of Helen's cottage, are you?" Lisa inquired anxiously, grill fork still in hand.

Kelly had to laugh. A few small comments about mountain property had morphed into a major conversation. It was almost like playing telephone, adult-style. "Folks, I'm not moving anywhere," she said with a laugh. "Curt's just planting seeds like he always does." She shot him a knowing look.

"Damn right," he affirmed with a nod.

"Make way for the chili," Jayleen called out across the lawn. "Do we have spoons and bowls?"

"Right beside the salad," Lisa said as she created space for the huge metal pot in Jayleen's hands.

"Whoa, Jayleen, that's a lotta chili," Burt observed, as she passed.

"That had better be hot," Curt warned.

"Don't you worry. Just be ready with the water," she said, settling the worn, scratched pot on the table, then glanced at Lisa. "Those steaks grilled already?"

"Almost. I'm letting the last one cook a little longer, so it'll be well-done."

Jayleen screwed up her face like she smelled something bad. "If you insist. I'll go take a look." Retrieving the long fork, she strode toward the grill.

"Boy, that chili smells good," Greg said, sniffing the air. "Maybe I'll take a bowl and pick out the meat. Save it for Carl."

"Better not let Jayleen see you," Steve warned with a laugh. "I have a feeling—"

The rest of Steve's sentence was drowned out by the loud sound of cursing. All conversation ceased in the friendly semicircle as Jayleen's colorful invective floated on the air, just like the chili aroma. All heads turned to the grill. Kelly took one look and froze as Jayleen paused to take in wind.

"*Damn* you, Carl! Drop that steak, right now!" Jayleen yelled.

There was Carl, huge sirloin dangling in his Rottweiler jaws, standing well out of Jayleen's reach—and the grill-fork. Instead of looking guilty, however, Carl looked positively triumphant. He'd finally caught something. At last. The fact that the steak couldn't run away from the grill was clearly irrelevant. Carl had stalked the steak, and when it wasn't looking, he'd pounced. It was his, fair and square.

Kelly was mortified. If only she'd taken him to puppy school.

Curt observed the scene with a wry smile. "That woman can sure call the dogs out from under the porch, can't she?"

Steve was shaking his head with laughter. "I'll say."

Everyone was laughing except Kelly. Even Curt's dogs seemed to be laughing at Carl. Whether it was Jayleen's ability or their natural curiosity, two border collies and a black Lab had suddenly appeared at Curt's side.

"Leave him be, Jayleen," Curt called out. "There's plenty where that came from."

"I should never have left the grill," Jayleen fussed as she stomped across the lawn. Kelly swore she could hear Jayleen's boots hit the grass.

"It's all my fault, Jayleen," Lisa confessed, trying to look contrite but laughter making it difficult.

Curt beckoned as he headed for the farmhouse. "C'mon, we'll get the rest of the steaks from the kitchen."

Jayleen followed, but not before she scowled one last time at Carl, who was clearly waiting for her to leave before he enjoyed his meal. "Carl, if you had a tail, I'd wring it off! I swear I would," Jayleen threatened once more, before she stomped toward the farmhouse.

Carl immediately sat down, obviously protecting the part of his anatomy most at risk, while he stared after Jayleen.

Kelly was beyond mortification. She sank her head in her hands. "I should never have brought him. I knew he'd get into trouble. He always does. Carl has absolutely no manners. It's all my fault."

"Kelly, he's a dog, for Pete's sake," Megan teased. "He saw a steak. End of story."

"If only I'd taken him to puppy school. Maybe he'd be better trained, maybe—"

"He could have gone to Harvard, Kelly," Burt spoke up, wiping his eyes. "He still would have grabbed that steak."

"I should never have brought him," Kelly continued, refusing to be consoled.

"Kelly, give it up," Jennifer needled. "I'm so hungry, I was about to grab that steak myself. Only reason I didn't was I knew Jayleen would run me down and stomp me flat."

Kelly had to laugh, joining the others as they each took turns adding to the picture of Jayleen chasing Jennifer across the grass, grillfork in hand. Steve appeared beside her with a plate loaded with chips, salsa, and guacamole, and advised her she'd "feel better" if she ate. She didn't need much prodding, and neither did her friends.

Soon, Jayleen was happily grilling again, and they all settled down to feast on picnic fare. Once or twice, Kelly caught herself staring out at the mountains for several minutes at a time, letting the conversation and shared laughter swirl about her. It felt good. Somehow, she already knew in her heart she was going to stay here. How, she didn't know yet. But she did know she didn't want to leave. She couldn't.

Glancing at the empty plates and the satisfied expressions, Kelly decided it was time for blueberry pie. "Okay, folks, find some more room, because I'm bringing out vanilla ice cream to accompany Ruth's blueberry pie," she announced and gestured to Megan. "Compliments of Megan, that is. She had the temerity to attempt Ruth's recipe."

Megan's cheeks colored as she rose to follow Kelly to the kitchen. "I hope you like it, Curt. I followed the recipe scrupulously."

"If it's half as good as your biscuits, it'll be delicious," Curt assured her.

Megan needn't have worried, Kelly thought a few minutes later, watching her friends devour the pie. Ruth would be pleased. The pie was truly delicious. Now, all that was needed was coffee. Strong black coffee. Kelly glanced toward the farmhouse, wondering if she should volunteer to make a pot.

At that moment, a delectable aroma wafted through the breeze, tickling Kelly's nostrils. Was she imagining it? She could have sworn she smelled . . .

"Coffee, anyone?" Jennifer asked as she approached, glass pot in hand. "I know your answer already, Kelly. I even brought a cup. We don't want you going without caffeine for too long. It gets ugly." She proceeded to pour a dark stream into a ceramic mug. "Curt, I hope you don't mind. I took the liberty of making coffee for Kelly's sake."

"Boy, I need some of that, too," Jayleen said, holding out a foam cup. "I'll probably be up late working tonight."

Kelly heard her cue and jumped in. "All right, Jayleen, tell us. What big decision are you thinking about? I hope you're going to hand off those accounting clients. It sounds like you no longer have the time for them."

"You're right, I don't," Jayleen said, leaning back in the lawn chair and resting a booted foot on her knee. "But I can't dump those folks. I have to find the right person to take on their business." She sent a sly grin Kelly's way. "I was kinda hoping you might be interested, Kelly. I heard you're looking for more consulting."

Kelly blinked. She wasn't expecting that. "Well, I am, but . . ."

"Didn't I hear you say you were looking for more clients?" Megan prodded.

"You know, I do remember your saying that, Kelly," Steve said with a grin. "You were there, Curt. Didn't we hear Kelly say she needed more consulting?"

"Damned if we didn't," Curt decreed, eying Kelly from beneath the rim of his Stetson, while Jennifer filled his coffee cup.

Kelly glanced around the circle of smiling faces. They had her, and they knew it. *Rats*. Trapped by her own words. Not an inch of wiggle room.

"Well . . . I guess you're right. I did say that," she admitted. "I just wasn't expecting to have it show up all at once. How many accounts are we talking about?"

"Well, I'll keep two or three of my oldest clients. They're getting on in years and are pretty crotchety now."

"Watch it, Jayleen," Burt spoke up. "Some of us here are in that category."

"Speak for yourself, detective," Curt countered with a grin.

"Hey, I'm not exactly a spring chicken myself," Jayleen agreed. "But these folks are used to me takin' care of their business, and they'd get their panties all in a knot if I left them."

"Senior citizen underwear," Jennifer conjured. "That's more than I want to think about right now."

Kelly had to laugh. "You still haven't answered my question. How many are you handing off?"

"About fifteen."

"Whoa," Kelly stared at her. "That's a lot. There's no way I could take on that many right now. I'm swamped with my own accounts. Maybe we could work into it gradually or—"

"Kelly girl, you're missing the picture here. Look again," Curt suggested. "If you take over Jayleen's accounts, you could quit that office job. Hell, you'd like the alpaca ranchers a whole lot better than those city suits you've been dealing with."

Kelly sipped her coffee as Curt's words danced in her head. Could she do that? Maybe. Maybe she could. It would all depend on the numbers.

"You can do it, Kelly," Megan encouraged.

"Shhhhh, don't disturb her, she's thinking," Jennifer teased.

"All right, all right, folks," Kelly conceded with a good-natured laugh. "I am thinking about it. But I won't know if it's doable until I see the numbers. Jayleen, you and I will have to get together and talk when we don't have an audience, okay?"

"Name the day," Jayleen said. "And while we're at it, I've got another consulting job for you, Kelly. I'm going to need financial statements for my business. I've never had those done before. But the bank says I need them. Hell, I can't even remember all the ones they said, but I've got it written down at home."

"Are you taking out a loan or something?" Kelly probed, noticing that Jayleen didn't seem to be the least perturbed about discussing her financial affairs in front of everyone. Polar opposite of Kelly's corporate clients who were steeped in secrecy.

"You betcha," Jayleen nodded, holding out her cup to Jennifer for a refill. "I'm gonna make an offer on Vickie's ranch. Well, Bob Claymore's ranch now."

Jennifer did an abrupt 360 degree turn, coffee pot in hand. "Hello? Did I just hear the words 'make an offer'?" She set the coffee pot aside. "Sorry, folks, waitress shift ended. Back to real estate now." She drew up a chair.

Jayleen laughed. "I figured that would catch your attention, girl."

"Are you serious about buying that Claymore ranch?" Jennifer probed.

"Hell, yes. I'm bustin' out of the corrals with this new herd. I've gotta have more space. And, I've done a little pencil-pushing, and with luck, I'll be able to swing it. I've got twice as many females now, not to mention the stud fees from Vickie's Raja." She swirled her coffee. "It's risky, but hell, I've never played it safe my whole life. Why should I start now?"

Jennifer turned to Kelly with a wicked grin. "Are you listening to this, Kelly? You should take a page from Jayleen's book."

"Would someone give Jennifer another piece of pie, so she'll stop," Kelly countered, joining the laughter.

"Jayleen, I've seen your place. Why don't I check out some comparables and work up an analysis for you to look at. That'll help you decide. As much as I'd like to do the deal, I don't want you biting off more than you can chew."

Jayleen grinned. "I appreciate that, Jennifer. Let's see what those financial reports come up with, then the three of us can have a talk."

"I congratulate you, Jayleen," Mimi said. "Expanding your business is a risky decision, but for some of us, it's something we have to do. I know exactly how you feel, and if you want to pick my brain for any advice, I'll be glad to help."

Kelly wasn't sure, but she thought she saw a trace of moisture glisten in Jayleen's eyes. "Thanks, Mimi. You're a sweetheart. I'll take you up on that offer."

"Uh, oh," Steve interrupted and pointed into the yard. "Look who's skulking in the background."

Kelly turned and spied Carl edging his way across the grass toward their friendly circle. Unfortunately, the grill was also nearby, so he may have been looking for seconds. "I see you, naughty dog," she accused. "If you're looking for forgiveness, I'm fresh out."

Almost as if she understood what Kelly was saying, Curt's black border collie jumped up from beside his chair and raced across the grass. She stopped right in front of the empty grill, fixed Carl with a doggie stare, and barked loudly.

Curt chuckled. "Katy's decided to guard the grill, I guess. Carl won't get within three feet of it now."

Sure enough, Katy patrolled the grill's perimeter, glaring at Carl and barking protectively. Carl, who outweighed the little border collie by at least fifty pounds or more, lay on the ground, face between his paws, sulking.

"Gutsy little gal," Jayleen commented.

"Oh, yeah. She'll get right in his face if she has to," Curt replied with a grin. "She's the best sheep dog I've ever had. Bossy as hell."

"You ought to let Katy come over for a visit some weekend," Kelly suggested. "Maybe she can teach Carl some manners."

Fifteen

Kelly pulled up in front of Megan's condo building and was about to leave the car when Megan raced up to the driver's window.

"Thanks so much for doing this, Kelly. I must have dropped my checkbook yesterday when I was checking Allison's apartment. I was looking under the desk and checking the cupboards, everywhere, making sure that none of Allison's things were left," Megan explained breathlessly, handing over a key. "Then my phone rang, and that's all I remember. My new client wanted to change a whole report section, so I had to leave right away and get back to the computer."

"Don't worry. I'll go over and check," Kelly reassured her. "I was already at the post office when you called, so it's no problem."

"You're a lifesaver. That new client had me on the phone all morning and demands a total redo of his report by tonight. Brother, I'm not sure this guy is worth the money."

"Take a deep breath," Kelly teased. "I'll be right back.

Go inside and get to work, so you'll be able to come to practice tonight."

"I'll try," Megan promised as she turned away. "You can drop the key back in the apartment office when you've finished."

Kelly gave her a wave as she pulled away from the curb and headed west towards Allison's apartment complex. Thanks to newly coordinated traffic lights, she arrived at the building quicker than she expected. As she approached the concrete steps leading up to the apartment, however, Kelly stepped back beneath the stairs, out of sight. Someone was at Allison's door. She peered through the stair opening. A dark-haired man, unshaven, dressed in jeans and dark sweatshirt rattled the door knob, again and again. He pushed forcefully on the door with his shoulder, and Kelly listened to him curse. Not as colorful as Jayleen, but it got the message across.

Suddenly Kelly knew who the man was. She didn't know how she knew, she just knew. That had to be Ray Baker, she decided, trying to see his profile. An idea darted through her mind. She'd been anxious to talk to Allison's former boyfriend, if for no other reason than to see what her antennae picked up.

The man stared at the door for another minute, and Kelly knew it was now or never. She popped out from behind the steps and grabbed the rail as if she was heading upstairs.

The man jumped and stared at her, clearly startled by Kelly's sudden appearance.

"Hey, are you coming to see the apartment, too?" Kelly chirped in her best Barbie voice as she climbed the stairs. "I got the key from the manager so I could take a look."

"Uhhhhh, uhhhhhhh, yeah," Baker nodded, his confused look mixing with surprise.

Kelly turned up the wattage of Barbie's smile. "You can come on in with me if you want," she offered. "I'm not sure if I want to be this far west or not. Kinda far from my job, if you know what I mean. But I'd heard this place was available from someone at the knitting shop in town." She watched Baker's reaction.

His bloodshot eyes widened, and he swallowed but said nothing. So, Kelly slipped the key in the lock and pushed the door open, chatting away in Barbie's high-pitched little-girl tone of voice. No one could be suspicious of Barbie, not even Ray Baker. "Isn't it sad what happened here? I mean, that poor girl died and all. Someone at the shop said it might be murder. That's just awful."

Baker's wary expression shifted immediately, staring at the floor. "Uhhhhh, yeah, it is . . . I . . . I knew her, kind of," he volunteered as he followed Kelly into the empty apartment.

"Really?" Kelly squeaked, excitedly. "She was a friend of yours?"

Baker walked to the middle of the nearly empty living room. "Yeah," he said quietly. "She was a good friend."

Kelly scrutinized Baker's expression. She wasn't sure, but something suspiciously akin to sadness crossed his face. "Oh, wow, you must be all broken up then. You miss her bad, I'll bet," she probed, waiting for his reaction to her words.

It came swiftly. Slight, but unmistakeable. Baker's mouth tightened then twitched before he turned his head, but not before Kelly glimpsed the distinctive glint of moisture in his eyes.

What was this, she mused? Ray Baker the violent, bad-news boyfriend was exhibiting signs of grief? Was he pretending? Kelly quickly eliminated that possibility. There was no reason for Baker to pretend in front of a stranger, especially not non-threatening, sympathetic Barbie. No. For one brief moment, Kelly had seen inside the troubled, drug-taking musician and seen something she hadn't expected. Baker cared for Allison. Was this what kept Allison tied to him for so long, Kelly wondered? Allison must have blocked out his destructive twin.

"Uh, yeah," Baker said as he stared at the floor. "I miss her a lot."

"That's really tough," Kelly sympathized as she started a slow stroll about the living room. Baker walked toward the windows, she noticed, then headed down the hallway. Kelly used his absence to search for Megan's checkbook. She glimpsed it on the floor beside the bookcase. Kelly quickly pocketed the checkbook and resumed her stroll.

Glancing about the kitchen, Kelly noticed Baker approaching. Curious, she asked, "Are you actually thinking of renting this apartment? I mean, that would feel kind of weird, wouldn't it? Your friend being killed here and all."

Baker paused at the edge of the living room, then stood and stared for a long minute, as if he was picturing the past and remembering. "Yeah, you're right. It wouldn't feel right. Not after what happened to Allison."

Kelly saw a chance and took it. "Do the police have any idea who killed her?" she asked in the wispy voice.

Baker's face darkened, and his thin mouth twitched once again. "The police don't have a clue," he muttered. "If they were smart, they'd go look in Denver."

Kelly stared at Baker. She hadn't expected that. Was Baker referring to Brian Silverstone? He had to be. Who else in Denver held a grudge against Allison Dubois?

Almost as if he'd surprised himself, Baker shot Kelly a self-conscious glance then hastened to the door. "Listen, I gotta go. Good luck finding an apartment." And he was gone before Kelly could say goodbye.

She'd been driving for five minutes before Kelly realized she was heading toward Wellesley, the tiny town north of Fort Connor. So immersed with the ideas that bounced around her brain, especially after she'd told Megan about her accidental encounter with Baker, Kelly had unknowingly slipped into autopilot mode. The car was driving itself.

Megan agreed with Kelly that Baker's comment pointed to Brian Silverstone. However, Megan clearly wasn't about to drop her suspicions about Baker. She tried to convince Kelly that he was only acting a part. Kelly had nodded in seeming agreement, so Megan could escape back to her consulting. Kelly, however, was looking at Ray Baker with new eyes. She'd sensed something when she was with him, something she never expected. Ray Baker didn't kill Allison. How Kelly knew this, she couldn't say. She just felt it.

There was something else, too. Baker knew about Brian Silverstone. Kelly sensed that Baker was well aware of Allison's feelings about Silverstone. Judging from the entries in Allison's diary, Brian had been harassing Allison for months. Ever since she'd attracted New York's attention. Had Allison shared her anxieties and fears about her former lover with Baker? Or had Baker found out the same way Kelly and Megan had, by reading Allison's diary?

Kelly slowed for a stop sign on the edge of Wellesley. Coming back to the present moment, she slipped out of autopilot with a rueful realization. There was only one thing in Wellesley that would bring her out here. The development of new homes that Steve was building on the eastern edge of town.

Why was she driving out to see Steve, she wondered? Running through the daytimer in her mind, she quickly found the reason. Dinner. Steve had mentioned their going to dinner this week. That was it, Kelly told herself as she pulled her car to a stop in between two pickup trucks.

Scanning the busy building site as she exited the car, Kelly spotted Steve talking with two carpenters. At least, she assumed they were carpenters. They were inside a newly framed house, holding drywall in place, hammers in hand.

Steve turned as she called his name, gestured to the men again, then walked to meet her outside what would soon be the front door of the house. Kelly sniffed the fragrance of new wood. She'd always liked that smell.

"Hey, what brings you out here?" Steve asked, tugging down the brim of his baseball cap to shade his eyes. Kelly wished she had hers. Noonday sun in Colorado could be brutal, even in October.

"I just wanted to check something. Are we scheduled for dinner this week? I seem to remember something about that."

Steve grinned. "Yeah, we are. For this Friday night. What's the matter, you need to cancel again?"

"No, no," Kelly replied with a grin, listening to the ring of hammers from several directions. "I just wanted to check. Friday's good."

"You could have told me that over the phone," Steve said. "What really brought you out here, Kelly?"

Almost without thinking, Kelly answered with the real reason she'd driven all the way to Wellesley. "I've been thinking about Jayleen's proposition. We're going to get together Friday morning to go over her records carefully, but she gave me a ballpark figure last night before we left Curt's. Whispered it, actually."

Kelly smiled, remembering Jayleen leaning over the trash can when they were all cleaning up after the picnic—despite Curt's protests. "I was awake most of the night thinking about it, Steve. I'm going to do it. Take the plunge, that is." Kelly let out a breath. "I'm going to give my boss two weeks notice. That'll give me time to save as much as I can. That plus doing the financial statements for Jayleen will keep me afloat for a month or so, until those alpaca accounts start paying off. Or, I get some money from the drilling company. I went to Chambers's office this morning and signed the lease agreement."

Steve's face lit up. "That's great news, Kelly. You're

making the right move. Now we'll really have something to celebrate on Friday."

Kelly felt lighter somehow. Hard to explain, but it was noticeable. "I wanted to tell you first, since you've been nagging me the longest," she teased.

"That's because I wanted you to stay. You belong here, Kelly Flynn, and you know it. This is your home," Steve said in a quiet voice.

An unexpected moisture appeared behind her eyes, startling Kelly, and she blinked. "Whoa, don't go all mushy on me. I'm not used to that. I like it better when you're giving me a hard time."

"No problem," Steve promised, his good-natured grin returning. "I'll start on Friday. Right now, I've gotta get back to the guys." He jerked his thumb over his shoulder before he turned. "Oh, and don't dress up for dinner. I'm taking you on another picnic," he called as he walked away.

"Where?"

"You'll find out Friday. Wear jeans and bring a sweatshirt. It gets chilly up there after sunset." He gave a wave then jogged back to his workmen.

"'Up there,'" Kelly repeated as she headed to her car. Darn it. Steve was true to his word about giving her a hard time. He knew she'd be puzzling over the picnic location from now till Friday.

Kelly fingered the plush fibers that lay temptingly on the knitting shop's maple table and squeezed. Soft, soft, soft. She squeezed again, letting the fibers slide between her fingers, caressing her skin. She felt herself weakening. She dared not peek into her knitting bag. The circular sweater would be frowning at her, she was sure.

The siren call of silky, lustrous fibers beckoned. Unmistakable. How would she ever finish a sweater when she kept getting seduced by these sinfully soft yarns? She'd be the only knitter in northern Colorado who had yet to make a sweater.

Kelly forced herself away from the lush, plush bundles and tried to make a run for the library table. She didn't get very far. Frothy mohair yarns stopped her at the doorway, spilling from an open bin, a kaleidoscope of color from bold to subdued. She fingered these as well, remembering how beautifully Lisa's shawl had turned out.

How long would that take, she wondered? After all, she deserved a present, didn't she? Weeks and weeks of stewing and deliberating about her future had finally produced a decision. She was staying and building a career and a new life here in Fort Connor. She definitely deserved a present for making a commitment at last.

Kelly fondled the colorful bundles. Choosing a rainbow of vermillion, sapphire, emerald, amber, and wine, Kelly dropped her knitting bag on the library table and headed for the front counter. She swore she could hear the circular sweater complaining. Did yarn cry?

Rounding the corner, Kelly nearly ran into Mimi, who was followed closely by Burt. "Oops, sorry," Kelly apologized. "You know me, when fiber fever strikes, I head for the register."

Mimi laughed lightly, her cheeks pink with amusement. "You're my favorite kind of customer, Kelly. A yarn floozy."

"Yarn floozy, that's me," Kelly admitted, remembering Jennifer's less circumspect term for knitters with absolutely no willpower when it came to yarns. For them, it was impossible to say no.

"Give me a minute, Mimi, and we'll go over that new class schedule," Burt said, turning toward Kelly.

"Sure thing. I'll be in the office." Mimi continued her quick pace through the shop.

"What's up?" Kelly asked, moving into a quiet corner beside a huge weaving loom. The Mother Loom.

"I thought you'd like to know that we located a record of Ray Baker's fingerprints," Burt said in a hushed voice. "Way back in Tennessee. It happened five years ago. Seems he got drunk in a bar and started wrecking the place. When the police came, he threw some punches their way. So, they got him for resisting arrest." Burt wagged his head, his expression revealing how many times he'd witnessed a similar situation.

"Have you matched the fingerprints?"

"Not yet. We're waiting for the local authorities in Tennessee to coordinate with our department. Unfortunately, you never know how long that can take. It all depends on their administrative procedures."

Kelly paused for a moment, wondering how best to tell Burt about her encounter with Baker. "You know, I met Baker yesterday," she ventured. "Megan asked me to retrieve her checkbook that she'd accidentally left in Allison's apartment. When I got there, Baker was trying to get in the door. So, I started a conversation with him."

Burt fixed her with one of his concerned stares, part fatherly, part cop. "Why in the world would you do that? I've been keeping you updated with everything we've learned about him. Keep away from this guy, Kelly. He's violent and unpredictable as hell."

Kelly stared at the yarn instead of Burt. "It was an accidental encounter, Burt, so I decided to use it to, you know, get a read on him."

"His life's pretty much an open book so far, Kelly. And it doesn't make for good reading."

"It's hard to explain, Burt," she replied, looking out into the shop now. "There was something bothering me about Baker being the murderer. I don't know. So, I took that chance to talk with him. I pretended to be looking at apartments to rent since I had the key from Megan. That way it appeared completely natural for me to ask him questions."

Burt's eyes popped wide. "You went into the apartment alone with him? Good God, Kelly, what were you thinking?"

She shrugged. "I was just going on instinct, Burt, what can I say. I played dumb and asked him questions. He readily admitted that he knew Allison, and I sensed he was still broken up about her death."

A scornful expression spread over Burt's face. "I'm sure he is. Particularly now that we're looking at him closely."

Kelly debated. She knew Burt would reject her feeling about Baker, but she had to say it anyway. "I don't think he's guilty, Burt. He didn't kill Allison. Someone else did."

Burt's expression softened a bit, and he reached out and placed a big hand on her shoulder. "I respect your instincts, Kelly, but this time, I think you're misguided. Baker has a violent history and we've got witnesses to prove that he was harassing Allison."

"You know, Burt, that's the thing that bothers me. Everyone always focuses on Baker's violent history. But the method of murder wasn't violent at all. It was sneaky and treacherous. It just doesn't sound like the method Baker would choose."

Burt pursed his lips, telling Kelly that he'd thought the same thing himself, but had probably been talked out of it. "That's true, Kelly. But we've learned that Baker stalked Allison. That takes a good degree of deviousness of character, don't you agree?"

"Yes, it does, Burt," she admitted in a softer voice, now that customers had entered the weaving room. "And you may be right. Keep me posted on those fingerprints, okay?"

"Will do," Burt promised with a mini-salute as he headed toward Mimi's office.

Sixteen

The crunch of gravel beneath her tires reminded Kelly to slow down. Sending a goodbye wave to Jayleen, Kelly stopped at the intersection of Jayleen's driveway and the county road. She hesitated before turning to the right and back into town, back to her computer. Instead, she made a swift left turn and headed up the county road that led into Bellevue Canyon.

She and Jayleen had spent the entire morning pouring over business records. Thanks to Jayleen's bookkeeping ability, the accounting records were in order. Kelly had gathered everything she needed to create the necessary financial statements of income, balance sheet, and cash flow. She'd advised Jayleen that it would take her at least a week to finish, since she was finishing up all her corporate accounting and closing the files.

Talk about 180 degrees difference, Kelly had to laugh. Most of her former office mates at the CPA firm would be shocked to learn she'd given up a high-profile corporate career to start a very low-profile and decidedly non-corporate career in the Colorado Rockies. Keeping track of alpacas, no less. They'd fall off their chairs in either laughter or shock.

The road wound past the open pastures of the canyon's mouth, then quickly started to climb. Rock-rimmed ravine walls closed in on both sides. Autumn's paintbrush was evident everywhere Kelly looked. She hadn't driven into this canyon since the end of summer and had missed the changing colors, so she relaxed and drank in the season's splendor.

Canary yellow and molten gold claimed the cottonwoods above her head. Slender aspens peeked out from hidden groves and shook their lemon-colored leaves, announcing the end of summer with their familiar rustle. Oranges as bright as pumpkin and as bashful as burnt umber danced through the treetops, hid beside deep emerald evergreens, and jutted from canyon walls. Reds from russet to ruby shouted between rocks and crevices, demanding attention.

Kelly felt herself relax even more as she drove higher into the canyon. The ever-present pressure she'd felt weighing her down was gone. She felt free. It didn't make sense. As soon as she gave notice, she'd be working twice as hard for several weeks while she wrapped up one job and started another. Why then, did she feel happier than she'd felt in a long, long time? She didn't know, and she didn't care. Kelly found herself smiling as she drove.

Rounding an aspen-lined bend in the canyon road, a familiar property came into view. Vickie Claymore's ranch. Sure enough, there sat the real estate company's sign proclaiming FOR SALE. Kelly slowed and pulled her car into the entrance to the driveway and stared at the impressive log home in the distance. The spacious pastures were totally empty of alpaca. Jayleen had bought the best of Vickie's herd, and other breeders had claimed the rest. Vickie had been one of the most successful alpaca ranchers in the region—while she was alive.

Kelly felt a poignant tug, remembering Vickie talking about her dreams, her plans. All snuffed out by a scheming killer. Now, Jayleen was spinning new plans and dreams. Vickie's beautiful house would be filled with laughter and friends, and the pastures would be covered once again with alpaca. Listening to Jayleen dream out loud, it was hard for Kelly not to start dreaming, too. Especially now that she was up in the canyon she loved.

Glancing at the road ahead, Kelly pondered for a moment, then turned her car back into the canyon. Climbing higher now, she glimpsed the mountain ranges in the distance. Finally, Kelly pulled into the driveway of the property she was heading for, shut off the engine, and left her car.

This property also sported a FOR SALE sign, but it was a different one. This property was being foreclosed on by the lender who held the mortgage. Once Geri Norbert had confessed and been arrested for Vickie Claymore's murder last summer, the entire house of cards she'd built around her struggling alpaca business collapsed. Now, all of Geri's dreams were for sale.

Kelly strolled over to the fence and stared at the modest ranch house and weather-beaten outbuildings. Geri's alpaca were still grazing in what used to be her pasture. According to Jayleen, someone had been hired to manage the animals until they and all the ranch equipment could be sold at auction.

She gazed past the ranch house to the mountain range that shimmered in the distance, set sparkling by October's snows. It always snowed earlier in the mountains. Kelly had loved this view the first time she'd seen it. This high up into the canyon, there was a different look and feel. More alpine, and the views more striking.

Kelly let herself gaze for several minutes while her mind began to spin dreams of her own. What would happen to this property? Who would buy it? A high-end developer would love to grab it and build a mega mountain home, she thought. How much would it sell for, she wondered? She could ask Jennifer. Surely a property as desirable as this would be scooped up by real estate investors, wouldn't it? Then again . . . Kelly remembered stories of people who wearied of the colder north-facing canyon roads where the snow clung far longer than in the sunny southwestern-facing canyons. Remembering the steepness of the drive, Kelly didn't want to think about sliding down an ice-covered canyon road.

Another little voice sounded in her head. *Are you nuts?* it asked. *You can barely make the payments on the cottage now, and you're about to quit your salaried job. Hello? Earth to Kelly.*

Was she crazy, Kelly wondered? True, she was about to relinquish her CPA salary, but she was also the owner of Wyoming ranch land. Land that held cattle, sheep, and alpaca. Land that also held something very valuable beneath. Natural gas deposits. Valuable gas deposits, according to Curt Stackhouse.

Kelly surveyed the ranch property once more, then turned and walked to her car. Revving the engine she turned her sporty car back onto the road and headed down the canyon. Jayleen would know what this property was worth. Jennifer could explain the foreclosure process and how it worked. And Curt, who'd planted this seed last weekend, would be able to help Kelly find the money to pay for this dream.

Kelly stretched out her legs on Steve's faded plaid blanket. As she leaned back on her elbow, she sipped the flavorful white wine, savoring it. It was good even from a plastic cup. Steve's surprise picnic was, well . . . surprising. Instead of standard picnic fare, Steve brought selections from their favorite restaurants around town, plus a baguette from the French bakery. He even promised a carafe of coffee was hiding somewhere in his truck.

Kelly nibbled a slice of Brie as she gazed out at the deep green-and-gold forested mountains that surrounded them on all sides. Aspens streaked their gold through the emerald evergreens in bold slashes. Kelly swore she could smell the snow to come. With its higher altitude, Rocky Mountain National Park's glorious mountain peaks usually began to sparkle in September, when low-hanging clouds brushed across the peaks and sprinkled white flakes.

Suddenly, a high-pitched squeal echoed across the valley where she and Steve and several others had spread out their picnics. The shrill sound hung in the air, floating through the twilight for a full minute, before it was followed by a series of guttural cries. Kelly glanced into the open meadow and spotted a huge bull elk anxiously patrolling the perimeter of his small harem. The cow elk grazed nearby or lay docilely on the grass, observing the autumn mating ritual as if they were bored with it all.

Elk bugling. Mountain music, Steve called it. Kelly had never had a chance to hear the eerie yet captivating sound until now. Just then, another high-pitched squeal trumpeted out of the surrounding forest. A young male on the prowl, anxious to start a harem of his own by raiding another bull's cluster of cows. Kelly watched the elder bull lift his magnificent antlered head and let out a belligerent bellow. Answering the youngster's challenge.

"I think he just told the other elk to 'bring it on,'" Kelly joked as she dipped a chip into the hummus.

"That's about it," Steve agreed, scooping up a handful of

cashews. "Boy, he's got a great rack. Looks like a twelve point."

"You know, this is the first time I've ever seen this," Kelly admitted. "My dad never took me when I was a kid, and I've been away ever since."

"Now you'll get to see it every fall," Steve said with a lazy grin. "It's like watching a soap opera. The bulls challenge each other, going head to head. Meanwhile, the cows do what they want. Some of them join a different harem every night."

"You're kidding," Kelly scoffed. "With all that bugling, they actually ignore old Harry and walk over to . . . to Charlie, over there." She pointed to another huge bull on the opposite side of the park road. His small group of cows grazed peacefully.

"Oh, yeah. They'll wait until Harry over here isn't looking, then they'll edge closer to Charlie." He pointed across the meadow to a cow elk that was grazing on the edge of the group. "See, there's one. She's starting to make her move. Just watch."

Kelly watched, and sure enough, when Harry turned his back and bellowed at an unseen male, the cow moved farther away from the harem, approaching the meadow's edge. "Well, look at that. Agnes is making a run for it."

Steve chuckled. "Now, watch old Harry. He'll notice she's drifting away and run after her, bugling like hell."

Almost as if he'd overheard Steve, Harry took one look at Agnes inching away and ran after her, bellowing raucously. Agnes seemed unperturbed, stopping her escape to graze in place. Harry gave several warning bellows until the younger male's challenge echoed from the encroaching forest once more, and Harry raced back to his remaining herd. Without so much as a backward glance, Agnes began her deliberate wandering, reaching the meadow's edge. With a quick glance down the road, Agnes trotted over to Charlie's domain and started grazing the greener grass. Steve and Kelly laughed out loud.

"So, what do you think about the canyon property?" Kelly asked, switching from elk soap opera to real life quandaries. "Am I crazy, or do you think I can find the money to buy it?"

"You're not crazy," he replied, pouring more Riesling into her proffered cup. "You've definitely got the assets to buy it. It's just a matter of which ones you choose to sell."

"Let's start with the cattle. How much if I sold off the rest of the herd?"

Steve grinned. "You really don't like the cattle, do you?" he teased. "Okay, selling off the rest of the herd will yield a fair amount, less expenses, of course. But you may not have enough left to buy the canyon property because Curt's still paying off past-due bills. And he may find more of those. It sounds like that ranch hasn't been managed well for years."

Kelly pondered. "How much if I sell off the sheep?"

"Still not enough. Besides, Mimi and the others would never let you hear the end of it. Selling off all those wool-producers."

"Yeah, you're right. I guess they have to stay along with the alpaca. Hmmmmm," she mused aloud. "That leaves the ranch land itself, or I may have to sell some of the mineral rights if I want to buy that canyon land."

"Better hold on to both," Steve ventured, snatching a slice of Brie. "You're going to need surrounding acreage for access roads when they start drilling, and those mineral rights provide the income stream you're counting on. Selling those would be like selling the goose that lays the golden eggs."

"I know. But I don't have anything else left to sell."

"Not necessarily," Steve countered. "You've got the cottage here, and you've also got the ranch house in Wyoming. But you can't sell the cottage without taking a loss, so that leaves the ranch house."

Kelly frowned. "I don't want to sell Martha's house. It doesn't feel right somehow."

"It would yield more than enough to buy the canyon place."

She shook her head. "I don't think I can. I mean, there are all those memories there. Family memories."

"Martha's family. Not yours," Steve pointed out, sipping his wine.

Good point. Kelly pondered for another moment. What was it about selling Martha's place that bothered her? She had no memories there. In fact, Martha had left it behind, too.

"Didn't you tell me Martha was planning to sell that house, then donate all the land?" Steve probed.

She nodded. "Yes, she was."

"Well, then. If Martha didn't even want her own house, why the heck are you holding onto it?"

Another good point. Martha had planned to sell not only the house but give away the furniture as well. Why was she holding on when Martha hadn't? Kelly wondered.

"I don't know," she admitted softly.

Steve sat up on the blanket and pushed their plates aside. "Let's take a look at what you've got," he suggested. Scooping up some chips, a handful of nuts, and the wedge of cheese, Steve began to place them on the blanket. "Here's the cottage," he said, indicating a potato chip. Plunking down the cheese, he said, "Here's the Wyoming land with gas deposits. You can slice it anyway you want." Sprinkling cashews next to the cheese, he added, "Here are the cattle and here's the ranch house." He plopped down a container of hummus.

Kelly chuckled. "What's your point, other than tempting me to snack again?"

"Let's analyze the assets," he suggested. "You can't sell the cottage yet, and the cattle might not yield enough after expenses," he said, pointing to the chip, then the cashews. He proceeded to slice the cheese into small wedges. "So, you could choose to sell ranch land instead of donating it or sell mineral rights and reduce your income." He pushed several wedges to the side. "Remember, those income examples Curt showed you were based on keeping all the mineral rights. If you sell them, there goes the money." He popped one then another wedge into his mouth.

Kelly studied the diminished cheese. "Good point," she admitted. Steve answered by snatching another wedge of Brie. "Hey, I didn't sell that one," she protested with a laugh.

"Sales commission," Steve teased. "So, that leaves the ranch house." He pointed to the container of hummus. "You could sell the house with several acres, and that should easily fetch enough to buy the canyon property. That would also leave all the rest of the land to use however you choose."

Kelly stared at the half-eaten container of hummus. Martha's ranch house. Of all the assets spread out on Steve's plaid blanket, that was the one she could sell without either breaking a promise to Martha or sabotaging her own financial future. She had to admit, it made sense. Kelly had no emotional attachment to the house. Neither did Martha.

Kelly remembered how her elderly cousin had calmly discussed selling off her family home, all the farm equipment, and the cattle without a trace of regret. Martha didn't even want the furniture, planning to donate it to the Sisters of Charity. Kelly pondered that last thought. She differed with Martha on that one, recalling all the beautiful antiques coated with dust that filled the ranch house.

She nodded. "I have to admit that makes more sense. I could sell the ranch house and keep the furniture."

"Why? The cottage is full already."

"Have you seen all those gorgeous antiques in Martha's ranch house? I can't sell those." She grinned at Steve, then popped the cottage potato chip into her mouth.

Steve laughed. "You just ate the cottage."

"I'm redecorating."

"Okay, then the cattle are mine," he teased and scooped up the cashews, popping them in his mouth.

Kelly snatched a stray potato chip, plunged it into the hummus ranch house, and gobbled it down.

"Hey, leave the ranch house alone. It's for sale," Steve protested, reaching for the container.

"I'm moving the furniture into storage."

"Okay then, I'll help." He snagged a chip and dug in. To-gether they laughed and hunched over the hummus, battling each other for the last morsel. Martha's ranch house was stripped clean in moments.

Steve looked Kelly in the eye and grinned. "I like the way you make decisions, Kelly Flynn." Then leaning over, he kissed her quickly on the mouth.

Kelly blinked. She certainly wasn't expecting that in the midst of a real estate discussion. Besides, it happened so fast, it was over as soon as it started. Steve had lingered only a second. He was quick, she had to give him credit. Now, how was she going to respond? Kelly retreated into the safety of humor. Always a good move.

She gave him a wry smile. "What was that all about?"

"I don't know," Steve replied with a genial grin. "It felt like the natural thing to do at the time. Kind of like the elk out there. They don't think about stuff all the time. They just do what comes naturally."

Kelly stared out at Harry, still patrolling his harem with bugles and bellows. "Natural, huh? Does that mean you're gonna run into the meadow and start bugling?"

Steve leaned back on the blanket and laughed. "Naw. I'll

save my bugling for the ball field. We play Greeley tomor-row. Big game."

Ahhhh, the safety of softball. Kelly jumped in without missing a beat. "And you play us on Sunday. So look out."

Steve fixed her with a wicked grin. "You guys don't worry us. It's Greeley that's out for our blood."

Kelly snatched up the gauntlet, feigning offense. "*We* don't worry you? Whoa, listen to that." She fixed him with a playful scowl. "Any more of that talk, and I'll go join Agnes over there." She gestured to the philandering cow elk across the road, grazing contentedly in Charlie's harem.

Steve chuckled. "Okay, I guess I'll have that dessert all to myself then."

Dessert? Kelly didn't remember any mention of dessert. She eyed Steve skeptically. "You didn't say anything about bringing dessert."

"I'm a man of surprises."

He was that, Kelly had to admit. "Okay, we'll take up this discussion again after practice some night when I have reinforcements," she bargained. "Now, what kind of dessert are we talking about here? If it's a package of Twinkies, I'm definitely going across the road with Agnes."

"It's a chocolate raspberry torte from Babette's bakery," Steve tempted.

Kelly's mouth started to water. Still, she hesitated, hat-ing to sell out for chocolate. Even chocolate with raspber-ries. "Hmmmmm," she deliberately stalled.

"Don't forget the coffee."

Rats. She'd forgotten the coffee. That did it. Team honor was one thing, but principles were another. And first among Kelly's principles was Allegiance to Caffeine. Agnes could keep Charlie and the grass.

She grinned across at Steve. "You get the cake. I'll get the coffee."

Seventeen

Jayleen reached over her corral fence and beckoned to a smoke-gray alpaca nearby. "You want some attention, don't you, little one?" she cajoled. The young male eagerly thrust out his face for a nose rub, and Jayleen obliged as she looked up at Kelly. "Thanks for bringing those reports out here," she gestured to the bound portfolio in Kelly's hand. "I could have gotten them."

"No problem, Jayleen. I've been stuck at home in front of the computer for the past week finishing up my corporate accounts. Believe me, I needed an excuse to get away and take a drive into the foothills."

"Have you told your boss yet that you're quitting?" Jayleen asked as she gave the alpaca a final pat and turned toward the house.

Kelly fell into step beside her, the late October breeze whipping her linen shirt. "I called him last week and promised to wrap up everything and have it into the Washington office by next week. So, I basically gave him two weeks notice."

"What'd he say? Was he angry or anything?"

"No, as a matter of fact, I sensed he was relieved." Kelly paused at the edge of Jayleen's front porch and clasped the portfolio of financial statements to her chest as she stared off into the foothills. The early afternoon sun was angling toward the canyon. A red-tailed hawk cruised atop the air currents for a moment then swooped toward the ridge top, hunting. "I had suspected he was loading on the work in hopes I'd either quit or return to Washington like a proper corporate CPA. Suit up and show up at the office." She smiled wryly. "So, I think my reason for quitting surprised him.

Jayleen hooted. "Lord, girl, you didn't tell him you were leaving to count alpaca, did you?"

Kelly laughed as she traced another hawk's flight against the yellow-brown background of cottonwood trees that bordered Jayleen's property. Late October's chill had stripped most of the trees already, especially in the mountains. The higher up, the colder the nights. Kelly had noticed Autumn's handiwork in the glistening pockets of early morning frost she glimpsed along the roadside. Winter was coming on fast.

"No, I avoided all mention of alpaca," she joked. "I told him I'd inherited a large property in Wyoming, which happened to contain natural gas, and I needed time to manage it properly. Oh, and I did mention that various consulting opportunities had also come my way." She winked.

"Good girl," Jayleen said, shoving her hands in her back pockets. "Make him sorry to lose you."

"I have to admit it felt good when I said I was quitting." Handing over the portfolio, Kelly added, "And it felt really good to finish these for you, Jayleen. The final numbers are even better than we talked about last week. You're in good financial shape."

Jayleen stared warily at the legal-sized black vinyl portfolio, as if it might bite. "Lord, you don't know how strange that sounds, Kelly. I've spent my entire life scrabbling around the edges. Working hard but never really getting anywhere. I still can't believe things are finally beginning to happen."

"Believe it, Jayleen," Kelly reassured with a grin. "The bank will take one look at these and happily lend you the money for Vickie's ranch. And if not, you let me know. I'll go talk to them myself," she promised as she turned toward the driveway and her parked car.

Jayleen followed after. Pointing to a real estate sign at the edge of her land which bordered the road, she said, "Jennifer was out yesterday with the listing contract. I sure hope it sells quick, because I'm not crazy about having strangers traipse through my house."

"I understand how you feel. I'm sure I won't like strangers prowling through Martha's house either, and I don't even live there." Kelly slipped into the car seat and started the engine.

"I kept my mouth shut about your wanting to sell that place," Jayleen added. "After all, you and I were just bouncing ideas when we talked. I figured you'd tell the others when you were ready."

"I appreciate that, Jayleen. I've been so busy this past week, I haven't had time to even think about Geri's place. Once I get those last accounts off my desk, I'll ask Jennifer to explain the foreclosure process. She'll walk me through it."

"Just like I'll walk you through those alpaca accounts when you're ready," Jayleen reminded her with a good-natured smile.

"Don't worry, I haven't forgotten," Kelly said with a goodbye wave as she drove down the gravel drive.

Turning onto the paved road, Kelly headed back into Fort Connor, her mind busily sorting through and rearranging items in her mental daytimer. The jangle of her cell phone interrupted.

"Kelly, here."

"Kelly, this is Sophia Emeraud. I wanted to call and update you on the design competition."

Kelly mentally smacked her forehead. She'd totally forgotten about the upcoming award in Allison's honor. Had two weeks passed since she'd spoken with Sophia? Wow. She had been busy.

"Thanks, Sophia, I appreciate your calling. I can't believe it's almost time for the award."

"That's right. I'll be flying in next Tuesday. Professor Jaeger has the award presentation set up for Wednesday night at the university," Sophia said.

"Did you get many submissions?"

"Boy, did I! Kelly, I had nearly forty submissions, can you believe that? Think how many we would have had if we'd had more time to promote the competition. Word must have spread around the area art groups like wildfire."

"That's amazing," Kelly exclaimed. "I'm so excited. This is exactly what Allison would have wanted."

Sophia's voice softened. "I agree. Somehow it's helped me handle Allison's death."

Kelly understood what Sophia meant. Somehow a living memory helped. She wheeled the car around a corner. "I'm curious. Did that Denver artist, Brian Silverstone, enter the competition? Or, did he refuse to submit with less experienced artists?"

Sophia chuckled. "Actually, he did submit a design. I have to admit, Kelly, his work was quite striking. Amazingly similar to Allison's."

I'll bet it was, Kelly thought, frowning in the car. *Wait until Sophia sees Allison's portfolio drawings. Then the "amazing similarity" will be made clear.*

"That's interesting," Kelly replied. "How was it similar to Allison's work? I'm curious."

"Ohhhhh, the drape of the sweater neck, for instance," Sophia answered. "Particularly the use of loose knitted yarns and ribbons threading through the design. And even some marvelous beadwork. Truly striking. He will most definitely place in the finals. I'm not sure yet which one will be the winner. There're two others who've submitted really original pieces. One is quite dramatic in its use of color."

"Beadwork?" Kelly repeated, the little buzzer in the back of her brain going off. "What kind of beadwork?"

"Well, the beads were woven in separately along with the yarn and ribbon. He created a very distinctive look, I must say."

"I'm sure he did," Kelly agreed, picturing the design exactly. After all, she'd watched Allison describe how she planned to use the beads in her next design for Sophia. Woven through the draping neckline along with the lacy yarn and ribbon.

That bastard. Brian Silverstone blatantly stole Allison's design, knowing that was the only way he could attract Sophia Emeraud's interest.

"What color were the beads?" she asked Sophia. "Were they colorful?"

"Actually, no. They appeared to be bone and were carved with interesting designs. Very likely Native American."

This time, Kelly's buzzer vibrated inside her. Those beads sounded exactly like the ones Allison found in Santa Fe. Son of a . . . sailor, Kelly fumed, invoking one of her dad's sanitized Navy curses.

There was only one way Brian Silverstone could have gotten those beads. He went to Allison's apartment that night after the banquet. Brian was the late-night visitor who crept up the stairs. And it must have been his dark car parked outside on the street that Allison's neighbor noticed.

"Why so interested in the beads, Kelly?"

"Oh, I'm simply curious. Allison showed Megan and me some beads she bought in Santa Fe that sound very similar to those."

Sophia's voice dropped. "Kelly, there's something you're not saying, I can tell. What is it?"

"Right now I don't know anything, Sophia. All I have is a whole lot of suspicions, that's all," Kelly admitted. "Perhaps I'm still too close to Allison's death. Maybe I'm seeing shadows. I don't know."

"Promise you'll tell me if you learn anything new, all right?" Sophia bargained.

"I promise, Sophia. Meanwhile, go back to being the brilliant designer and judge of talent that you are. Award the prizes and call me when you arrive in Fort Connor, okay?"

"Okay, Kelly. I'll talk to you next week. Bye." Sophia's phone clicked off.

Kelly pulled into the parking spot in front of her cottage and exited the car, her mind spinning at warp speed. Suspicions. That's all she had. Nothing more. Beadwork and designs. Scary phone messages. They all proved nothing. Even Ray Baker's hint that the police should look in Denver for Allison's killer meant nothing. After all, Baker was the chief suspect. He'd say anything to deflect police scrutiny, wouldn't he?

Carl came running to the fence to greet her. Kelly leaned over and rubbed his shiny black Rottweiler head. Carl slurped her wrist with six inches of pink tongue. Kelly was so lost in thought, she forgot that it tickled.

Police. She needed something the police would pay attention to. Even Burt would laugh at what she had right now. Think what Lieutenant Morrison would say. Recalling

Morrison's dour and dismissive demeanor, Kelly didn't want to be in that situation.

She dug into her pocket for her cell phone and dialed Burt's number. No harm in picking Burt's brain. Who knows? The police may have learned something new. Maybe she was completely wrong. Maybe . . .

"Hey, Kelly, you must have been reading my mind," Burt's friendly voice came on the line. "I was about to call you."

"Really?" Kelly perked up. "Did you find more evidence? Did Baker confess or something?"

Burt sighed. "No, I wish it were that simple. In fact, they're having to take another look at everything."

Kelly's pulse quickened. "What's happened?"

"Baker's prints finally arrived from Tennessee, and they don't match the print on the coffee cup," he said. Kelly could tell from the tone in his voice that Burt was definitely disappointed.

"Whoa," Kelly said softly. "Does that mean that Ray Baker is no longer suspect number one?"

"Well, not exactly," Burt hedged. "The print could always be from the clerk in the coffee shop, you know, the bar—whatever."

Kelly chuckled. "Barista."

"Yeah, whatever that is," he continued. "Anyway, Baker could always have worn gloves. I mean, he probably would have thought out the entire murder, including wearing gloves."

Pondering that for a moment, Kelly couldn't resist saying, "That's a stretch, Burt. Baker still doesn't impress me as someone who'd plan out a murder in all that detail. This crime required a really devious mind."

"Well, he's shown himself to be pretty devious," Burt countered.

Kelly let it drop. Once again, a crazy idea was forming

in the back of her mind. Talking with Burt had stimulated her thinking, that's for sure. And stimulated her into sticking her nose in police business again, despite Burt's admonitions not to.

"Have your partner and his colleagues ever seriously considered anyone else as Allison's killer?" she probed.

"Now, Kelly, you know I can't answer that," Burt scolded gently.

She knew it. She just needed a way to maneuver into her next question. "Tell me, Burt. Do you know if the department has camera surveillance around the various playgrounds around town? You know, to help decrease vandalism."

Burt paused. "What are you getting at, Kelly? I know you're going somewhere with this. You're not really interested in playground vandalism."

"You're right. I was wondering if you guys had ever checked to see if there were some photos taken of the cars parked outside Allison's apartment that night. If you remember, Allison's observant and reliable neighbor said there was an unfamiliar dark car parked across the street from the apartment building practically all night. It didn't leave until early in the morning, according to her."

"May I ask how come you know all these details about the neighbor's comments?"

Kelly took a deep breath. "Because I spoke with her, too."

"Kelly, what have I told you about getting into this?"

"I'm sorry, but I couldn't help myself, Burt," she replied cheerfully. "I was curious about the comment that she'd heard someone come in late at night. Anyway, she told me all about the unfamiliar dark car staying way late that night."

"We already knew about that, Kelly."

"Well, I was simply curious. After all, if those playgrounds have cameras, maybe they caught a glimpse of that dark car and the license plate. You know me, Burt. When I get an idea, I have to run with it."

"That's what scares me. What other ideas do you have bumping around in your mind?"

Burt, you don't want to know, Kelly thought. "Don't worry, Burt. I've got to get back on the computer. Finishing up the CPA stuff," she reassured as she headed into her cottage. Carl had already returned to chasing squirrels.

"You do that, Kelly," Burt advised. "And stay out of trouble, okay?"

"I'll do my best," she lied before she clicked off her phone. She'd better do her best, because Kelly knew she wouldn't get a second chance.

...

Eighteen

Kelly paused briefly before she knocked on Diane Linstrom's apartment door, hoping the website designer was true to her word and always at home. No answer, and no sound at all for a full minute. Kelly forced herself to count before knocking again.

Then the metallic click of door locks sounded, and the door partially opened. Diane Linstrom peered around the wood and stared out at Kelly, surprise and recognition in her pale eyes.

"Kelly, it's good to see you. Is everything okay?"

"Everything's fine, Diane," Kelly reassured. "I just came by to see how you were doing and to ask you a couple of questions."

At the word "questions," Diane's eyes popped even wider and she held the door open. "Oh, sure, of course. Come on in, Kelly."

Kelly sniffed the aroma of cinnamon and cloves perfuming the air and wondered if Diane were a secret baker or simply enjoyed scented candles. Observing Diane Linstrom's skinny frame as she led the way into her immaculate-and-barely-touched living room, Kelly was betting on the candles.

"Coffee?" Diane asked, pausing at the entry to the kitchen.

"I'd love to, Diane, but I've got a boatload of errands that I've got to run this afternoon, so I won't be able to stay." She made an offhand gesture. "Actually, two things brought me here. First, I wanted to tell you that the New York designer, Sophia Emeraud, will be here Wednesday night to present a design award in Allison's honor. There's a small ceremony at the university at seven if you'd like to attend."

Diane's pale face flushed with obvious pleasure at being included. "What a wonderful way to remember Allison," she said softly. "Thank you so much, Kelly, for inviting me. I'll think about it."

"I thought you might enjoy seeing Allison remembered in this way. Sophia's going to make the competition an annual event. And the winner gets to work in her studio for six months. Exactly like Allison was planning to do."

This time, tears glistened in Diane's eyes, then trickled down her face. "That's . . . that's wonderful. And so . . . so sad at the same time." She blinked then grabbed for a nearby napkin.

Kelly waited for Diane to wipe her eyes then added, "Give me a call if you decide to come, and I'll tell you which banquet room at the university. I won't know until tomorrow."

Diane nodded wetly, so Kelly continued.

"I also wanted to ask you a question, Diane. You've got this fantastic memory. Even my friend who's the retired cop is impressed with the level of detail you could recall about the night of Allison's death."

Diane's head came up. "Really? Well, I was simply trying to help. It's the least I could do for Allison."

Kelly nodded. "I guess that's why I'm still poking around myself. Anyway, I'm still curious about some things, and I remember your saying Allison had a late night visitor before midnight. Can you remember more precisely what time that was? Was it before eleven or after?"

"I remember exactly when it was," Diane spoke up. "It was 11:45 at night. I recall because I was working on my client billing statements, and I keep scrupulous track of the time. The sound of more footsteps upstairs and muffled voices caught my attention right away. I glanced at the clock out of habit."

Diane's response was even better than Kelly had hoped. "Excellent. Thank you, Diane," she said. "And do you remember if the unfamiliar dark car appeared on the street about that time?"

This time, Diane shrugged. "It may have. I didn't check out the window until after midnight, when I was getting a cup of coffee."

Wow, Diane's caffeine tolerance was even greater than her own, Kelly thought in semi-admiration. Even she didn't drink coffee after midnight.

"But it stayed parked through the night until the early morning, you said," Kelly prodded.

"Yes, that's right."

"Thanks, Diane, you've been a great help," Kelly said, giving Diane a big grin before she turned toward the door. "Let me know if you can come Wednesday, okay?"

"What are you looking for, Kelly?" Diane called after her. "New evidence or something?"

Kelly opened the door and paused. "I'm not sure exactly," she admitted. "That's why I'm sticking my nose where it doesn't belong. Wish me luck." And Kelly was out the door before Diane could ask another question.

• • •

Kelly idled her car engine at the stoplight, waiting for it to change. She glanced at the beige office envelope on the seat beside her and the color photo that lay atop the envelope. Thanks to the neighborhood copy shop, Kelly had done an excellent job of enlarging the glossy gallery brochure's publicity photo of Brian Silverstone. It looked exactly like him, she thought, scowling at the photo.

Kelly had been driving around town for over four hours. Coffee shops were everywhere. Boutique and corporate, warm and fuzzy, and cold as glass and chrome. By now, Kelly was so full of coffee she could float.

She'd started her search at the university events center, using that as the hub of a directional wheel. She figured Brian would have left the university and headed toward Allison's apartment, stopping for a specialty coffee on the way over. Driving one spoke of the wheel after another, Kelly carefully searched each street for anything resembling a coffee shop. She was amazed at how many she found.

Unfortunately, Kelly found no answers. She'd driven every one of the main streets that led to the western part of town where Allison lived. She was able to eliminate all national chain coffeehouses because of their distinctive cup designs. The cup that lay beside Allison had a yellow and green plaid design. Kelly remembered it exactly, and she had yet to see it after four hours.

Disheartened, Kelly had even asked shop employees if they'd switched cups lately. The puzzled replies always came back in the negative. In shop after shop, the green and yellow plaid cup was nowhere to be seen.

Kelly pulled in front of the university events center for the sixth time that afternoon. Checking the dashboard clock, she noted it was nearly dinnertime, and while she could always keep going with more coffee, Carl could not.

Picturing Carl staring balefully at his empty doggie dish, Kelly knew she would have to return home soon.

Staring out the windshield at the nearby tennis courts, Kelly drummed her fingers on the steering wheel. What had she missed? She'd covered every main street leading to the west side of town. Why hadn't she found the coffee shop? What had she overlooked? Obviously, she'd missed something. What was it?

She closed her eyes, trying to concentrate. Then the sound of a cyclist calling to a friend as he zipped by her open window caught her attention. The cyclist slowed and waved to his friend, who was leaning his bike against the corner street sign. Kelly glanced at the sign across the street out of habit. TYLER STREET, it read in neat black letters against white.

Tyler Street, she repeated to herself. That name is similar to Allison's street, Taylor Street. Taylor. Tyler. Something buzzed. Was it possible that Brian Silverstone confused the street names, she wondered? She surveyed the street which ran past the university events center and bordered various athletic fields. Impossible, she decided. This street deadended into a parking lot only a few blocks away. Even if Brian was confused, he'd quickly discover Tyler was not Allison's street. And then, and then . . .

Kelly sat up straight. *Damn!* she cursed herself. She was only familiar with the section of Taylor Street that ran west from the university past Allison's apartment and deadended into the foothills. What if there was another section? Kelly had been away from Fort Connor for years. The city was filled with little streets that wound around one another, especially in Old Town. She'd been driving around Fort Connor for six months now, and she still didn't know all the streets. Brian Silverstone didn't know Fort Connor at all. He could have easily gotten lost.

Grabbing the street map in her car-door pocket, Kelly

quickly scanned the index for Taylor. Sure enough. There
were two Taylor Streets. One that ran west, and another that
ran east through Old Town. Kelly tossed the map to the seat
beside her and peeled away from the curb, startling the
chatting cyclists. Winding through the university streets,
she finally reached the main north-south avenue that bi-
sected Fort Connor east and west. She followed it straight
to Old Town. According to the map, Taylor Street jutted off
one of the diagonal streets that bordered the older section.

Kelly's hunger interrupted her navigational plans, and
she decided to stop at the first coffee shop she saw on the
way over. She needed food and coffee. Now. Her cell phone
jangled, and she answered as she turned onto one of the
main streets that traversed Fort Connor's Old Town.

"Well, hello, Kelly Flynn," Eugene Tolliver's voice
sounded. "It's wonderful to hear from you. I just got your
message. Today has been a zoo. There must be a full moon
tonight. All the animals escaped their cages."

Kelly felt like one of them, driving around Fort Connor
on a wild coffeehouse chase. "Be nice to the animals, Eugene. They bite."

"Don't I know it. Now, what's on your mind, Kelly? I
can practically hear the wheels turning all the way to Denver."

"Oh, I simply had a question. I was wondering if you
knew what kind of car Brian Silverstone drives. And what
color?"

"Oooooo, sleuthing again, are we?"

Kelly chuckled. "I'm afraid so. Do you remember seeing his car anytime?"

"I most certainly do. How could I miss it? Brian would
park his black Lexus right in front of our gallery whenever
he'd drop in for a 'chat,' as he called it. I always called it
spying. Every gallery owner has had their display ideas ap-
propriated by Brian at one time or another." Eugene heaved

a dramatic sigh. "I suppose imitation is the sincerest form of flattery, so I never got too upset."

Kelly's pulse speeded up. "Black, huh?"

"Black as an assassin's heart."

"Thanks, Eugene. You've been a real help." Kelly spied a small coffee shop wedged between two boutiques and slowed, searching for parking.

"Not so fast," he countered. "I want details."

"I don't have any details yet. But I'm hoping I'll know more by Wednesday." She spied a space between cars and angled her way in. "The designer, Sophia Emeraud, is giving an award Wednesday night at the university for a design competition. It's in Allison's honor."

"Ah, that must be the same competition that Kimberly entered. She's one of the finalists, I understand."

"Really? How wonderful," Kelly exclaimed, shutting off the engine. "She's so talented. Now I have someone to cheer for. Besides, I don't want Brian to win."

"Brian entered?" Eugene's surprise was evident. "With all those youngsters? My, my, he must be getting desperate."

Kelly couldn't agree more. "You're right, Eugene. In fact, he's so desperate he used one of Allison's designs. I'm sure of it. I saw her portfolio drawing in his studio when he showed me around the gallery."

"*No*"

"Oh, yes. I distinctly remember Allison showing us a drawing like that when we were all in Santa Fe." Kelly flicked her door lock and crossed the street, heading toward the coffee shop. "And I intend to show Sophia Emeraud those drawings. Let her decide if Brian's stealing Allison's designs or not."

Eugene chuckled. Kelly could almost see the wicked smile. "Brian will be furious. He's very confrontational, you know."

"That'll make it even better," Kelly said, feeling a competitive surge. "Because I intend to confront him, and I don't back down."

This time, Eugene laughed loudly. "Ah, what I wouldn't give to see that. Perhaps I'll tag along with Kimberly after all. She'd asked me to only yesterday."

"Good. Being embarrassed in front of his colleagues will put even more pressure on him," Kelly said, pausing outside the coffee shop. She spied colorful round tables and chairs scattered inside the shop along with huge bags of coffee beans and assorted brewing paraphernalia.

"Exactly what are you hoping to accomplish with all this pressure, may I ask?"

Kelly exhaled a deep breath and rubbed her neck, trying to relax the tension that was building between her shoulder blades. "I want him to incriminate himself. Confessing would be better, but he's too wily to do that. I'm hoping to get in his face and make him so mad, he'll trip and let something slip."

Eugene was silent for a few seconds. "You've got brass, Kelly. I'll give you that."

"I'm afraid that's all I've got, Eugene. But I'll push it for all it's worth."

"That's not all, Kelly. You're a hell of a lot smarter than Brian. You've got brains *and* brass. Go get him."

Kelly smiled as she clicked off her phone and strode into the cozy coffee shop. Brains and brass. She'd take it.

Sniffing the addictive aromas, Kelly wound past the crowded tables and scanned the chalk board menu that hung against the wall. Her stomach growled when she read "bagel and herbed cream cheese," so she ordered it and an extra large coffee to go. Kelly checked her watch. Any plans for office work were off the table for now. Who knew how long this search would take?

"Here you go, ma'am," the young man behind the

counter spoke behind her. "One bagel with herb cheese and one extra large coffee black."

Kelly reached for her order as she handed over her debit card, then froze. She stared at the takeout cup in the clerk's hand. A yellow and green plaid design covered the cup. After nearly five hours of searching, she'd finally found the cup that matched the one that carried the lethal caramel coffee to Allison.

"Is there something wrong, ma'am?" the young man asked, peering curiously at Kelly.

Realizing she was standing there with her hand outstretched, staring at the cup, Kelly grabbed the bagel and coffee. "Uh, no, no. I'm fine. It's fine." She signed the receipt without even looking, her brain spinning a mile a minute.

Kelly headed for a nearby table and devoured the bagel with the help of surprisingly rich coffee. Hunger made her antsy, and she didn't want to spook the coffee shop clerk any more than she already had. She needed food before she attempted questions. Glancing at the menu board again, Kelly scanned the selections. One in particular jumped out at her: Caramel Coffee Supreme. That had to be it, she decided, her pulse racing despite the bagel.

Taking a deep breath to relax, Kelly returned to the counter and brought her brightest client smile. "Hey, that was delicious. I was starving. Do you think I could have one of those special caramel coffees? The supreme?"

"Sure thing," the young man said with a nod and went to the espresso machine.

Kelly watched him prepare the sugary concoction with fascination. Clearly not a drink for diabetics "How late are you guys open at night?" she asked, digging in her purse for cash.

"Eleven, usually."

"Who works the late shift? Do you guys take turns?"

The clerk gave Kelly a quizzical look before he handed over the Caramel Coffee Supreme. "It depends on our class schedules. I work days till six."

"I've got a friend who used to work in a coffeehouse in Seattle. She's looking for a job here and was wondering what kind of schedule you guys have at night. Is there a lot of cleanup afterwards? That can stretch till midnight, she says." Kelly made herself take a sip. Whoa. So much sugar, her teeth hurt.

He shrugged noncommittally. "Yeah, I suppose."

Kelly dropped a ten dollar bill on the counter. "Keep the change," she said with a big smile. "Anybody here that works nights? Maybe I could ask them."

He pointed toward the girl in the corner who was bussing tables. "Wendy works nights. Ask her."

"Thanks. You've been a big help," Kelly said as she headed for the young blonde woman in the corner. Wendy was loading coffee mugs and assorted dishes into a big plastic tub. Kelly strolled up and smiled. "Hi, there. The guy at the counter said you work nights, right?"

"Yeah," Wendy said, glancing at Kelly as she wiped a table. "What's the matter? Did you lose something? We've got a lost and found I could check."

"No, no, I promised a friend that I'd ask about your night shifts. She's looking for a job and used to work coffee shops in Seattle," Kelly said. "She wanted to know what time you finished up at night. Is it real late, like midnight?"

"Naw, not that late," Wendy replied. "I'm usually out of here by 11:15 or so."

Kelly made herself take another sip of sugar in an attempt to appear relaxed. In actuality, her pulse was racing. Of course, it could be the sugar. "Do you usually work on Tuesday nights?" she probed.

"Yeah, why?" Wendy peered at her, with the same curious look the clerk had.

Kelly decided it was time to stop circling and go straight for the information she needed. She fixed Wendy with a somber look and dropped her voice. "Listen, would you mind looking at a photo and telling me if you recognize the person? I think he came in here on a Tuesday night about a month ago."

Wendy's eyes widened, clearly curious at the request. "Sure, I guess so."

"Thanks, Wendy, I really appreciate it. The photo's in my car. It'll only take a minute," Kelly said and hurried out of the shop. Retrieving the photo from her car, she raced across the street to find Wendy standing outside the door, lighting a cigarette.

"What's this all about, anyway?" she asked between puffs.

"I'm looking for somebody," Kelly replied as she handed Wendy the photo of Brian Silverstone. "I'm curious if he came into your shop late one night. It would be a Tuesday night. First week of October."

Wendy studied the photo as Kelly held her breath. She studied Wendy's face, hoping for a glimpse of recognition. Kelly saw more than a glimpse. Wendy's eyes lit up, and she smiled broadly.

"Yeah. Oh, yeah. I remember him. The big spender," she said, nodding. "He came in one night just as I was turning off the lights. Begged me for one of our special coffees. The caramel one. He went on and on about how his girlfriend had to have it." Her freckled face spread with a smile. "Offered me fifty bucks for a five-buck coffee. You bet I stayed open."

Kelly's heart skipped a beat this time, and it wasn't the sugar. "So, you recognize him, huh?" she repeated.

Wendy nodded, then drew on her cigarette. "Why are you looking for him?"

Kelly gritted her teeth. If she thought the sugary coffee

tasted bad, it was nothing compared to what she was about to say. "He's my boyfriend, and he told me he was in Denver with his mom that night. Not up here getting caramel coffee for another girl." She deliberately screwed up her face as she took the photo from Wendy.

"Uh, oh."

"Uh, oh is right," Kelly replied in her sternest voice as she started across the street. "Let's just say the big spender is in big trouble. Thanks, Wendy," she said with a wave as she headed for her car.

Nineteen

Burt's light blue sedan turned into the driveway between the knitting shop and Kelly's cottage. Kelly was already seated at one of the cafe's outdoor tables, waiting. Despite the sunshine, Kelly found the morning chillier than usual, forcing her to dig through her closet for—of all things—a sweater. Now, she really felt guilty for not finishing the sweater in the bottom of her knitting bag.

Kelly held that same knitting bag in her lap, waiting for Burt to approach. "Thanks for coming, Burt," she greeted.

"You couldn't keep me away, Kelly," he said as he settled into a wrought iron chair across from her. "I could tell you've been up to something from the sound of your voice." He smiled genially. "I don't know why I even bother to warn you."

"Well, this time I think you'll be glad I didn't pay attention," Kelly replied. "I've found something, Burt. Something important that will help with Allison's case."

"I figured. What is it?"

Kelly withdrew the beige office envelope from her knitting bag. Opening the flap, she gingerly pulled the glossy gallery brochure halfway out of the envelope. Pausing deliberately, she looked Burt straight in the eye. "This brochure has fingerprints on it. Some are mine, but there are other prints as well. And I'm betting those prints will match the ones found on the coffee cup at Allison's apartment."

Burt stared at Kelly, then at the brochure, then back to her. His eyes narrowed. "Where did you get this, Kelly?"

"From Brian Silverstone. He gave it to me when I visited his gallery in Denver. I watched him take the brochure from a file cabinet, so hopefully there won't be too many other prints there, aside from Brian's and mine." She grinned. "I'll be glad to come to the department and be fingerprinted, if you'd like."

"I don't think that will be necessary," Burt said dryly.

Kelly slid the brochure back into the envelope and handed it over. "And just so you won't think I'm obsessing on Brian Silverstone—"

"Now why would I think that?" Burt retorted, eyebrow raised.

Kelly ignored his comment and continued. "I thought I'd fill you in on some new information reported to me by other people, mind you. Not the figment of my imagination."

Burt tapped the top of the envelope, eyeing her expectantly.

"Sophia Emeraud, the New York designer, told me a few weeks ago that Silverstone called her and volunteered to create a design in Allison's honor. Sophia took the idea and expanded it to a regional competition for new artists. The award is tomorrow night at the university, and Brian Silverstone entered. He's even using one of Allison's designs. I saw one of her portfolio drawings in his studio when he was showing me around. I remember Allison showing us that same drawing in Santa Fe."

Burt's bushy gray eyebrows conferred with one another, but he said nothing.

Kelly leaned over the table. "I recall your saying that police found fingerprints on the portfolio drawings in Allison's apartment. They matched the print on the coffee cup, right?"

"Correct."

"I think Brian Silverstone took that drawing from Allison's apartment the night he killed her. He also stole the antique beads from Allison's desk. Sophia says Brian's submitted a design 'just like Allison's' and it even has beads."

"Kelly, all of that could be easily explained away," Burt countered. "Allison may have shown him the drawing earlier, getting his prints on it at that time. And, beads . . ." He made a dismissive gesture. "You can't prove they're the same. I know you're trying hard, but all of that is circumstantial. Even if you throw in the phone message. It proves nothing."

Kelly figured Burt would say that. "But there's more. Someone saw Brian Silverstone at the awards banquet that night, so he was here in Fort Connor."

"So?"

"And I've found the coffee shop with the exact same cup design as the one found beside Allison. The one with the lethal coffee. I talked with the girl who worked late that Tuesday night and showed her a copy of the brochure photo. She remembers Brian. He paid her fifty bucks to stay open so he could get a Caramel Coffee Supreme for his girlfriend." Kelly paused, waiting for Burt's reaction.

It came quickly. Burt's eyes widened as he stared at her. "What's this girl's name, and when did you speak with her?"

"Yesterday about six P.M. Her name's Wendy, and she works at the Coffee Retreat on Emerson in Old Town. She's short, blonde, looks to be a college student. Sorry I didn't get her last name. I didn't want to spook her."

"I can't wait to hear what excuse you gave her for asking questions."

"I told her Brian was my boyfriend, and I suspected him of cheating on me." She grimaced.

He chuckled as he pushed away from the table. "Okay, Kelly. You've definitely got my juices running with this. Let me take it to Dan and see what he thinks."

"That's all I'm after, Burt," Kelly replied as she rose to leave. "Let me know what you find, okay?"

"Will do," he said, giving her a wave as he hurried to his car.

Kelly followed the leaf-strewn flagstone path around the shop to the front door. She definitely deserved a knitting break. Yesterday was consumed with anxious searches through coffee shops. Kelly figured she was due for some low-key relaxation. Besides, she needed some instruction before starting that frothy shawl.

Mimi was in the foyer, straightening yarn bins, and turned at the sound of the tinkling doorbell. "Kelly, how great to see you here so early," she exclaimed, smiling broadly. "I've missed chatting with you. It feels like ages since we've had a good talk."

"I'm sorry, Mimi. My workload was unreal for a couple of months," Kelly apologized. "But that should improve, now that I'm switching careers, so to speak."

Mimi beamed, clearly pleased. "I can't tell you how happy I am that you're staying, Kelly. But you already knew that."

"You're one of the big reasons, Mimi," Kelly replied. "You and all the others. I couldn't leave all my friends here. So, you're stuck with me." She winked.

"We'll stay stuck, too," Mimi promised. "Say, have you

started that shawl yet? You bought the wool over two weeks ago."

"You're reading my mind, Mimi," Kelly said, heading toward the library table where she dropped the knitting bag and sat down. "I could really use your help getting started. I glanced at the pattern briefly, but I can't remember much. Do I use a circular needle for the shawl?"

"Yes, you do. Why don't I snag one from up front? Or, we could use the one from your circular sweater if you've finished."

Kelly hung her head in mock shame. "No, it's still sitting in the bottom of my bag, pouting," she confessed. "I was seduced away by the frothy yarn."

"Be right back," Mimi said with an indulgent smile.

Settling into the chair, Kelly lifted her coffee mug and took a long drink, purposely not allowing herself to conjure images of police checking fingerprints or Brian Silverstone emptying sleeping pill capsules into a Caramel Coffee Supreme.

Instead, she reached into her bag to withdraw the scrumptiously soft frothy yarn that had led her astray. It wasn't there. Funny, Kelly thought, she could have sworn she'd placed it on top of the pouting circular sweater. She felt around the silk and cotton half-finished sweater, her fingers remembering its softness. Where was that other yarn, she wondered?

Setting her coffee aside, Kelly opened the bag wide and dug beneath the sweater. There, at the bottom of her knitting bag, was the frothy yarn. Kelly couldn't figure out how it wound up shoved into a bottom corner. Perhaps the envelope with brochure shifted the knitting bag's contents. Or . . . maybe the silk and cotton sweater staged a preemptive strike and "yarn-wrestled" the froth to the bottom of the bag. Kelly decided she had enough weird images running through her mind. If yarns were conducting guerrilla warfare in her knitting bag at night, she didn't want to know about it.

"Here, we go," Mimi said, scurrying back to the table and settling beside Kelly. She held up two needle tips attached by long plastic twine. "This pattern uses size fifteen needles, so it'll go faster."

"That's good to hear. I'm sure I would be finished with the circular sweater by now if the needles were bigger. Now, how many do I cast on with this?"

"Let's see, I think the pattern says to cast on three or four," Mimi said, shaking the frothy yarn loose from its wrapper. "After that, you'll increase each row one stitch at a time."

Kelly frowned. Because of some yarns' capricious tendencies to add more stitches to a row than required, Kelly had had ample practice knitting decreases, but not increases. "How do I do that?"

"There are several ways to do an increase, but this pattern also calls for a yarn-over near the end of every row, so we'll use that method. That's what produces the lacy pattern you see in the shawl." She pointed to the wall and the grayish-blue frothy shawl draped there.

"Whoa, hold on a minute." Kelly held up her hand in concern. "I've heard about yarn-overs, but I haven't a clue how to do one."

Mimi grinned. "Not intentionally, you don't. But you've been doing them ever since you started knitting."

"Huh?"

"Whenever you've seen a hole in your knitting that wasn't supposed to be there, that was a yarn over."

"Oh, so it's a mistake."

"Well, when we first start out, it is," Mimi agreed. "But there are many patterns that call for yarn-overs deliberately, in order to create an open, lacy effect, like that shawl."

Kelly stared at the lacy froth draped against the wall.

"Hmmmmmm, patterns that call for mistakes. I can do that. In fact, I oughtta be real good at that."

Mimi laughed. "Well, it's not a mistake if we're doing it on purpose. Here, let me show you."

"Good. I've always wondered how I managed to get all those holes in my pieces."

"The yarn simply got wrapped around the needle and you didn't notice it. Now, watch, here's how you intentionally create a yarn-over."

Mimi shifted so Kelly could watch over her shoulder, as if the needles were in her own hands. "Now, I'm going to start the knit stitch, but watch. I'm about to do something different." Mimi brought the yarn from behind the right needle in its regular starting position and moved it in front of the needle. She then proceeded with the knit stitch as usual, wrapping the yarn around the needle, and slipping the finished stitch from the left needle to the right needle. "See? There's now an extra stitch on the right needle."

"Whoa," Kelly remarked. "So that's how it happens."

"Now, I'll move the yarn to the back as usual and knit two stitches to finish the row." Her nimble fingers quickly finished the stitches. "Now, we turn it, like we normally do, and begin the next row. Once you get to the last two stitches, stop. Do a yarn-over, then knit the last two stitches normally. That way, you'll not only increase each row by one, but you'll also obtain the lacy effect you want."

"Do the next row, so I can watch again."

Mimi obediently worked the next row, stopping before the last two stitches. Kelly watched her wrap the yarn to the front, then knit a stitch, then return the yarn to the back and knit two regular stitches.

"Boy, I hope I can remember that."

Mimi repeated the process for another row as Kelly studiously observed. "Now, you try," she said, handing Kelly the needles and yarn.

"Okay, I might as well start botching it while you're still here."

"You'll be fine," Mimi promised with a smile.

Kelly slowly began to imitate Mimi's motions, finishing one, two, then three rows. "Wow, I did it," she said, amazed.

"Of course, you did, Kelly. Stop doubting yourself," Mimi scolded playfully.

Rosa appeared in the doorway, beckoning. "Mimi, that distributor is on the line."

"I'll check on you in a minute," Mimi said, giving Kelly a reassuring pat before she left.

Kelly was about to continue her beginning efforts, when she had her own interruption. The cell phone jangled insistently until she dug into her bag and answered.

"Kelly? Sophia, here. My plane's landed, and I'm renting a car. Can you give me directions into Fort Connor?"

"Of course, Sophia," Kelly said, an idea forming as she glanced around the riot of colorful yarns and fibers surrounding her. "I'll direct you straight to your hotel, then I'll meet you there. I want to show you someplace special."

"Fantastic," Sophia said, her voice sounding tired. "Can we have lunch first? I'm living on airline food and candy bars. And coffee."

"Absolutely, Sophia. In fact, this place has a cafe attached. So you can feast on fibers and food in the same setting."

"Oooooo, you've got me curious, Kelly. I can't wait. Now, let me grab a pen and paper for those directions."

Kelly paused until Sophia was ready, then rattled off the easiest, most direct way to reach Fort Connor and the hotel. Sophia hung up, after promising to call Kelly when she arrived.

Perfect, Kelly thought to herself. Sophia and she could have lunch at Pete's Porch beneath a canopy of cottonwoods, then indulge themselves in a colorful Lambspun dessert.

Sophia Emeraud caressed the fluffy antique gold yarn that lay atop a chest spilling over with equally vibrant colors. "This is unbelievably soft," she remarked, her fingers sliding through the fibers. "Do you have Rapunzel spinning for you at night?"

Kelly and Mimi both laughed, but Kelly noticed Mimi's cheeks color with pleasure as she replied. "We've actually got several talented Rapunzels spinning for us."

"And Mimi is a wonderful spinner, too," Kelly spoke up. "She teaches everyone, then goes on to create all those marvelous combinations of yarns you see." She reached into a basket and held up a skein that contained at least three different yarns in colorful combinations.

Sophia examined the yarns intently for a moment. "Mimi, I will definitely be ordering some of these yarns you've created. New designs are popping up in my head already, and I'm tired. Can you imagine what will happen when I'm rested?" She looked up at Mimi and smiled.

Mimi flushed, clearly delighted at Sophia's comments. "That would be wonderful. We would love to work with you, Sophia."

The sound of the doorbell tinkling in the foyer caught Kelly's attention, and she peered around the corner of the main yarn room. Burt gestured in the open doorway, beckoning for her to join him outside.

"Sophia, Mimi, will you excuse me for a moment?" Kelly asked before she left to follow Burt. She found him standing on the patio beside the flowerbeds, which were all mulched brown for winter. Kelly could read the expression on his face. He had news. "What's up?" she asked, keeping her voice down.

"The prints matched," he said in a deep voice. "Now, tell me, when is this award ceremony at the university?"

Kelly felt the exultation run right up her spine. "Tomorrow at seven o'clock," she said, keeping all trace of gloating from her tone.

"And you're sure Silverstone will be there?"

"Absolutely." Kelly nodded toward the shop. "Sophia told me he's one of the finalists for the top award. Don't worry, he'll be there. Expecting to win, probably."

Burt folded his arms and observed her with a careful smile. "I'm sure I'm going to regret asking this, but do you have some plan in that fertile brain of yours? Given your feelings about this guy, it's a safe bet you weren't going to applaud politely while he receives his award."

Kelly grinned. Burt knew her too well. "Well, I'll applaud, but I also plan to talk with him afterwards."

"Talk with him?" An eyebrow shot upwards.

"You know, in my usual in-your-face, confrontational, accusatory style."

"Figured as much. What do you expect to accomplish?"

"Shake him up, get him so mad at my accusations that he lets something slip. He's too clever to actually confess," she admitted. "But he's also vain and arrogant and probably thinks he's too smart to ever be caught. After all, he's completely avoided suspicion so far. And his arrogance is his weakness. That and his vanity. I plan to work on that, too." She grinned slyly.

"Okay, Kelly, you've earned some points with my partner, Dan, on this, so we'll let you set this up. But this time you won't be working without a net. I'll be there and so will Dan. We'll be close at hand."

"Not too close, Burt, or we'll spook him." She gave him a mocking frown. "Besides, I work best alone."

Burt returned a real frown. "Not this time, Kelly. If Silverstone lets something slip, Dan will want to take him to the department for questioning."

"Okay, make sure you and Dan mingle with the other art lovers then. Look interested." She winked.

"We'll pretend to be proud parents. That's a role we've each got down pat," he said with a twinkle in his eye.

Twenty

Kelly glanced about the banquet room as she and Megan strolled along the edges of the crowd that had gathered for the award presentation.

"This is a wonderful turnout," Megan said, looking at the proud parents, excited design students, and professors that filled the room.

Kelly observed the faces as she sipped the nondescript Chardonnay. She was surprised how much her palate had evolved over the last few months since she and Steve had been sampling different wines at their favorite cafe.

"It's a fitting tribute to Allison," she said, choosing a morsel of cheese from the appetizer table.

"Which one is Kimberly Gorman?" Megan asked. "Now that I've seen her work, I understand why you were so excited about her talent."

Kelly surveyed the ten design entries at the front of the room. Kimberly's dramatic entry definitely stood out from the others that were displayed on headless, white mannequins. Fire-engine red silk and wool, woven with jagged streaks of black fibers, Kimberly's bold poncho dominated the other designs in Kelly's opinion, and she wondered how the daring young artist would fair in the competition. Ten finalists and only five awards. Scanning the room, Kelly spied Kimberly standing with a group of professors and Eugene Tolliver. Kimberly's flushed cheeks spoke of her excitement.

"Kimberly is the tall brunette in royal blue standing near the podium. The really sharp dresser is Eugene Tolliver, and the others must be professors or parents."

Megan smiled. "So, that's Eugene. You're knitting him a scarf, right?"

"Well, I've threatened to," Kelly teased, then gestured again. "Look, there's Brian Silverstone, trying to weasel into the conversation."

"Smarmy bastard," Megan decreed.

"Arrogant bastard is more accurate. Stealing Allison's design after he kills her," Kelly muttered, watching Brian turn on the charm for the professors.

Megan's scowl darkened. "Boy, I hope he finishes last."

Remembering Sophia's obvious surprise when Kelly and Megan showed her Allison's portfolio drawings, Kelly added, "I've got a feeling that Sophia reevaluated the list of finalists after she saw Allison's last drawings. That woven top Brian submitted is the exact copy of Allison's design down to the beads."

Megan gestured toward the podium and the stylishly dressed woman stepping to the front of the room. "I think the suspense is almost over."

Kelly felt her pulse speed up, partly catching the excitement of the occasion and also in anticipation of her confrontation with Brian Silverstone. She scanned the crowd again and spotted Burt, looking every bit the proud parent, hovering on the edge of Brian Silverstone's conversation.

Burt's former partner, Dan Jacobsen, was strolling nearby, ostensibly watching the proceedings.

Listening to Professor Jaeger's greetings and Sophia's remarks with half an ear, Kelly searched the room for the student reporter/photographer she'd invited to the occasion. Bribed him, more accurately. She spotted the young man, attired in latex shorts and soccer shirt, angling through the crowd, his digital camera catching the assembled eager artists in unguarded moments. Excellent, Kelly thought with a smile, watching the photographer insert himself right into a conversation as he grabbed a shot.

Ripples of applause floated around the room as Professor Jaeger and Sophia described the design competition guidelines and the grand prize awaiting the first place winner. Kelly could almost see the excitement arc over the heads of the finalists who stood waiting, some patiently, others not. All fidgeting stopped, however, when Sophia explained her reason for offering the award. In a somber voice, Sophia related her delight at discovering an exciting new talent and the shock of losing her so suddenly. The Allison Dubois Award for Wearable Art was in memory of a "talented designer, an innovative artist, and a wonderful young woman," Sophia finished and held up the bronzed plaque.

This time the applause that started as a ripple grew into a wave, which flowed around the room. Kelly blinked away the beginnings of tears, brought on by Sophia's words. Focusing her attention on the crowd again, Kelly spotted Brian Silverstone conveniently positioned near the podium. Burt and Dan had also moved closer to the front as well.

Professor Jaeger read the list of ten finalists, and Kelly watched them all line up at the front of the room. Six women and four men stood expectantly as Sophia pointed out each of their displayed designs and the reasons they were chosen as finalists. Kelly observed Brian Silverstone carefully, the studied posture and tilt of his head. Clearly, Brian was awaiting coronation as the superior talent, she thought with a wry smile, and wondered how he would respond if he didn't win.

Kelly had her answer quickly. Sophia began to read the names of the five winners, starting with fifth place. Brian Silverstone. Kelly had to bite the inside of her cheek to keep from laughing at Brian's expression. Utter amazement. Gone was the studied poise and posture. Brian's face went from smug to shocked in an instant. In fact, he seemed dazed when Sophia shook his hand, offering him the small plaque. Polite applause rippled around the room as the crowd stirred restlessly, awaiting the next winner.

Brian Silverstone stood rigid, face flushed now with what Kelly could only surmise was unbelievable humiliation. To be held up for comparison with untried and unseasoned artists, only to lose. For someone of Brian's arrogance, the shame of having to stand there while lesser talents reaped the rewards must be unbearable.

Looking over the crowd for the student journalist, Kelly found him rifling the appetizer table. "See the guy who took fifth?" she said, sidling up to him, then pointing at Brian. "That looks to me like the Agony of Defeat. What do you think?"

The student popped another cheddar morsel into his mouth, then zeroed in on Brian. He gave Kelly a knowing smile before he merged into the crowd again. Meanwhile, Kelly noticed that Sophia had finally reached the top finalists. Maneuvering her way through the excited guests, she paused as Sophia read the first-place winner's name.

"Kimberly Gorman," Sophia said with a big smile.

Kelly burst out in joyous applause while she watched Kimberly's expression change. If Brian's shock had been humiliation, then Kimberly's face shone with the radiance of validation. At last, Kelly thought. Somehow, she knew

Allison was pleased, and Kelly clapped even louder as a glowing Kimberly accepted the award. Eugene Tolliver stood at the front of the crowd, looking even more parental and proud than Burt and his partner.

Spotting Brian Silverstone start to back away from the assembled contestants, Kelly watched in delight as the photographer suddenly blocked Brian's stealthy escape, relentlessly shooting pictures. Brian scowled angrily at the student, as Kelly drew closer.

"That's quite enough," he growled as he pushed past the young man.

Kelly recognized her chance and jumped at it, intercepting Brian before he could pick up his stride. "Mr. Silverstone," she announced as she planted herself directly in his path to the door. "Congratulations on winning fifth place."

Brian scowled at Kelly for an instant before his expression changed. Clearly, he remembered her from her earlier performance as a visiting reporter. "Miss Flynn, what brings you here?" he asked in a tight voice.

"I couldn't miss the awards," Kelly explained, gesturing at the celebrating designers and friends. "Once I came up here to Fort Connor, that story about the young designer who died just wouldn't let me go. My editor gave me permission to cover it." She forced herself to smile into Brian's angry eyes.

"I see. Well, I wish you the best of luck," he said, clearly wishing nothing of the sort, and started to walk away.

Kelly quickly stepped in front of him again. "If you don't mind, Mr. Silverstone, I'd like to ask you some questions. After all, you and the young artist, Allison Dubois, were well acquainted. In fact, I was told you two lived together for a couple of years. I was hoping you'd be able to answer some of the questions that have been bothering me."

Brian peered at Kelly. "Whom have you been talking to, if I may ask?"

"Various Denver artists," Kelly replied with a smile and a shrug, deliberately continuing her affable pose for the time being. "Reporters have to protect their sources, you know."

Glancing over his shoulder in the direction of Eugene Tolliver, who was chatting with some professors, Brian sneered. "Common gossips, that's what they are."

"I was wondering if Allison abused sleeping pills when she lived with you?" Kelly probed. "Did she ever overdose while you two were together?"

"No, of course not!" Brian snapped.

"Don't you think it strange that she overdosed on the night before she was to leave for her dream career?"

"Allison always was an emotional girl. Unstable, actually," he replied, eying Kelly.

"You know, I've been studying Allison's portfolio drawings, and I can't help noticing the uncanny similarity between her designs and your entry." Kelly let her smile fade. "In fact, you even used beads in the same pattern she sketched."

"I believe I told you that Allison drew heavily on my ideas when she developed her designs," he retorted.

Kelly nodded. "Yes, you did. But a friend of Allison's remembers her purchasing those exact beads in Santa Fe last month." She pointed toward Brian's entry. "Allison told her she was planning to use them on her first design for Sophia Emeraud. That same friend was at Allison's apartment before she died and saw the beads on the desk. Yet, they had disappeared when she walked in and found Allison the next morning."

"It sounds as if this friend was emotionally distraught at finding Allison had killed herself," Brian remarked in a cold voice.

Ignoring his comment, Kelly stepped over the line. "Did you take them when you were in her apartment?" she probed. "Allison's downstairs neighbor told police that Allison had a late night visitor. She also noticed an unfamiliar dark car parked outside the building. It was under the streetlight, so she was able to get a good look at the car. I was told you have a black Lexus, right?"

Brian's dark eyes turned jet, and Kelly detected a slight twitch at the corner of his mouth. She fervently hoped Burt and Dan were close enough to observe, and was about to press Brian further when the student photographer suddenly appeared beside them.

"Congrats again," he chirped as he clicked away at Brian.

"That's enough!" Brian snarled as the student retreated into the crowd.

Now that the photographer had pushed Brian's button, Kelly leaned on it. "I heard that phone message you left for Allison. Pretty ugly, Brian. You were really mad at her, weren't you? Allison's friend let me listen to it before she gave the phone to the police. You realize the police have reopened the investigation into Allison's death, don't you?"

Brian's mouth twitched again, but he made no reply.

"That's why you came to her apartment that night, wasn't it?" Kelly's voice dropped lower. "You came for revenge, didn't you? Your career was over and hers was just beginning. You couldn't stand that, could you, Brian? So you poisoned her, figuring it would look like suicide."

Conflicting emotions flashed across his face, before he curled his lips in a practiced sneer. He fixed Kelly with a hateful gaze. "I don't know what kind of rumor-mongering rag you're writing for, but I do not intend to stand here and be slandered in public." He started to push past Kelly, but she braced herself, refusing to yield.

"We know you were there," she accused. "The girl at the coffee shop identified your photo, Brian. Remember the photo in the brochure? She said you came in at eleven o'clock that night and paid her fifty dollars for a five-buck Caramel Coffee Supreme. That's the same coffee that was in Allison's cup. What'd you do? Go to the car and dump the sleeping pills? Do you think some of the pills dropped in your car? What do you think the police would find?"

It was only an instant, but Kelly caught it. A flicker of fear darted through those black eyes. Then, it was gone.

"Either you're insane, or you've been paid by someone to slander me. You'll hear from my lawyer shortly," he snapped, the mask of arrogance firmly in place once more.

Kelly leaned in closer. "You'll need that lawyer, Brian. Your fingerprints were found on the cup of poisoned coffee."

The mask slipped, as all color drained from Brian's face. As conniving and clever as Brian had proved to be, arrogance had indeed been his downfall. Obviously, he'd been so convinced Allison's death would be ruled a suicide that he had failed to worry about something as basic as fingerprints.

Brian stared at Kelly for a long moment, then stammered, "I . . . I . . . I . . ."

Suddenly the photographer was back, inserting himself between them, clicking away, right in Brian's face.

Fury returned with a vengeance, and Brian swung the award plaque at the student. "Damn you! Get away from me!"

Kelly's quick reflexes kept her out of Brian's reach. But as soon as she stepped back, Dan Jacobsen stepped forward, placing himself in front of Brian Silverstone.

Holding up his identification, Dan spoke in a quiet voice. "Take it easy, Mr. Silverstone. There's no need to make a scene and ruin this nice ceremony. I'm with the police department here in Fort Connor. Why don't we go over to our office so you can answer a few questions, okay?"

Brian's mask dropped to the floor this time as Kelly

watched panic claim his face. She swore she could feel the fear radiating from him.

"Wh—wh—what? Wh—why?" he stammered, his gaze darting from Dan's face to Burt, who appeared behind his old partner.

"It'll only take a few moments, Mr. Silverstone," Dan explained as he placed his hand on Brian's elbow. "Remember that job as a security guard you worked in college? Well, your fingerprints were still on file, and they matched prints found at the scene of Allison Dubois's death."

Brian's face went chalk white, and he stared disbelieving at the police detective. His mouth moved, but only a plaintive whisper came out. "I can explain—I can explain—"

"I'm sure you can, Mr. Silverstone. Let's go to our office," Dan reassured him in a gentle tone, as he guided Brian toward the doorway, Burt following behind.

Kelly watched them all the way out the door, a huge feeling of relief settling over her. Whether Brian Silverstone chose to confess or freeze up and wait for his attorney—it was out of her hands now.

"Maybe I can sleep at night now," Megan's soft voice spoke up beside her.

"At least we've done what we could for Allison. What happens next is up to the police and the lawyers."

Megan released a long sigh. "Yeah, you're right. Time to let it go."

Kelly glanced to the clusters of excited artists and friends mingling throughout the room. Their enthusiasm was palpable. Kelly felt the last of the dark clouds dissipate at last. She turned to Megan with a smile. "I've got an idea. Why don't we congratulate Kimberly and say goodbye to Sophia and Eugene, then head over to the field. If we're lucky, we'll have only missed a couple of innings. Maybe they'll slip us in the lineup. I don't know about you, but I could use some fresh air, even if it's got snowflakes in it."

Megan's eyes lit up. "Fantastic idea. I'll buy pizza on the way over."

Mimi rocked rhythmically, her nimble fingers working a vivid shamrock-green wool into a sweater. Kelly sat beside her at the Lambspun library table, enjoying the quiet. Four other knitters sat around the table, all knitting colorful yarns into a variety of garments. Most of the yarns were wool, Kelly noticed. Warm, wonderful, versatile, forgiving wool.

Forgiving. That was the quality Kelly appreciated the most about the fiber, and she sincerely hoped the silk and cotton yarns in her lap were equally charitable. She held up the oft-neglected circular sweater and examined the rose-colored yarn. Row after row of neat stockinette stitches. She was going to finish this sweater at last.

So far, the silk and cotton yarns proved as forgiving as wool. Of course, it had helped when she'd placed the frothy shawl yarn in an empty "stash" bag and let it sit beside her sofa. Stroking the deep rose sweater, Kelly recalled what had drawn her to this yarn at the start. The seductive soft-ness of silk.

"Look, I see snowflakes," Megan spoke up, pointing outside.

Kelly turned and stared through the windows. Sure enough, tiny white flakes were skirting through the air, whirling, dancing.

"Just in time for Halloween," Lisa said, looking up from her lemon yellow yarn.

"That reminds me. I have to buy candy," Kelly said.

"Oooooo, please do," begged Jennifer, fingers moving at warp speed. "But bring it here first, so we can taste-test it. You wouldn't want to give away bad candy."

Soft laughter bubbled around the table.

"Well, personally, I'm glad it's snowing," Mimi remarked with a teasing smile. "Maybe cold weather will slow down Kelly's sleuthing. Maybe she'll stay inside and keep warm until spring."

"Fat chance," Jennifer observed.

"Hey, I'm taking a leave of absence from detective work. I've got too much on my plate learning Jayleen's consulting business." Kelly grinned across the table. "Megan and I will both turn in our junior detective badges."

Megan laughed. "I'll gladly turn in mine, but I have a feeling you'll keep yours. You like this detection stuff, I can tell. And you're good at it."

Kelly was about to reply, when the October wind blew a visitor into the shop and straight to the library table. Jayleen breezed in, snowflakes in her hair and dusting her denim jacket.

"Whooeee," she exclaimed, brushing off the flakes. "Winter's dying to come, you can tell. It's breathing down our necks."

"Hey, Jayleen," Kelly greeted her with a smile. "Did you come to nag me about your clients?"

Jayleen gave a dismissive wave. "Hell, no. I gave up nagging after my last divorce. I came to invite all of you to my place this Friday night. Night before Halloween. Bring your own pumpkins, and we'll have a jack-o'-lantern party. Whaddya say?"

"Count me in," Jennifer said. "I haven't been to a pumpkin party since college. And that's been so long ago I can't remember."

Kelly chimed in along with her friends, as everyone responded to Jayleen's offer. Glancing out the window again, she noticed the snowflakes were getting heavier. Wow. Maybe it would stick this time. Where the heck were her boots, she wondered? Picturing the unpacked boxes of winter clothes still sitting in the cottage garage, Kelly shuddered. Better to buy some new ones than face the boxes.

Watching her friends laugh and joke with Jayleen, Kelly felt herself relax. This was home now, and she was happier than she'd been since she was a kid.

Joining the lively conversation that was going on around her, Kelly asked, "What else can we bring, Jayleen? Aside from the pumpkins?"

"Oh, whatever munchies you like snacking on," Jayleen replied. "I'll have a pot of chili and some cornbread."

"Sounds great," Kelly said, tasting the chili already.

"I'll tell you what you *can't* bring." Jayleen grinned, hands in her back pockets in trademark fashion. "You've gotta leave Carl at home. Replacing a steak is one thing, but if that hound stuck his head in my chili pot, there goes dinner."

Kelly threw back her head and laughed out loud at the image of Jayleen chasing Carl throughout the canyon.

Lambspun Easy Triangle Shawl

MATERIALS: Bulky yarn or any combination of yarns to obtain gauge.

Sizes:	S	M	L
Main Color (MC) (yds)	525	610	700
Accent Color (AC) (yds)	186	186	186

NEEDLES: US Size 9–32-inch circular needle (or size necessary to obtain gauge)

ADDITIONAL SUPPLIES: Tapestry needle

GAUGE: Approximately 3 sts = 1"

INSTRUCTIONS:
Using MC, CO 3 sts, turn.
Row 1: Holding MC and AC together, k3, turn.
Row 2: With only MC, Inc in first st, k1, Inc in last st, turn. (5 sts total)
Row 3: With only MC, K3, yo, k2, turn. (6 sts total)
Row 4: Holding MC and AC together, k4, yo, k2, turn. (7 sts total)
Row 5: With only MC, k5, yo, k2, turn. (8 sts total)
Row 6: With only MC, k6, yo, k2, turn. (9 sts total)
Row 7: Holding MC and AC together, k7, yo, k2, turn. (10 sts total)
Row 8: Continuing color pattern as established (2 rows MC, 1 row MC & AC held together), knit to the last 2 sts, yo, k2.

Repeat Row 8 until shawl measures 28 (32, 36) inches or desired length from the beginning. Stop before you are ready to use MC and AC together.

FINISHING:
TOP EDGE: Use both MC and AC together.
Next Row: K1, *yo, k2tog* Repeat from * to * until 1 st remains, yo, k1, turn.
Knit 2 rows even.
BO. Sew in loose ends.

Pattern courtesy of Lambspun of Colorado, Fort Collins, Colorado.

Two Recipes for
Chiles Rellenos con Queso
(Chile Peppers Stuffed with Cheese)

Anne Murphy, a native and lifelong resident of New Mexico, was kind enough to share her family's recipe for Chiles Rellenos con Queso. Anne and her family now reside in the Washington, D.C., area.

Note from Anne: Chiles Rellenos con queso are like lasagna. Everyone has a different idea as to what they are. This recipe is from my aunt Beatrice "Bea" Vigil Lopez, who is ninety-three years old. Her great-grandparents started a ranch in northeastern New Mexico, and her family has remained New Mexico residents since then. I believe it is authentic.

Rellenos de Chiles Verde

Whole roasted Hatch green chiles
1/2 pound shredded Longhorn cheese
1/2 cup flour
Salt to taste
1 egg, beaten

Remove excess liquid from chiles by sponging with a paper towel. Fill with the shredded cheese, roll in the salt-flour mixture. Dip or roll in the egg mixture and fry until egg browns lightly. Drain and serve. (*Author's note: Use medium hot oil or bacon grease for frying.*)

AUNT BEA'S SAUCE FOR THE CHILES:

Heat 2 tablespoons bacon fat until bubbling. Add 2 tablespoons flour, stirring with a whisk until it is medium brown in color. Add 2 cups of hot water all at once and stir. Add one teaspoon salt and 1–2 cloves of crushed garlic. Heat until the sauce comes to a slow simmer and let it simmer until thickened.

The second recipe comes from Richard Dolph who lives in Silverton, Colorado, and was kind enough to share his favorite recipe.

Note from Richard: Big Jim's or Hatch chiles are grown in the Southwestern part of the United States. Hatch is a town in New Mexico that is famous for its chiles. This chili has a unique and wonderful flavor and can be used in many dishes. I have used it in stews, eggs, and pasta sauces. Fresh chiles need to be roasted, peeled, stemmed, and seeded. When eaten, green chiles produce endorphins, pain blockers that give a sense of well-being.

Baked Chiles Rellenos

10 whole green Anaheim chiles, peeled (also called Big Jim's or Hatch chiles)
1/2 pound Monterey Jack cheese, cut in ten-inch strips
1 cup grated Cheddar cheese

3 eggs
1/4 cup flour
3/4 cup milk
1/4 teaspoon salt
1/4 teaspoon black pepper
Dash of liquid hot pepper sauce

Preheat oven to 350 degrees. Cut green chiles in half, seed, leaving a few seeds for extra flavor. Spread chiles on paper towel and pat dry. Put a strip of Monterey Jack cheese in each chili. Lay them side by side in a greased 9 inch by 13 inch baking dish. Sprinkle with Cheddar cheese. Beat eggs with flour until smooth. Add milk, seasonings, and pepper sauce. Carefully pour egg mixture over chiles. Bake uncovered for 45 minutes or until knife inserted in custard comes out clean.

Maggie Sefton
Knit One, Kill Two

A Knitting Mystery

Kelly Flynn never picked up a pair of knitting needles she liked—until she strolled into House of Lambspun. Now she's learning to knit one, purl two, and untangle the mystery behind her aunt's murder.

"You'll love unraveling this mystery!"
—Laura Childs

"This is a clever, fast-paced plot, with a spunky sleuth and a cast of fun, engaging characters."
—Margaret Coel

0-425-20359-X

penguin.com

B070

PO #: 4500349367